BRIGHT LITTLE GIRLS

A NOVEL BY
LORNA HOLLIFIELD

Black Rose Writing | Texas

This is a work of fiction. Names, characters, businesses, places, events, and incidents are either the products of the author's imagination or used in a fictitious manner. Any resemblance to actual persons, living or dead, or actual events is purely coincidental.

ISBN: 978-1-68513-573-7 (Paperback); 978-1-68513-632-1 (Hardcover)
LIBRARY OF CONGRESS CONTROL NUMBER: 2024949818
PUBLISHED BY BLACK ROSE WRITING
www.blackrosewriting.com

Printed in the United States of America
Suggested Retail Price (SRP) $21.95 (Paperback); $26.95 (Hardcover)

Bright Little Girls is printed in Georgia Pro

PRAISE FOR
BRIGHT LITTLE GIRLS

"Lorna Hollifield's prose and story shine. Drenched in southern atmosphere, and rich in character, *Bright Little Girls* is a testament to the great lust for life that can both harm and heal. Through gasp-out-loud twists, we watch Eliane reach her own crescendo in both life and writing. Evocative and suspenseful, *Bright Little Girls* will keep you turning the pages and guessing until the very end."
–Patti Callahan Henry, NYT Bestselling author of
The Secret Book of Flora Lea

"In *Bright Little Girls,* Lorna Hollifield immediately hooks the reader with deliciously voyeuristic and subtly ominous narration. This tale of murder, obsession, and self-discovery is sure to keep fans of Southern suspense turning the pages in search of answers about Eliane—and her mysterious stalker."
–Stephanie Alexander, award-winning author of
The Tipsy Collins Series* and *Mean Low Water

"A wonderfully suspenseful novel with quirky characters and gasp-out-loud plot twists, *Bright Little Girls* is a binge-worthy read that grips the reader from the very beginning and commands attention until the very end."
–Sarah Rose, journalist for *Charleston Post* and *Courier*

"A clever, suspenseful work..."
–*Kirkus Reviews*

This one is for too many people to name. It is for the ones who uplift and the ones who tear down. Without either group, I wouldn't be here now, my words on a page. So maybe, this one is for everyone who was part of the ride. It is especially for every person who crossed my path between 1990 and 2005, when it seems that everything in the whole world happened—and also nothing at all. You were all my muses in some way, those who helped me grow up, and for that, I thank you. Eliane, much embellished and more peculiar than any of us, but full of glimpses, thanks you too. You all are her existence.

"I am really only myself when I'm somebody else whom I have endowed with these wonderful qualities from my imagination."
– Zelda Fitzgerald

BRIGHT LITTLE GIRLS

CHAPTER 1

Sometime before now, but after back then
The Blue Ridge Parkway

Her story is more important than mine—Eliane's. It seemed that it always was. She was the star, and I played mean fiddle for her in the background from the moment we met. It doesn't matter who I am or why I watch her, not yet. Time will tell if any meaning at all is assigned to my existence. Not so long ago, she became my reason when I had no other left, which is why I was in the woods that day, too—about three or so years after I started trailing her. I was always where she was, in some shadow at least. I'd only looked away for an instant I thought, but it was an instant too long, because what little was together about her was coming undone like a sweater that had unraveled after one too many threads pulled. And I'm afraid I might have pulled one or two of them myself.

I wasn't sure she was alive when I first saw her in that place. It wasn't the first time I ever saw her of course, not by years, but for some reason that's where she begins for me, somewhere right in the middle of the whole story. What happened before and what happened after is probably more important but seeing her there in that cursed mud where the other girls had lain as well—the girls who'd only made it out in pieces—that's always her opening image for me. It's probably because that's where she was stuck for a very long time, long after a hand had reached in and pulled her out.

Her face was so covered up with mud that I had trouble seeing it was her at all when I first peered into the little mountain grove at dusk. I'd hoped it wasn't her, and if it had been, I knew that I only had myself to blame for it. It might have been more than an instant, but I'd only let her out of my sight for a matter of hours at most. After that terrible email came and I all but heard *his* disgusting voice in it, I had to get out for a while. So, I did. I left her alone. I should have known better after everything I'd seen in the days leading up to this, but I did it anyway. I was selfish, and I left, it never occurring to me that she might be in danger, that she might end up in that particular spot on the Blue Ridge Parkway that smelled like water and leaves and the metal of blood draped onto honeysuckle.

It isn't her anyway, I told myself as I peered from behind the newly blooming rhododendron bush. But then I was able to make out her identifying marks in the dimming light. There was the odd ankle bone that protruded out abnormally from her old cheerleading injury. Then there was the silhouette of a dainty eye and arched eyebrow—that no one ever knew was from Zelda Fitzgerald's right profile—tattooed on the inside of her left wrist. It was perfectly visible with her arm splattered out over top of her head like it was. It was her, my very best creature.

"Where are you at?" A male voice, but not so masculine called out to her. "I didn't sign up for this. This isn't fair to me." The slight man wearing all black appeared, huffing, his hands on his notably narrow hips.

She didn't move, nor did I. I simply stayed put, waiting in the shadows for him to notice her. I wanted him to notice her, to catch a glimpse of her white tennis shoes lighting up the brown soil. I wanted to scream at him that she was just a little farther ahead of where he'd given up to pant and grimace in some brush and dirt. I wanted to instruct him to check her pulse, to pick her up out of that cold hollowed-out dip in the earth where she lay. But I couldn't do it. I couldn't say a word, the feeling of a phantom hand around my throat stopping me. I wasn't the kind to speak up, not ever.

He marched on, kicking at leaves with boots that looked too heavy for him. There was paint on one of them as well as on both of his bony hands. There always was. I'd seen him before, back at the studio apartment they shared as roommates in the river arts district. His hair was always combed straight down and gelled into a helmet. He always wore black, and it looked like he'd never met the sun. He was interesting to look at. Though, I'd rarely heard him speak. He was a painter, not a talker. He had a rather androgynous look about him, but with less sex appeal than he was capable. I learned that word, *androgynous*, reading an article about Ruby Rose in *People Magazine*. I'd never met anyone else it applied to so much, but still, he was no Ruby Rose. It was better when he didn't speak, for sure. It helped him. His voice was higher pitched than I liked and always pissy. I don't know why I even thought of that then, in such a heavy moment. I wondered if other people had such pointless thoughts while their hearts pounded blood into their ears.

Finally, he turned the right direction. "Oh my God." He jumped big but spoke small.

Then he ran to her. "What have you done? Oh my God. What in the—" He kneeled beside her but hadn't gotten the nerve to touch her, unsure that he should. His thoughts must have raced like mine. Should he help? Was he at a *crime scene*?

Her eyes popped open, but she didn't move. "I'm fine, I'm fine. Calm down." She said quietly and almost indignantly while pulling mud-caked air pods out from her ears.

"What is wrong with you? Why would you ever do something like this? I thought you were dead. I thought someone had done something to you out here. And they could have. You know what this place is. It isn't safe. Of all places, you shouldn't be out here.

I shouldn't be out here." He crossed his arms around himself, making him appear even skinnier.

"I just had to. I needed to come out here, exactly here. I thought it would help me deal with some things."

"With mud all over your face, sprawled out like a corpse? Come on, let's go," he looked all around, the blonde hairs on the back of his stained hands raising to their tiptoes.

"I just needed to feel it, what they felt lying in the thick of it like that. I needed to let it in, to connect to it. Maybe then, it will leave me, if I *experience* it the best I can."

"Why would you want to connect to *murdered women,* Eliane? He could be here watching us right now. The police have made it clear that this is his dumping site. This isn't safe. This isn't some controlled environment where you can experiment with weird therapy you've made up for yourself."

"I don't expect you to understand. It's just me facing some things I need to...so I can feel better, respond better, than I have lately. There are things you don't know about my past. I have to get close to the parts that scare me sometimes when I'm melting down, expose myself to whatever it is so it can release its power over me. It's a basic, Psych 101 coping mechanism. Exposure lessens fear. If you're scared of dogs, pet a dog, you know? I'm just having trouble getting it to work this time. It's too heavy."

"So, you're trying to pet a serial killer so he won't bite you?"

"No, no. You don't get it."

"You're right. I don't get it. I don't understand at all. You don't expose yourself to something like this to get over it. That's a death wish. I think psychologists would agree that avoidance is good in this case. This is your craziest stunt yet, coming out here to lie down in a murder field...and *me* having to chase you. I hope you never start fearing mustard gas." He brushed the dirt off his long black jacket as demonstratively as he could.

"I knew someone connected to this, Zen—I just, I want to escape it all."

"You have a funny way of showing it," he paused to huff dramatically.

"I was trying to face it, go to the scariest part of it, fight the dragon in his lair, slay him. But I can't."

"Look, I'm sorry about whatever tie you have to this freak. I'm guessing you knew him or a victim, maybe. But I can't be a part of it. I've tried to ignore all of this over the past couple of weeks with whatever's been going on with you. I don't mettle in people's lives. I don't involve myself. I don't want to involve myself. I don't chase people into the woods. This is why I never wanted a roommate to begin with."

"You won't have to again, I promise. I'm fine." She believed what she said in that moment, though I knew she'd never come through.

He reached his hand down and helped her onto her feet, always more loyal than he wished he was.

"You. Are. Not. Fine."

CHAPTER 2

Asheville, NC
Now

It didn't start like this, but I've been watching her for a long time now—years, though I'm not sure exactly how many. I'd been watching for a long time by the time she put herself in the dirt that day as some sort of strange therapy, and I've been watching for a long time since. Today I saw her sitting at the white antique vanity in her childhood bedroom putting her wildly curly hair up into a proper ballerina bun. It took her seven tries to get it right. She was red in the face by the last attempt, her arms starting to get heavy from holding them over her head for so long. It was perfect on try number six, but I knew she'd go for one more. She never liked even numbers; that was one of her *things*, one of many. She considered the idea that perfection always had to mean symmetry to be manmade, and it went against her. She didn't believe in perfect like that. She was known to preach sermons about it to anyone who would listen, and I always listened. I liked that she wore her compulsions on her sleeve for everyone to see, claiming that whatever weird thing she did was the correct way all along.

From those come-to-Jesus meetings with her, I learned that perfection, if it existed, would include the things that are messy, like prime numbers, remainders, and equations never to find balance. Life is sticky on a good day, and everything else reflects that, so to be true, at least to her, was to be perfectly *imperfect.*

For instance, sometimes ends that had once been tied into a nice little knot would become loose again. The breaking news headline she'd just read on her phone proved that much. And by breaking news, I mean one of the most followed criminal cases in Asheville's history highly syndicated throughout the Facebook statuses of soccer moms, neighborhood ladies and wannabe social commentators who weigh-in between loads of laundry. One of them had shared the story, with her two cents, "Excuse my French, but when will they get this son of a bitch?" added to the post. The headline read "After lengthy silence, The Blue Ridge Ripper Strikes Again." That was one of those ends which El thought had been tied up once upon a time, yet there the threads were, flying all about.

"I can't," she spoke out loud, still a little tempted to click on the article. "No, it isn't good for me. I won't. This doesn't concern me. This is none of my business." She took a deep breath and fidgeted with her bun again.

I gave her about fifteen minutes, give or take. She'd try not to look at the article. She'd try to make herself late for her appointment by dawdling around just long enough so she didn't have time to read about the latest antics of the unnamed man who had eluded the police for the past nine years, well longer than that really, just nine years that had affected her—the same man that compelled her to desensitize herself by lying where his victims once had. But I knew eventually she'd find herself with just enough time on her hands, and she'd have to click on it, pick the scab that was healing, and see it bleed again.

If nothing else she'd comment on the name, *"Blue Ridge Ripper.* How ridiculous? That sounds like some corny villain from a film noir. This is serious." She found it disrespectful that any serial killers were given catchy names, and she voiced it every time. She believed they enjoyed such things too much and shouldn't be given the pleasure.

I'd been watching long enough to predict all her tendencies. I'd been watching long enough to know everything. And for now, that's what's important. I'll think about the news story another time, because unlike her, it does somewhat concern *me*. But this isn't about me. This is about her, though bits of me are part of her—whether she likes it or not.

The parts I didn't see for myself, I'd heard about in her tales. I call them tales because that's what they were, yarns. She spun them even when it was on accident. Speaking, to her, was never a casual thing; she had too much to say, and she said in all in a *manner*. It wasn't how the rest of us just...talk.

She was a natural-born storyteller, better than any in Appalachia, and could never keep her own secrets. She would have loved to have been mysterious, but she wasn't. However, that didn't make her any less alluring. Mystery isn't always necessary to hold attention; an awe-inspiring mess will do just fine. There's no mystery to watching a volcano erupt over a quaint village or a tornado ransack a heartland town. Destruction is certain, but the power—from that, we can't tear our eyes away. It's the same with everyone who watches Eliane. I'm not alone; I'm just the only one who watches like this. I haven't been many places where someone wasn't looking at her. She was meant to be examined, like a butterfly with a unique pattern on her wings. People like the idea of catching her, putting her in glass and examining her intricacies with a magnifying glass. I, however, find her more interesting in flight, however hard to follow she can be.

She didn't know that people admired her, the way she owned all that she was, good or bad. But they did. She assumed they only egged her on for sport, to watch someone take a dare that had been laid out in front of them. People who are too scared to take any chances themselves love watching others give the outlandish things in life a go. Think about it. Have you ever stood in a crowd cheering on a drunk dude break dancing at a wedding, or urged your buddy to leap off that rock that's just a little bit too tall? It's because it's brilliant to watch others do the things which we're scared to do ourselves, and sometimes that's just being bold enough to shine. So many of us are afraid of light; I know I am. So, everyone egged her on for their own benefits, being near the light good enough for them. But they also envied her. I envy her, still—the boldness. I saw her skinny-dip once in broad daylight that spring when I met her. The water was too cold, but we'd gone with a group to Sliding Rock, which is exactly what it sounds like. Everyone toed the water a little bit, squealed shaking their heads.

"Dear God, that's freezing," the boy with shaggy hair said. "I'm glad I don't have my suit. It gives me a good excuse not to get in *that*."

"That's not a good enough excuse. You'll only have so many chances to experience the thrill of sliding down a rock on your belly like an otter into cold mountain water." Eliane responded while she disrobed.

And everyone started to cheer. I was there, not how I'm here now, but *really* there where people could see me. Still, I hugged my knees close to my body and watched from underneath a tree, careful not to draw attention to myself, even then, in those very different times, attempting to hide. My biggest fear was that everyone would start to follow. And I'm only bold in the shadows.

This isn't really who I am, the one who voices what they've observed, but it's the way I wished I could have been, and it's how I am able to be from here where no one can judge me or offer their opinions. Maybe that's why I watch all the time now...well, among the other reasons I'll get to later.

Like those forces of nature I mentioned, I cannot take my eyes away from her, and I wish so much that I could tell her, because she'd appreciate it. We all have egos. But that would ruin it. It would upset her to know that I'm still here. So, I'll attempt to tell her story instead, for no other reason than the fact that it brings me that amusement I long for so much in being *near* to her. I was never a storyteller the way she is, until now I suppose. If I'm any good, it's just because of her. She is my muse. I've never had a talent of my own, even though I was told I was a decent singer growing up. Even with that, I just learned to mimic others' voices so I could dance like a circus elephant with a ball on my nose whenever I was told to. So, what I really was, was an impersonator, I suppose. It didn't come from me; this is the same as that, just a regurgitation of someone else's charisma that I sew into a scarf and pull over my own shoulders. But it looks good on me when I wear it, and it's the best I've got.

CHAPTER 3

When I knew Eliane best, she was young, a little scrawny, and desperately beautiful. I say desperately, because she was the broken type of beautiful people always felt a little bit sorry for, like an alley cat with big sad eyes. She was just a little bit too hopeful, a little bit too hungry. Though, despite her being feral, everyone wanted to take her home. In some ways, I'm surprised *he* didn't want her, the killer with the catchy nickname. I'm curious how it is that Eliane didn't end up in that muddy hollow that became the most infamous cemetery in Asheville. I know he watched her, as much as I watch now. She was there, always under his nose, close enough for him to lean in and smell. Maybe she was even *too* special to become his trophy. Perhaps he preferred punishing the more classically beautiful flowers, the irises and the lilies; Eliane was a Middlemist's Red Camelia, the rarest wildflower in the world.

But I need to back up for a moment before I talk about our short-lived friendship, or the poison-in-a-person we both fell addict to, or the ugly color of murder that we wish didn't spill on us like a stain we'll wear forever. First, I need to explain just how particular her rarity is—because it matters. Eliane Pangolin has a bit of a prologue to her life. Her story cannot exist without at least the brief knowledge of someone else's.

To know Eliane (should be pronounced El-ee-ahn, but because it's the South is pronounced Ellie-Ann) is to know Zelda, a long-dead woman whom she never knew, first. It's important that I introduce you to her before I follow Eliane to her mandatory therapy and watch her screw mercilessly with her therapist for an hour.

"I think I might be Zelda Fitzgerald's reincarnate. I mean, think about it. I was born in Asheville like a mile away from where she died, and I've listened to jazz since before I knew who she was," she'd said to me all those years ago. "I think something of her was left here when she burned to death and the ash stayed in the breeze until my mother inhaled it with a drag off her cigarette while she was pregnant with me. I think it's why I'm like this."

"Like what?" I laughed like I didn't know.

"Like, strange. I don't think like most people. I don't handle things like most people. Maybe I wasn't born in the wrong era, maybe I was born in another era first. Or, like I said, the ash got in somehow," she joked to me one afternoon when we walked through the botanical gardens by UNC Asheville after one of those rain showers where the sun still shines and old ladies say the devil is beatin' his wife.

But I think she believed it, that she was a little bit Zelda, at least to some degree. She casually smelled a bright yellow flower she should not have picked and then unceremoniously tossed it into the creek, shrugging. She thought the body language would convince me she was kidding, but who is ever really kidding about anything?

"You would love it if you were, but you are *not* Zelda Fitzgerald." I scoffed, which was always my role. "You're nowhere near that tragic."

But I lied. I might have believed it a little bit, too. She was the only millennial I ever met who listened to Duke Ellington and drank Gin Rickeys in corners at parties—and she wasn't doing it for attention or just to be different. I met a lot of people who did things like that, and it never came off right. We've all met the kind. They claim to love *Citizen Kane* and always have a streak of blue in their hair. They go door-to-door registering people to vote and never know the issues. They always wear fishnet stockings with boots that they got at a Goodwill even though their parents are rich. That's not Eliane. Whatever it was that seeped out of her pores the way it did, was just in her, who she was at birth. And I could feel the tragedy on her, too. It just hadn't happened, whatever the tragedy would be...yet. And I'm glad that I didn't know then all it would be, but I could feel it—what's that Shakespeare line—by the pricking of my thumbs...

She often referenced Zelda; it wasn't just that day. I think she adored the dead woman because she knew her, and not because she tried to become her. Her affection didn't tip over into emulation, not at all—Eliane was no woman's fangirl. It was more one of those connections that must have involved the planets, and the stars, and other bits of matter scientists don't *really* understand. Eliane had discovered some woman in the history books who made her make sense to herself. She even wrote her letters; it didn't matter that the woman had been dead for almost 80 years. She started writing them after watching a documentary on The Fitzgeralds when she was home sick with strep throat in the fourth grade. Most kids just watched *Maury* and *The Price is Right*, learning who was *not the father* and how to estimate the cost of washing powder, but not Eliane. She watched the History Channel, then pulled out a pen and piece of paper to write a letter to the woman she'd just learned fancied handwritten letters herself. That's how she began writing to Zelda and mailing the letters to the address of the home she'd grown up in. It didn't matter that they went unanswered, or that most of them showed back up in her own mailbox. It was her connection, and she kept doing it. Then it became a habit. She'd pen a letter to anyone she ever wanted to reach, dead or alive, close or distant from her. It could be a family member, a friend or one of Henry the VIII's wives. If she had thoughts, questions, musings, or rants, the appropriate person got a letter.

Maybe her letters were art, because they certainly weren't written in the hopes of ever getting answered. So, it's possible that her recipients were simply her artistic mediums, her muses, like she's mine. Everyone has a muse, and just about everyone *is* a muse. That's probably why people are rarely happy. They spend all their time being used by one person and impossibly enamored with another. It's an endless cycle that never makes a complete circle and is full of dead ends and events that never really find any closure. It makes sense in Zelda's case—and in Eliane's—and probably even in mine. But this is Eliane's story, so we'll start by examining the first of her kind, Eliane's Eve, and the original recipient of her letters.

Zelda Sayre Fitzgerald had been a fan of choice gin and delicious words, too. Though she was never alive the same time as Eliane, not by almost a whole century, she is her source, the mother of her kind. They are part of a species that exists in plain sight in small numbers but is never positively identified like some strange mammal in Australia or The Sudan that almost never shows it face. There have been a handful of girls like the two of them throughout time. They never go unnoticed when out of their dens, are almost always misunderstood, but rarely become famous (which just kills them, though they'd hate it either way). However, because Zelda was indeed famous, she *still* carries an enormous responsibility on her long-cold shoulders to represent this group. It's a group that has certain attributes, but no word that describes them properly—unless there's one unknown to English speakers in some other fabulous language in which people their roll r's then wash them down with better wine than ours. It's important to get to know them whenever one can be spotted in its natural habitat. That habitat could be anywhere, even some dive bar if there's one charming thing about it—like it only plays real vinyl records or something. It's hard to pinpoint what might draw one of these creatures from hiding, but you'll know when you see one. Zelda Fitzgerald is simply the poster child, her picture beside the missing word for her kind in the dictionary.

Her wit made her famous more than anything else, even more than her author husband everyone adored, at least in my opinion—or maybe it was Eliane's. Sometimes in our entanglement I forget what's mine and what's hers. But I'm the one telling the story, so I'm the one who gets to have the opinions.

Anyway, Zelda's tongue was like her birthplace in Alabama—drawled, hot, and fiery. But it was more than just her speak...it was everything...the essence, the aura, the things that could be touched and the things that couldn't. She had too much art in her for her own good...just like someone else I know. She could dance, she could paint, she could write, and was almost great at all of it. Almost. She must have always been in a state of *feeling* so deeply, so much that it burst out of her and jumped into every artistic medium it could, two parts beautiful, one part awkward. The emotion swelled into elixir from somewhere inside her body and then seeped out into these other things in some attempt to show itself to the world. It had nowhere else to go, no other way to make it underneath the spotlight it coveted so much. But that spotlight was reserved for her husband, who will not ever fall out of it. He *is* history now, and no eraser could ever touch him. He is Americana; he's who Taylor Swift would had been if she were a prohibition-era man. He was the author of all that was his *or* his wife's story as far as pop culture is concerned. He was F. Scott, and I'd had no idea who he was when I first met Eliane. But this, for once, isn't about him. It's about the girls, Eliane and Zelda.

Maybe if Zelda had poured it all into one thing—that intangible "it-factor" she had—it would have been strong enough to be something, and it would have been about her all along. But it wasn't. Instead, "it" divided itself like the angriest cancer cells do and splattered onto everything in the form of paint, words, and awkward dance moves while her husband spit out novel after novel, his steady girlfriend. Zelda's arts became rampant and inoperable and insistent. The concoction became spread too widely, the pattern erratic and undiscernible by the layman. Zelda had created pieces of everything that could be seen, heard, or touched in the world, but she'd crafted nothing whole, not even her own life. Even the most beautiful things she wrote, the love letters to her always somewhat estranged husband, couldn't have existed without him. She needed his pain and hers to produce the pieces she did. She was born a yin in need of the yang, and that might have been the whole problem to begin with. With Eliane, it's far too soon to tell. But she does cry like a baby when she sits in dimly lit rooms reading those famously doomed love letters.

Girls like the two of them cannot help but to be what they are. People elevate them, which they love like an addict loves good blow. But the fans never admire them in the sweet spots where it's healthy and flattering. They like all the wrong parts of them. They love to see the break downs, the mascara-infused tears, the rough sex after an argument, the boldness to pop a pill in polite company. The onlookers keep celebrating it, and the addicts keep providing the entertainment. They keep taking that dare, leaping off the bridge no one else will. And, damn, people like to tell their stories. Just look at me.

Zelda, perhaps, would have preferred to have been the author of the stories, the architect of her own legend. Some conjecture that she was, that she penned many of the words written in those time-honored books. But her husband, arguably the greatest American writer of all time, got all the credit either way. In and out of sanitariums her entire adult life, she would only be credited with being a symbol for rebellious women or a public case study for mental illness. She just was what she was, a favorable bone structure in an obstinate haircut—a strong but misunderstood woman in a drop-waisted dress, the original American flapper.

The confidence and glamour that came with her absurdities made it all look so damn delicious, too. So, everyone grabbed a spoon. That was largely the problem; it all seemed so fucking fabulous. *She* seemed so fabulous. She indulged on the delight she brought herself too often, got drunk off the taste of her own ambience, then offered the spirit to everyone else for a swig. Like my Eliane, Zelda had just burned so brightly. She was smart. She smoked and drank and cursed. She was the nerve other people wished they had. Everyone wanted to be close to her to feel her heat on their own cheeks, always taking, never giving. They lingered near the bonfire just to watch it burn bigger and bigger, never helping to contain it.

But sometimes such powerful things are also threats to themselves. A nuclear power plant is full of all the energy in the world, but with the wrong push of a button, it melts itself down and takes everything nearby with it. Zelda stumbled through glamorous parties, French riviera scenes, sanitariums, and extra-marital affairs for the same reason a bird flies through the forest. Then her life ended in an Asheville, North Carolina sanitarium on Zillicoa Street in the famed Montford historic district, about a mile from where Eliane first came screaming into the world. The institution caught on fire and took Zelda's life when she was 47 years old. A large fire is always capable of engulfing a smaller one, and it turns out there were flames too great for even Zelda to conquer.

The place where she burned in the Blue Ridge Mountains, the little hill on Zillicoa Street hiding among the Queen Anne and Colonial Revival homes, is now home to many other things: a lot of non-profit organizations, those same now much older homes, Southern hippies drinking out of mason jars and even one of

Asheville's most well-known psychiatry practices. I spend a lot of time watching there; it's where I'm headed now. It isn't the place where Eliane's story starts for me, but it's where it starts for her, caught right in the middle of what was and what will be, her destiny to live, or her fate to burn. And while *her* future remains unclear, I can confirm this fact: not everyone involved in the story of Eliane Pangolin will get out alive.

CHAPTER 4

Eliane fidgeted with her leotard while she waited on her therapist to speak. It was black, the tights pink, as they should be for a serious adult ballerina. The bun was right too (after the arguable six or seven times she constructed it). The important thing is that it was tight, high on her head, and without any dirty-blonde strays trying to escape and fall onto her pale face. It pissed her off when the other women rolled into class in yoga pants and sock feet like the let's-not-keep-score, never-compete, hobbyists they were. I could tell by the way she gave them the side eye, something she normally tried to avoid. But this was serious. This wasn't a time to be whimsical...journals and vlogs were for that. Her natural hair was for that. It could be whimsical on a windy day, or hanging from her head while she gazed down at a lover from up top where she had all the control. But not for this. This was training; this was putting in the effort to get something that she'd made a goal. This was a time for uniformity, to strip away the self and become something she'd chosen to become. No one told her she had to do it, but because she'd selected it, she held herself to the rules of the craft. Now, had someone forced it on her, she would have marched in wearing blue jeans and street shoes, her middle finger waving in the air with a smiley face painted on it. Everything had to be her own choice, her natural proclivities, her own whims turned into committed effort. This was the time for precision, which Eliane took seriously and only in certain circumstances that would somehow color her life a little bit brighter than the dull grey it had been the past decade.

"I was waiting on you to speak first today, but I don't think you're going to." The therapist said with a lightness like it was over a glass of Chardonnay.

"I never speak first. You say something, and then I respond to it." No emotion.

"I was hoping you'd want to, that perhaps you had some thoughts you were eager to explore together. That's how we will get to the place where you're exploring on your own, which is your goal, I'm sure."

"I wouldn't read too much into that. I just feel weird in forced situations like these. Trust me, *all* I do it think."

"Well, tell me, what progress do you believe you've made since we last spoke?"

Eliane thought for a second. "I guess that I've been driving. I drove here without my mom in the passenger seat today. It was my first time without my 'just-in-case' person with me. I felt a little panicky at first, but I got here."

"That's an enormous stride, Eliane. I'm so proud of you for that. And you know to do your steps should the panic show up again. Don't forget your breathing and tapping techniques just in case. They will ground you. They *will* stop the panic because the rhythm will let your body know you're safe. But it sounds like you're doing well."

Eliane worked up a small smile.

"The panic was never about driving itself. It was about being trapped, like in a circumstance, feeling like I can't escape. It just showed up when I was literally trapped in the car. But it wasn't about the car. It was about what I'd been through. Once I realized that, that part of *all this* got a lot better. I don't think I need the coping skills for that anymore."

"Just keep them in your back pocket. Trauma has a tendency to tap us on the shoulder in strange places." She scribbled, *put that in the book*, on her note pad.

"Noted." Eliane was annoyed at her therapist's reluctance to ever see anything as cured. She only saw remission, and shaky remission at that.

"Do you have dance practice after this?" Dr. Vitale asked, adjusting her winged vintage glasses, which were her attempt at fun. They didn't match her, which Eliane hated. Trying too hard never paired well with anything.

She didn't answer the question at first. She hadn't seen the glasses before and she got distracted in evaluating them. The weirdness must be authentic to come off. This was not Eliane drinking expensive gin from a solo cup. This was blatant costuming on a hard rule follower—someone looking not to color their own world but hoping that others would perceive them as color. The glasses were a lie, which made Eliane's skin itch. I could see her physically scratching at her arms, which meant she was reluctant to trust Dr. Vitale's advice at all—the glasses, the aquariums, and the two dozen plants taking over the whole office were just décor, not personality. The doctor wanted Eliane to divulge everything, when she, herself, was willing to divulge nothing. Also, there were so many things in there to keep alive. The therapist clearly had a savior complex. She had something to prove to somebody, and it wasn't herself.

"Eliane?" The doctor nudged her.

"Oh, dance practice. No, no. I'm wearing this to appear less crazy. Is it working?" Eliane leaned forward on the slick leather sofa, eyes wide like she was actually seeking the affirmation.

"Well, you haven't lost your sense of humor, clearly." The doctor paused for Eliane to interject, but she didn't. "Believe it or not, I'm a fan of your dancing goals so long as you keep it all light and fun. It could be a great outlet for you. It's good to have hobbies, and the endorphins don't hurt, either."

"You meant distractions, not hobbies. It's good to have distractions to keep me from obsessing." Her voice was cute and perky as she talked with her hands, lightening up her words. "Let's just go ahead and say the real thing. Semantics don't get me worked up. They annoy me. A spade is a spade. People almost always understand connotation. Semantics hall monitors only analyze words down to the arrow to manipulate people or twist facts. You want me to keep my mind busy. I get that." Eliane's distaste for bullshit was well above average.

"Hobbies are distractions for most people. Good distractions, so sure, we can say that." The doctor humored her. She'd clearly not heard or at least retained any of the soapbox speech.

Eliane almost rolled her eyes at her therapist's need to grant her permission to use whatever word she liked, but instead she sighed knowing it was futile, "It keeps my mind busy. And my body looks great now. A nervous breakdown goes nicely with ballet. I haven't been this trim since high school...and don't start worrying that I'm not eating or something. I'm at a healthy weight. Anorexia isn't my poison."

"Duly noted. And your other distractions?" The Doctor, who tried her best to be quirky instead of pretty, though she was in fact pretty, raised her thin dark eyebrows over the desperate glasses.

"What? Watching *Friends* reruns on repeat? Laughing like it's the first time every time Ross tries to pull his leather pants back up?"

"No. The other one."

"Ask me what you want to, Dr. Vitale. You're like that old Saturday Night Live skit where they all whisper the words no one likes like "cancer" or "divorce.""

The doctor looked to the side trying to recall the skit she knew damn well she hadn't seen because she wasn't an SNL aficionado. I think she didn't want Eliane to know and think she was more a square than she already did for not being familiar with the "hard words" bit. But there was no way. This woman was the kind who went to bed at 8:30 p.m. and woke up early just to make her bed because she read somewhere that successful people always do that. Eliane, however, would never waste such precious time to be alive straightening sheets she would mess up again in mere hours. I was a bedmaker. It was what I was taught. Until I met Eliane. After that, I never made another bed again. And guess what? It hadn't mattered either way.

"Never mind. I'm just saying, you don't have to tip-toe with me. I like the scary words as much as any." Eliane encouraged with a little grin more than she scolded. She had a way of making the bitchiest comments sound cute and harmless.

Dr. Vitale chuckled and asked the question she'd wanted to begin with. "Are you still reaching out to your friend?"

"Yeah, I'm still communicating with Lux." She blurted, hoping it would encourage the doctor to mirror her bluntness.

"When is the last time you wrote to her?"

"Days ago, maybe a week even."

"So, the recent news about the girl they found didn't make you want to talk to her?"

"I didn't read the story." She wasn't lying, and I was as shocked as anyone. I was rarely wrong about her.

"Well, that in itself is huge, Eliane. I'm happy to hear that."

"I knew what it would say. It would say that they'd found another one, or at least some part of her, in a remote area off the Blue Ridge parkway somewhere in between Asheville and Brevard. It would say that there was, as usual, no DNA and no leads. I used to read it over and over, but the fact that it never changes just frustrates me now."

"Yes, but the fact that you are following that logic and not compelling yourself to read it though you know the outcome is a step in the right direction. But let's get back to the letter from a few days ago. This is the area you've not been able to employ that same logic. Did you mail this one?"

"Of course I did." Eliane sighed.

"And has she answered you?"

"No. You know she never answers me. I've made that clear. And I know you think I shouldn't be talking to her. I've stopped the texts and emails. It's just the letters now. I'm a big fan of the handwritten letter. It's just writing. I've done this for years with all sorts of people, and it's never been such a problem—people I know, people I don't. She's just someone I can get everything out to. You know that. Writers need unique ways to express themselves. We were best friends once upon a time. She's one of the few people I was able to open up to all the way. I can't just turn that off."

"But you've been asked to stop writing. More precisely, you've been asked to stop any kind of contact, formally. That's why this person is different. Don't you think you should respect that?"

"It takes my creative medium away if I stop."

"I thought dance was your creative medium."

"I have a lot of them. You can't ask a dancer not to dance or a writer not to write any more than you can ask a bear to stop shitting in the woods. It's not going to happen. My expression is my expression. I'm a writer first, then a million other things. But it's all part of the whole. I can't just cut off an appendage and walk away." Her voice was calm, never showing inflection. She didn't apologize for the swear either, another thing I envied. I could swear to myself just fine, but I always blushed and offered a half-hearted "I'm so sorry" in front of people if I let a "damn it" or "oh shit" slip out. No one is ever actually sorry for when they curse. They fucking mean it. Eliane always just let it fly, no matter whom she was around. Because she wanted them to know she meant it.

"Perhaps you could start by writing letters and simply not mailing them." Dr. Vitale shrugged casually, though she'd made the suggestion at least twice before. "Then it's just a creative process and doesn't affect anyone else."

"It isn't the same. If it were that easy, I would have already done that one of the other times you've advised me to. I like that it connects, because otherwise, I feel like I've tried to draw a circle and ended up with a horseshoe. It isn't finished that way. You know that. I don't know why you just keep presenting it like I've never rejected that idea. Is it that you don't have any other solutions?" Again, her words seemed light, though they were accusatory; and it wasn't passive-aggressive. It was just Eliane.

Dr. Vitale didn't bite the friendly but sharp hook. "What isn't the same about it? If it's truly just to "get it out" as you say and not to get a response, then why isn't it good enough to just write it and then put it away? You could save the letters in a journal if you like. Hell, scrapbook them, even. Just don't mail them. Save all the money you're spending on stamps." It was clever for the doctor to try to match Eliane's energy with cursing herself.

"It just doesn't work." Eliane spoke quietly, wishing that something like scrapbooking *was* good enough.

"Is it because you think there's an off chance she *will* reach out to you one day?"

Eliane picked the hardened skin on the corner of her thumb's nail bed.

"Eliane?"

"No." She clenched her jaw this time. "I'm not crazy. I know the friendship is over, and I don't expect anything. It just feels less unhealthy to me if it's real. I can't write a letter never to be mailed. It completes it, mailing it. That's the connection. It was at least intended to be read. It wasn't futile, I guess."

"That sounds like hope to me, Eliane. That sounds like refusing to admit that your relationship with this person, in any form, is over."

"It isn't. It's just authenticity." She licked the drying gloss on her full lips.

"Or if it's not hope, is it a compulsion? You *must* mail it, or it isn't 'complete' as you say. Have you explored that possibility?

You appreciate bluntness, so here it is. You have the official diagnosis of obsessive compulsive disorder. You know that, and you're highly intelligent. Doesn't this act seem consistent with that diagnosis?"

"Not really. It's just another form of therapy to me." Eliane dug her heels in, truly believing what she said in that moment, deciding not to acknowledge that *everything* she indulged in had a dash of compulsion on top. This was hardly enough to taste, like a pinch of salt to set off the flavor of chocolate milk.

"Still, don't you think, at the very least, you need to respect other people's boundaries even though you're working on your own healing? Your process should be yours, not a burden to someone else. The way you're behaving now involves other people and blatantly defies their wishes. That isn't therapy. That's invasion."

"Yep, I get it," she said standing up and straightening the sheer skirt layered overtop of the leotard. "Our time is up. I have a one-on-one dance lesson in like 15 minutes. I can't be late for it. Auditions are soon, and my technique still needs polished. I've really gotta run."

"Keep it fun, Eliane. Don't let the goal become the next obsession. Remember how far you've come and be proud of starting something so new in your late twenties. A lot of people wouldn't have the guts. You're strong. Just don't let the goal ruin the accomplishment by letting it become stress. *Good* distractions."

"Yeah, sure. Of course." Eliane smiled and hurried out the door.

She made it out of the building and into the parking lot on Zillicoa Street. She always swore she could still find patches of bizarre dirt from where the earth was scorched there back in 1948. She'd claimed that since long before the therapy started. That theory dated back to when she had a fresh driver's license and would drive friends—who could not have cared less—

downtown to see the alleged "burn spots." Eliane claimed that the life just never seemed to come back to those areas all the way. She insisted that not everyone could see it after all this time. But she could. She was sure. There were places where the grass swayed opposite of the wind, certain blades defying its other conforming family members. There were spots where the dirt never seemed damp enough, even after a good rainstorm. They were still there to her, though I think in spirit only, the energy of the blaze that took Zelda. The scars. Maybe she felt them instead of saw them. Maybe she made the whole thing up, but I don't think so.

"And now for my favorite part." Eliane glanced at her phone for the time. "But damn, I've got to hurry up."

She settled down into what she had declared as one of the burn spots, in her mind *the* spot. She pressed her bare back that the U-shaped leotard exposed, against the sparse ground, then put her hands behind her head. She could feel it, all that had been alive, all that had been so alive it had eventually erupted into fire, still there. She inhaled her favorite drug, five deep breaths in and out, each one getting her a little bit higher. Then she waited until the time turned to a prime number, 1:13, her favorite, and let the sun burn into her cheeks for a moment. And she smiled.

CHAPTER 5

Ballet wasn't Eliane's favorite. I had learned her expressions by now. The furrowed brow meant she hated the concentration that it took. She wished she were freer in her practice, but dance only came to her *almost* naturally. The sigh before walking into the studio meant that she just wanted to get it over with. Perfect it and move on.

She preferred jazz and hip-hop, and she was good at those. The rhythms suited her better. Her attitude matched the shift in the beats perfectly. I understood why that was her preferred poison. Dancing like that, she could stomp out any bad memory, overpower it, and beat it to the ground, the delight showing on her indignant face. But her technique needed refining if she wanted to be any kind of real dancer. It couldn't stay the simple release it started as; she had to get better.

She moved a bit clunky, her feet never landing catlike enough, her transitions a bit too jerky. She didn't know how to glide her arm through the air like a case knife through warm butter. She didn't know how to be soft or how to move without force. Despite her little frame, she didn't dance like a dandelion caught in the wind, but more like a large predator ready to pounce. It worked well for some genres. Usually, dancers struggled keeping tight and executing sharp motions. But that wasn't Eliane, not ever. She was nothing if she wasn't sharp as a steak knife.

She had the raw part down—the reaction, the passion, the emotion of the music expressed on her face. Always had, with everything she did. She'd made straight C's in high school English for poor grammar and mechanics. But the teacher would have her read the essays aloud to the class for content. No one could beat her there—her observations, her analysis, her take on the material no one else understood. She could dissect poetry or prose just like she could dissect people—well, people who weren't *herself*.

The teachers would tell her how the writing shined, but that she had to get in line with the spelling and punctuation to at least some degree. They said similar things to her in college when they kept rejecting her from the creative writing program ever so gently until she dropped out. At least that's why I think she dropped out for good. I might have had something to do with her leaving the first time, but we'll get to that later.

What they didn't know was that she had tried, but that her other proclivities always interfered. Some of the punctuation looked strange to her on the page and didn't land at the "right spots." She couldn't stand to indent the paragraphs. She decided it was unnecessary as long as she skipped a line. An indention created a ledge, and the edge of it seemed sharp. It hurt her to imagine dragging her wrist across the phantom pointy edges on the paper. She didn't like sharp corners, but rounded edges. The sharpness eked her, except when delivering the truth. Seeing an indented paragraph would remind her of the feeling, an imagined needle jutting into the middle of her wrist, and then she'd have to tap each wrist three times to cancel the nagging thought. But the thought would come back, so she'd be tapping her wrists all class long, and someone would notice. She thought it better that she just make her own rules to indicate the transitions. So, that's what she did. She made her own rules about most things.

Eliane also liked any written piece to end in a prime number of sentences. If it didn't, she might just have to let it run-on, or she'd add an extra one that made no sense. She tried to change the obsession to be about the grammar, to perfect it, but she couldn't. She tried to tell herself that flawless grammar as directed was the new rule and attempted to compel herself to practice it by convincing herself of weird things like using perfect commas meant she would never get into a car accident. But it didn't take. The obsessions chose her, not the other way around. She couldn't re-route them to work *for* her no matter how hard she tried. So, she followed her own rules of grammar despite the consequences. At first, she traded A's and B's for her sillier rules, then, eventually, things much more costly for stronger compulsions she couldn't shake, things like her freedom.

In dance, it wasn't as bad. She hated that everything came in perfect counts of eight. Even numbers being perfect, seemed planned-out and inauthentic. They stroked her similarly to the doctor's glasses. Everything shouldn't just wrap up into perfect sets according to Eliane. A lot of people with her condition might beg to differ, but Eliane's obsessions tended to reflect life, and life was never perfect.

I once asked her, "What about snowflakes? Sand dollars? Butterflies? They're perfect and they're real."

She responded, "Naturally occurring outliers. The exception, not the rule. The rule is a gnawed-on baloney sandwich with jagged edges."

That might be when I wanted to know her more than ever. That answer sold me. No one had thoughts like Eliane Pangolin's.

With Eliane's logic, it stands to reason that if dance were to run freely, it should really occur in all sorts of bizarre rhythms...and sometimes more advanced routines do. Still, it's usually double time or half time...subsets of perfectly even counts. However, she felt so fabulous doing it that it worked to some level, better than the grammar had for sure. To cancel out all the dainty sets of eight, she would count to 13 before removing her ballet shoes. That seemed to fix everything, and to also feed the disorder in her head a little cookie to satisfy him. He was less aggressive if he felt full. If he got too hungry, he wouldn't shut up, and she'd have no peace. So, she counted every time she unlaced them, clicking her tongue up and down slightly with each number, the movement allowing her to really feel it.

"Remember, pretend a string is attached to the top of your head, pulling you up to the ceiling. Look the direction of your turn; do not try to rotate your body. Your eyes will take you there." The teacher called out as Eliane performed her double pirouette, spinning twice on the ball of her left foot.

"Dammit." She scoffed, falling off her leg when the teacher spoke. "I have to get better at that. I only have a couple of weeks left. There will be loud music. I can't get distracted by a little bit of invasive noise."

"You'll get there." The pixie-like girl-woman five years Eliane's junior replied. "Just get out of your head about it. Let's do something else for a second. Get in position for your chaine turns."

Eliane nodded and walked to the corner of the room to prepare for the chain of spins she'd complete across the floor, almost smoothly enough.

She heard her instructor's voice, "...five, six, seven, eight."

And she began. She tried to spot the opposite corner of the room, careful not to fall out of the straight diagonal line.

However, she'd catch glimpses of her face in the mirror along the way. Flash, flash, flash. Something about it felt like the past ten years, the way they'd shot by so quickly, spinning, struggling for control. She'd tried to keep every twist and turn in line then, too, but had ended up drawing a maze with her feet—one she'd gotten horribly lost inside. Sometimes she thinks she's still in it, and maybe she always will be to some degree. Other times she believes she barely made it out, but that she's safe now. I don't know which it is either. But she always has her eye on the exit. She knows where it is, and that makes it feel a little safer. She always has an out; she has control through her rules.

"And one, two, three, four..." Her teacher's voice became distant, and she stepped out of what felt like rotating doors. I knew what faces she was picturing, and what events. I'd been there for some of it. I'd seen the letters she wasn't supposed to be writing. I'd seen the tragedy that made her start writing them. The faces I knew she imagined now probably looked like fuzzy slides trading places like flash cards, showing her images of Lux, of her mother, of the man they'd first arrested as the Blue Ridge Ripper, of the man she imagined him to be now, of herself...and, of course, Jett, the boy with the shaggy hair. *Fucking Jett*, more haunting than any of them.

"Whoa, I got a little dizzy there." Eliane put her hand to her head, to the golden fly-aways forming at her sweaty temples.

"You OK? You need to take a water break?" The teacher said revealing her snapping green gum.

"You know, I think I'm good for today. It's almost time to stop, anyway. We can pick it up where we left off in a couple days if it's all the same to you."

"OK, if you're sure. You paid for another 15 minutes, you know. We could work on some balance exercises." The younger girl shrugged.

"Nah, I'm good," she panted. "Thank you so much. It's been a long day for me. A lot going on. You're right. I need to get out of my head, or I won't improve anymore."

She is never out of her head.

"Sure. I'll see you Thursday, then?" The snap of the gum again.

"Sure thing." Eliane panted as she sat down, counted to 13, removed her shoes, then spoke aloud to no one, certainly not to me. "Thursday, the fifth day, a good prime number. Thursday will be a better day."

CHAPTER 6

Somewhere just outside Asheville, NC
Back Then

I know the stories from before now because I was there for most of them, but not this far back. The others, she or Jett told me over time. And if they hadn't told me, I'd heard about them by carefully listening in on El's therapy sessions. I never missed one. The blanks? Well, I know Eliane enough to fill them in with my own colors. What I'm not sure of, however, is how Jett entered the picture for her. But I don't think anyone ever knew exactly how they ended up in Jett's world if they were to find themselves in it. I didn't really, and I doubt Eliane knew either. He tended to breeze around like the wind. And who knows where the hell wind comes from? All I know about Eliane's early years with Jett was that he was Jett...even way back then.

"I think it's creepy that you have such a fucking crush on a dead dude. It's 2013, El." Jett pulled the book out of Eliane's hand. Typical. "You know, many people in our age group engage in relationships with their peers. They go on dates. They touch each other in the back seats of cars. You're like over here dry-humpin' a ghost."

"Well, I think it's creepy that you think you're so artsy and shit with your Indie band, but have your hair cut like Justin Bieber." (I loved that comeback).

"Eat me." Jett flopped down on the couch next to her.

"See, Fitzgerald would never have said that. He might have needled me a little bit, but he would have made it sound so delicious, I'd think I was eating dessert. I was born in the wrong era."

"Says the girl wearing skinny jeans and cut-off Chuck Taylors." Jett grabbed the book out of her hand, *"Tender is the Night."* He read it like a sports announcer. "Sounds like some sappy chick book. I thought you were better than that, El."

"You're an idiot, Jett. It's not a love story at all. It was super ahead of its time. It's about mental illness, and infidelity, and hedonism—wait you don't know that word—I mean always seeking pleasure, and maybe like a thimble full of really ugly love. I'd think it would fit your image," she flashed air quotes, "to be well-read. Since your music is *so deep*." The quotes again.

"Umm—I know what hedonism means—and I don't understand why it's bad."

"You wouldn't."

"Is the dead dude who wrote this book the one you write letters to?"

"No," she snapped. "I write to his wife, mostly..."

"Is she dead too, or just like some really old lady in a nursing home trying to knit who you're probably freaking out?"

"She's dead too. I don't expect you to understand. I just like to write letters. They seem like they're going somewhere. I write them to a lot of people, not just to dead people."

"Anyone who has the ability to respond? Or are the live ones in like comas or something?"

"My Mom maybe. She could respond, but she doesn't. Sometimes it's *like* she's in a coma." Eliane answered dryly.

"You live with her, El. Why waste the paper?"

"You'll never get it, Jett. Your parents are from a 1960s sitcom. You have a casserole dinner at 6 before time for them to cheer you on at the game. My mother won't even tell me who my father was. She's not really an open book. I can't just *talk* to her. But I still have shit to say."

"Well, speaking of books," he changed the subject, "that one sounds like it sucks."

"I don't know why I'm explaining it to you. Any of it." She hated biting his baited hook.

"But I like watching your face when you explain it. All pissed off like that. I could write a song about just that expression. That one you're trying not to make right now. It didn't take much, but I made you move. I like to watch you move." He grabbed a magazine off the coffee table and propped one foot up.

And then he'd say shit like that so casually...that was Jett. He played guitar in a band that was textbook Emo even though they said it wasn't. But he *did* wear his hair like Justin Bieber 1.0 and was still the apple-cheeked starting pitcher from a nice blue-eyed family. He was as all-American as it got without a damn thing to be mad about. But he liked being *near* madness, intelligent, smart, alluring, destructive, witty, can't-quite-put-your-finger-on, Eliane-special, madness. He wished like hell he had problems, but he didn't. Not one. His parents were happily married, he'd never had a zit in his life, and the sun shined directly out of his ass where all the pretty girls in school liked to sunbathe.

"What do you want? I know you didn't just stumble into the library for no good reason."

"What are you doing after school today?"

"Cheerleading practice. It's basketball season."

"Oh yeah. I love that you make fun of me for my hair, then you're all 'rah rah ree, kick em' in the knee'."

"I like the dancing. It's fun. It's just art that moves."

"Then why not be a dancer?"

"No dance team at this school if you haven't noticed. Wait, of course you have noticed. If there were, you would have nailed them all already. Their pink tights would be fashioned into a dream catcher around your rearview mirror."

"True story." He nodded.

"Plus, I haven't taken real dance since I was a little kid. They offered cheerleading in the rec league for free. So that's where I wound up. It's hard to raise a kid with no man…Mama did what she could." She let her voice wax more southern than it was.

"See right fuckin' there. That's the name of your song. "Mama Did What She Could." It's about a girl who controls everything and loves smart dead dudes and makes these scrunched up faces and wants to be more than a small-town cheerleader and gets all squirmy over the shit I spew for giggles. I'll start on it tonight while you're practicing your splits wondering what I've come up with about you."

Eliane wanted to say something clever back, something to shift the power back to herself, but she couldn't. She could have been charming any other time, but not with him. With him she just flared her nostrils and tried to look more disgusted than annoyed, hoping her recently dyed black hair would help her sell it to him. It's all she had.

"I gotta go." Jett stood up. "I told Taylor I'd walk her to class. She's fussy about it. Loves the basic-bitch high school decorum."

"Why don't you write about that? There's you a title, *Basic Bitch*." Eliane rolled her heavily lined eyes. There was that sass.

"Because then she might put a lock on her jeans, and we can't have that now, can we? But don't be mean. She *is* your cheer captain." He poked. "Have a little respect."

"So, what did you want with me, exactly? As much as I adore the chit- chat, I'd rather read."

"You're busy. Doesn't matter."

"But what did you want?"

"Doesn't matter. You can't do it."

"So, you're just not gonna tell me, then?"

"Sucks, right? It was probably nothing. But you'll wonder." Jett winked, threw his backpack on his almost-manish shoulders, and walked out.

Eliane shook her head and went back to her book. Then she read the same page four damn times.

CHAPTER 7

Asheville, NC
Now

Eliane plopped down on the big blue velvet couch—which was the most fabulous part of therapy—to declare, "I'm going to Paris in a month. I found a job. I'd like to just Zoom with you if it's all the same. No use getting to know a new face, but if you're not into that, I'll need a referral to another therapist. But post-Covid, most of you work like this anyway. You tell me what to do."

"So, you are going, then? You're going to that audition you mentioned a couple months ago?"

"Yep. I'm doing it. But I was always doing it. I wasn't putting in all that practice for nothing. I don't change my mind on things like that." Eliane always declared things so suddenly in therapy. It was either for her own amusement, or because she didn't have the ability not to. She wasn't sure which, but I could tell. She did it for some kind of control. It always cultivated a reaction, and by controlling others' reactions she could steer the conversation. And Eliane liked control even more than she liked leftover green beans cold from the fridge at 1 a.m. She also enjoyed wearing her own quirks like a kid with a sticker on her shirt. She put it out there and waited for people to exclaim.

"And you think it's wise to relocate before you know if you make it? Can't you audition, then prepare to move later if it goes well?" And Dr. Vitale loved to appear nonchalant, but the scrawl that graffitied her notepad proved otherwise. She had all the concerns. Some were genuine while others were covering bases because she was always afraid a client would off themselves, and then she'd get sued. It's intriguing to watch the games that people play.

"I can't be here anymore. If it wasn't there, it'd just be somewhere else. I hate living with my mom. I don't have a boyfriend, well anymore. I had to quit my job, and they weren't interested in hiring me back when I finally put the cuckoo back in the clock. I mean, it was a shitty gig; I was waiting tables, and who the hell wants that job back anyway? The job I found in Paris seems fun, and I'll get to write. That's the best part."

"What's the job?" Dr. Vitale asked, her voice unable to project the optimism her expression had also poorly attempted.

"I'm ghost writing for a lifestyle blogger. It's some rich girl who shops and travels and promotes large events. She's one of those influencer types...takes good pictures and does interesting things, but she can't write well enough to even caption a photo. She needs someone to do the articles for the actual blog and make them interesting. You know, "Mykonos' Top Ten Best Kept Secrets According to Skyla", who of course is the only person on the planet who could know such juiciness. Whatever. It's writing. I'll find ways to get creative with it."

"And you're OK with that? Being the ghost? That doesn't sound like you."

"She's not the first person to take my words and use them as her own. You know that. At least she's upfront about it and paying me for it. I'll be able to afford a one-bedroom easily enough off it. She's pretty big. She was one of the rejects on *The Bachelor* a couple years back, so the money and opportunity to meet people is the draw. Plus, it's professional writing experience. Her name is Skyla Free. Look her up. That's her real name, too..."

"You don't like playing second fiddle normally, Eliane. This is as 'support staff' as it gets. Have you considered that?"

"She could help me get in front of people I'd never be able to get in front of and be a part of things I would never get to be a part of. She's in with whatever it is we all want to be into. I'm human too. I want all the pretty things as much as the next girl. I'd think you'd understand that, *Doctor* Melissa Vitale. Didn't you dream about having the best parking spots and getting special mortgage rates? Didn't you prance in front of mirrors in a white coat and blush the first time you wore one for real in your residency?"

She continued, no desire to answer Eliane, which proved more things about her. "What if this isn't a ticket into her world? What if this is less high-society meet-and-greets and more an office without a view? Can you be happy with that? Have you tried to think of this without romanticizing it?"

"Everyone always tells you to be optimistic until you are, then they tell you to become a slave to all the drawbacks. Everyone thinks pessimism is prudence when it comes down to acting on a decision. This thing is promising, and it's OK to dream a little. This is something real. No one else has ever wanted to pay me to write, and she thinks I'm good. Just look her up, like I said."

"Will do." Dr. Vitale nodded and scribbled something in her prized notes again. "So, this move...let's talk more about it."

"To talk me out of it? I'm not interested in that."

"No, just to navigate it."

"OK." Eliane relented, her tight bun pulling at the temples so much that she could feel it when she nodded. She liked the bun though. It pulled her face from 27 back to 21.

"What do you hope to accomplish from this move? What are your expectations?"

Eliane thought to herself for a second. She knew what Dr. Vitale must think. She was looking at a patient with severe obsessive-compulsive disorder, pushing 30 years old, who'd recently endured a trauma, then had suddenly taken up ballet after a short stent in the psych ward. Now, only one calendar year later, the bent geriatric ballerina had decided to move from the only town in which she'd ever resided to take a shot that was a long one for even incredibly talented, younger, and more normal people.

"I'm not manic. I don't get manic." Eliane replied. "I'm motivated."

"I didn't ask if you were manic."

"Didn't you, though?" Eliane smiled sweetly to temper her words, though no matter what she said, it almost never came off harsh. She came off like a safe space. "A spade is spade, Dr. Vitale. Just show me your cards."

"So, you've said," Dr. Vitale sighed, but reluctantly continued. "OK. I wanted to know your expectations, because I am concerned this is a snap decision that you believe will fix all your problems. Some women suddenly change their hair. You are suddenly changing your address and going a long way from a place where you have any support system."

"What support system? I just told you I have no job and no relationship."

"You have your mother."

Eliane rolled her eyes. "No one has ever had my mother. My mother belongs to herself."

Dr. Vitale sighed, "I just want to know, why now?"

"Why not now?"

"Are you running?"

"From what?"

"What's happened. The memories. The intangible, of course, but also, the fact that *he* still exists."

"Who? Jett or the serial killer? Not that it matters. Neither one is interested in me. But, to answer your question, no. I'm not running. I'm—I'm growing."

"I was referring to the murderer still at large. He came very close to your world, likely knows who you are. I don't know anyone who would be comfortable with that." Eliane never revealed to the therapist that she knows *exactly* who he is, not his name, but enough. She couldn't because it involved the thing she should have told the police long before now, the piece of information she got just before she was hospitalized, something she wasn't equipped to deal with then and was afraid it was too late to tell now.

"I'm not afraid of him. He won't come for me." This part was true. She wasn't afraid of him, just afraid of the memories of what he did.

"It would be normal if you are. Eliane, he murdered your —"

"I know what he did. And I know my meltdown came soon after realizing the police had the wrong guy. But honestly, it was more about what Jett did that pushed me over the edge. Because that made me have to face what *I did* to cause all of this. And you can tell me it isn't my fault a million times. I didn't kill the girl, but I *did* have a role in it. That's just the truth. But I've faced it. Now I just want to move on with my life. I want to do something free and different and fun where I'm not the crazy girl and nobody knows me."

"I get all of that. I do." She leaned in, elbows on her knees, ready to level with her patient. "But Eliane, you must realize that there is a list of cons for such a big change. This time last year you were in a mental rehabilitation facility. Those are the cards in your hand, so look at them. That is my goal. You've come so far, but it was one year ago. You still have your habit of writing the letters, which tells me that you aren't completely healed. I don't say any of this to be negative, but to examine the situation. Have you examined it? Have *you* seen the spades and called them spades?"

"I've always been a dreamer. I've always wanted out. My problems have kept me here. My circumstances have made me cautious, and it's changed nothing. Then there was, you know, the big things, then the things that followed that. It was a lot, and it was terrible. It did hold me back, but I'm finished with any of those things dictating my life. I realized that on about day three in the hospital. I saw where the bondage had left me, and I didn't like it. I need to decide where I go next, and I've decided on Paris. If I hate it there, I'll go somewhere else. I'm not stopping therapy. I'm just taking a job and changing some scenery. What's so unhealthy about that?"

"Nothing, necessarily, it's just—"

"Fear. Your concern is just fear. I realize that I've had plenty of problems in the place I've always been. I have problems here; I'll have them there, too. I know that. Hell, I'm only looking at apartments with odd numbers in the addresses. I know I'm a little bit batshit. I know I'll count the stairs every time I leave my apartment. I know I'll have a panic attack at some point. I'm just not scared of that, and you're paid to be. It would be reckless medical practice for you to encourage me to take a chance. I get it. I just need to you to be my therapist, not my gatekeeper. I don't think I'm making a move to Heaven. I'm only moving to Paris."

CHAPTER 8

The entire room was filled with boxes, mostly with Jack Daniels and Grey Goose written on the sides of them. Leftover liquor boxes are, of course, the way any true southerner moves their things from point A to point B. I'd had a shirt or two shoved into a Malibu Rum box myself. I didn't realize that there were stores which sold bona fide packing materials until I was an adult. I thought that anyone making a move just showed up at the local liquor store, called the ABC Store in North Carolina, and begged for boxes. If they were out, you just had to come back in a day or two. No one was going to pay for packing peanuts and collapsible boxes.

Eliane lucked out on her first try and hit the motherload. The boxes were already filled mostly with her clothes—not at all neatly folded, but all in odd numbers of stacks. OCD wasn't about neatness. Eliane heard people say it all the time. *I'm so OCD* about this or that, mainly because they liked order or had some sort of quirk. They didn't understand that OCD isn't about keeping things neat. It's about the underlying issue. Keeping shoes in even rows because one likes the aesthetic of it is being a Type A personality. Keeping shoes in a certain order because you're trying to create a rule in hopes to control something is OCD. If eight shoes in each row means your husband won't die in a plane crash, its OCD. If eight shoes in each row means it looks pretty to you, chances are, though you're probably a little bit anal, you're OK.

Eliane wasn't one of those late-era-millennial-borderline-gen-zers who stayed at home until she was almost 30. She'd been on her own plenty. But she'd been staying with her mother again since *everything* had happened. In some ways, everything had sort of always been happening, been culminating into what it all is now. But she moved back into her childhood home, an aging doublewide with a crippled trampoline out front since the chaos machine all overloaded and blew up the factory. Before that, she'd had a couple different roommates in different seasons of life. She'd had a college roommate, then later, Zen, the one whom she lived with in a studio by the river in West Asheville. I enjoyed watching him when he got in the way of her. He was an eccentric young gentleman (it would be weird to call him "guy" or "dude") who wore boys' sizes in suits and painted strange pictures. He fit the area well. Eliane only halfway did. I always thought of West Asheville as Asheville junior—for people who wanted to be downtown but weren't willing or able to pay for it. It's a charming little community, half full of hippies and half full of older natives. It's where liberals and conservatives hate each other the most, yet still leave homegrown cucumbers on one another's doorsteps. And the whole place, indoors and out, smelled like pachouli and sweet tea. Welcome to the weirdest place in The South. It fit Eliane well enough because it was conflicted and adorable, just like her. If she were a house, she would have been a circa 1920 arts and crafts bungalow like the ones that lined those streets. Her existence had all been so sweet before it was sour, a bottle of wine left to turn to vinegar. But now, there was a new season, a new wine, bottled differently. Maybe this one would keep—like the little refurbished cottages.

Eliane made her way to the back of her closet, which was still 75 percent full of childhood items, like beanie babies and Disney VHS tapes whose value never panned out or old cheerleading uniforms stuffed into cracked plastic totes. She dragged three boxes out awkwardly, balancing them one on top of another underneath her skinny arms. She knew what she'd find there inside the one she stuffed to the back of the closet behind a dollhouse that looked like it had barely survived an earthquake. The boxes pressed against the unfinished wall back there weren't as old as some of the others and had only been shoved away with the nineties to get them out of her sight. However, she knew it was time to unearth them. It wasn't because she stumbled upon them. They didn't surprise her; she'd seeked them out after years of leaving them untouched, and she knew she had to pack them. They couldn't stay there, left behind like a buried pet. But finding them made her itch, even though it had been on purpose. And when she itched, she had to scratch—in very specific ways.

She went to her desk and pulled out a pen and a piece of paper. She always used a good pen—well fabulous, more than good. She wasn't writing with a famed Mont Blanc or anything. The ink was standard, and the mechanics of the pen as simple as a Bic from the office supply aisle at Target. It was probably ordered from Amazon, truth be told. But it was pretty, and it mimicked a vintage quill. It mimicked *her*. With it, she began writing another letter she wasn't supposed to write anymore.

> *Dear Lux,*
> *I found the dead flowers when I was packing.*
> *I found the ones Jett gave you and then the ones I had later-on. Jett's bouquet was huge. I wonder if he ever knew how they pissed you off so much when they showed up at the door. You knew they weren't 'I'm thinking of you' flowers as much as they were 'I still want to sleep with you' flowers. He didn't know you were smart. He knew you were pretty, but he did know that you were something else too, I'm sure of it, even if you*

weren't...even if he said you weren't. That's how he screwed up the most. Had he dug into your head, he would have known that you were beautiful because of your mind, not despite it...you just had trouble showing it to him. He was a hard guy to reveal things to. I knew that, despite some of the things I said that were taken the wrong way...used the wrong way...but I don't want to talk about that again. You've already heard all of the apologies you're ever going to for the trouble I brought into your world, too—I know I'm not the only one affected by all this. You're not interested in any more of them, anyway. I know that. That's not what this is about.

I'm still smiling thinking back to that bouquet he sent. I don't remember what he'd done. You'd been on maybe one or two dates. The whole thing was so short-lived. It was unlike him to send flowers, and I knew they meant that you'd impressed him in some way—even if he never had the guts to say it or the sense to admit it. I remember they'd wilted and died altogether. You left them sitting in that old Princess House vase from the '80s that had belonged to your mom. You'd finally decided to trash them, but I stepped in.

"No! Don't do it!" I bounded across the room like Roxy on a scent. Roxy was the bird dog we had while I was growing up. She killed squirrels more than birds, then left them on the porch as gifts for us like a cat with a mouse. Did I ever tell you about Roxy? Anyway...

"Why? They're dead." You laughed.

"I don't believe in dead. They're beautiful," I responded. "We're just conditioned to think they are only good while they're perfect." I took them and pressed them into a book for you.

So, I kept them all. I thought you might want them one day. Maybe you do? I could bring them to you, if so. I want to, despite everything.

More than that, I thought it was a shame for them to only be beautiful for a week or two. I also kept them to admire them myself, so it was partly selfish. I appreciated them. Maybe it was because no one had ever gotten me flowers. Still haven't, actually, not even precious Jake who I'm sure I also ruined. Jake would have been more suited for you than me—but I have no idea where he even is now. I can't believe I didn't even get any get-well-soon flowers when I was...in the hospital. I hate even writing that.

I've always felt like I was something like a wilted flower, never quite in bloom, though that's not what other people saw—still don't. Maybe that's why I always liked them all shriveled up that way. Maybe it was all sad. It certainly is looking at them now. Still, I think I'll put them out in my new place when I get to Paris. I know you'd hate that. You'd find something morbid and gothic about the whole thing. You'd tell me to toss them, especially since most of them are from Jett. But, like my story, he's part of yours. Good or bad. Jett is the tie that binds us. And I will probably frame his dead flowers alongside mine and hang them on my wall. At least that way they have purpose; they've meant something. And isn't that what life is all about, just to have meant anything at all?

"Hey El—" Her mother came around the doorway.

"Yeah?" Eliane quickly folded the paper in the fashion her pre-teen self would have and slammed her journal shut.

"What are you doin'?" The woman somehow even skinnier, but an otherwise twin version of Eliane asked.

"Packing. Going through things. Making this happen." She rifled through her belongings, trying to appear as resolute as she could.

"Were you writin' somethin'?" She pursed the once-full lips that were now drawn from sucking on the end of one too many cigarettes.

"Oh yeah. I do that, you know..."

"Only with an ink pen and fancy paper when you're writin' those letters. Was that what you were doin'?" Her voice was calm but sharp and painted more Appalachian than her daughter's. The sharp part wasn't just for this though. It was always sharp. She was accusatory even when she had no reason to be. She could sound that way asking someone if they wanted a glass of ice water.

"I don't have to mail it," Eliane whispered.

"Except that you will. That's the problem. You will be compelled to do it, and you'll give in. It completes that cycle for you. You think that will undo the fact that you feel guilty for—"

"Mom—"

"I'm tired of tiptoein' around this, El. You say you're fine and you're ready to move out on your own and write and dance and do these great big things. You say you're in control. But you're still doin' this. I thought you might could stop it once you started to feel some better, but you won't. You're goin' to get in serious trouble. There's a restrainin' order in effect, Eliane. This is literally considered stalking. *You* are considered the *stalker*. Maybe you should say that out loud with me. My name is Eliane Pangolin, and I am *stalk-ing* someone." She pronounced the *ing*, so she was serious. "Do you understand that? It's time to face this. If you don't stop, you could literally go to jail."

"Nah, they'd probably just send me back to the nuthouse."

"Don't be cute with me. It ain't funny." Her mom's chest turned splotchy, the dots blending with the sunspots. "And they might. Have you forgotten what a treat that was for ya?"

"I get it. And I can just feel your enjoyment in your moment to give me that famous go-wash-your-face-Pangolin-women-are-tough love."

"Don't start with me, El. I don't have the energy for it." She ran her bony fingers down her cheeks like she hoped her face would slough off with them.

"What am I startin'?" Eliane mocked the accent and shoved the files of pressed flowers into a box.

"Don't start makin' this about me. Don't pick a fight to get out of answerin' to me."

"I just don't want to be 'handled.' I'm not some crazy stalker. I just have a process. I know that you get that. But then you start treating me like I'm insane. I have OCD. I have anxiety. I've been through some really bad things and had to take a little mental vacation. I think anyone might have. But I'm not insane. I'm aware of action and consequence. I don't follow the directions of voices that don't exist. I am right here in reality with you. And reality might be harder than insanity. It's why I cope how I cope. It would feel like a million bucks to be blissfully ignorant of all the shit I go through, trust me. But I'm not. I feel everything, and I'm painfully lucid for all of it."

"I know that. But you've got to admit that everything you've been up to lately seems a little bit off-the-wall. I'm your mother. Can you fault me for bein' scared for ya? Can you blame me for watchin' closely?"

"No, I can't," Eliane softened. "It's because it *is* off the wall. I'm not a brick in that wall you speak so highly of, that wall you would have done anything to have been on. Never was. That part isn't the OCD; that part is me. But when you pair it with mental illness, everyone freaks out. I change from talented and unique to crazy real quick. But I'm not. I just need some freedom. I never longed to be normal, with the good paper towels and better brand of spaghetti sauce like you did." Eliane turned back to her task and started whistling Pink Floyd though she knew her mother would never understand the reference. Her mother didn't understand many references. She understood nine to five. She understood asking bosses for permission. She understood working her way up from bank teller to assistant manager. She understood enjoying life at the same beach, in the same mediocre hotel, two weeks each year, on paid leave. She understood the fight to be average, a height she could never quite climb to reach.

"I'm not sayin' to be like everybody else—"

"Yes, you are." Eliane looked at her time-worn face that had once mimicked her own, without expression, begging for a moment of truth between them.

Her mother only rolled her eyes and rubbed her hands over the splotches on her forehead those two-week paid vacations in the sun had given her. "I made spaghetti, by the way, if you want some. Don't worry, it's the off-brand sauce, nothin' better."

CHAPTER 9

The University of North Carolina Asheville
Back Then

The University of North Carolina Asheville is a hippie school. On any given morning in late January—despite the temperature—at least a handful of students can be seen walking barefoot to class while drinking something weird out of a mason jar. But the writing program is good, and the sports teams are division one. These are precisely the reasons why both Eliane and Jett ended up there for their freshmen years of college. Those are the practical reasons anyway. Their complete codependency on one another was, of course, the other reason. This is also where I went to college, the place where I first met the both of them, the place where my part in whatever all this is, began.

Though Jett had loved football the most, his stature was built more for baseball. And though he also claimed he only cared about music, and would soon choose it for his major, it was baseball that got him to college at half price. By the time I met him, his hair was long enough to be pulled into a manbun underneath the baseball cap, and his tattoo of Dave Grohl pole dancing (Grohl on a pole—he thought it was *so* clever) snuck out from underneath the sleeve of his uniform. But that wasn't for another couple of weeks.

I met Eliane first, on the day she moved onto the second floor of Mills Hall. She came in the 2014 spring semester, though I believe Jett had started on time back in the fall. I later discovered Eliane had spent six months—from her high school graduation till the day before she stumbled into my world—determined to finish a novel about a teenager in foster care who wrote a novel about a teenager in foster care. I can't remember how many levels deep the book about a book got. It was very *Inception*, and I never got a chance to read it myself. She had indeed finished the novel, but decided it was complete garbage, threw the thumb drive it was on into the ocean during family vacation, and accepted her offer for admission to UNCA. That's where she met me. It was before I was watching her and before she was writing the unwanted letters to me—before we'd began following each other. It was before she hated herself for continuing to interlope into my world, no clue that I'm doing just the same. It was when there was no tangled web that I'm not ready to explain, when things were just...simple...for a moment in time.

"This entire place smells like a number two pencil," she remarked, her tiny nose scrunched up. That was the first thing I ever heard her say.

She stumbled into the dorm room dragging three things with her: an oversized shoulder bag that I imagined held her dainty clothes, an inflatable palm tree, and a poster of a man with a strange middle part and sunglasses on. The words on the poster read "Drop it like F. Scott."

I knelt down to help her roll up the poster that had fallen on the ground as she ambled into the room. She'd reluctantly let go of it in the struggle through the doorway. I could tell she didn't want to, and that maybe the poster was even more valuable to her than the pseudo palm.

"Who is this?" I asked her in my small voice, looking at the poster without a clue.

"That's the great American dreamer," she answered like I'd asked her favorite color—a simple answer extended, no inflection, no explanation. I knew then that I was to find out who he was on my own and ask no more questions until I was prepared to discuss it with some intelligence. Yet, at the same time, there was no judgment. She was extending me the time to prepare properly.

"I think you're in room B," was all I could come up with after she spoke. I was already intimidated by her. There could have been no poster. There could have been no words. I would have still been affected by her. She had an air. I wanted to know her, and I wanted her to like me.

"Who used to be in room B?" She eyed the door.

"I don't know. I mean, I know. Her name was Brittany something. She didn't want to be called Brittany, though...she had some nickname like Ice or Frost...something winter-sounding. She always kept the door shut and never went to class. I guess she unenrolled. She was never happy about anything." I rambled while I lurked like an enamored toddler who'd discovered an older little girl who wore lip gloss.

She made her way passed me and into the perfectly square room with white walls, brown carpet, and a single window that could be hand-cranked opened.

Eliane looked around the room, unimpressed, then looked and me and said, "Chill."

"I'm sorry?"

"Chill. Was that her nickname?"

"Oh, yeah, that was it. How'd you know?"

"It's carved on the headboard of the bed." She threw her stuff down on the bare mattress.

I still lingered in the hallway, though I wanted to see her unpack. I'm interested in the things people keep. It says a lot about them.

"What the hell am I doing here?" She mumbled under her breath, throwing a stack of vinyl records, then three or four super old books onto her bed.

I then watched her reluctantly plug the palm tree into the outlet by her desk. She never took her sunglasses off and then laid down underneath the out-of-place tree that would have looked like a pool toy had it not been adorned with white Christmas lights. It was like she was at Myrtle Beach on spring break—if Myrtle Beach had a love affair with some beach in France which I knew nothing about.

I tip-toed around the corner to get a better look but wasn't planning on getting caught. I'm much better at that now.

"Want to join me?" The large sunglasses that looked like they belonged on a rich vacationer in Monaco lowered to the bridge of her nose for an instant.

"Oh—umm, no thank you." I replied hesitantly but didn't look away.

"You, darling, are about the most perfect thing I think I've ever seen," Eliane returned the sunglasses to her eyes and spoke like a Hollywood starlet far past her prime. "Look at that long strawberry blonde hair, but with tan skin—eyelashes women would kill you to snatch off your body. You are shockingly gorgeous."

"Thank you," I laughed nervously, though I'd heard it a million times. People said I was beautiful. They had since I could remember, since toddlerhood when I'd began my reign as a pageant queen winning Baby Miss Greensboro. I could picture the sash around my chubby infant body, drool down my chin, in the frilly dress.

I thought she was beautiful too, offbeat of course, but I would have rather been that kind of beautiful where someone might have wondered about a thought I'd had, or a dream maybe. I would have loved to have been the kind of beautiful that makes people want to ask questions, the kind that makes men who've tired of sleeping with super models stumble over words and wonder what has captured them so much. But I was regularly gorgeous, no doubt a classic beauty, but typical. I wore

Abercrombie & Fitch when people still wore Abercrombie & Fitch. I ate Easy Mac. I watched Glee and crushed on Cory Monteith; God rest his soul. I liked what people liked and did what people do. I dated dumb boys and never spoke to them before I'd let them paw at me in front seats before my father flashed the porch lights. And I sang only nice songs when people told me to sing.

As I continued to look at my new creature kicked back beneath the fake tree, I wondered if she knew she was fascinating. I probably should have told her, but I didn't have the guts. I never had the guts to say anything. I can only be insightful when I'm the one looking on, but never when I was the one being observed in return. I was groomed to please judges, but for this, I'd had no training. I wasn't sure yet how to please her, so I stood very still, and I took my vow to watch.

"I'm Eliane. I'm not French, just the name—and my mother didn't even pronounce it right." She began to tap the ground as if there were music playing. I noticed an odd rhythm to it even then.

"I—I'm Lux." I said in an almost-whisper, not knowing then that I was destined to become *that Lux*, the one watching her while she writes me letters which she's been asked by a court of law not to write. It's...*complicated* now.

"Like in The Virgin Suicides." She nodded, approving. "Right on."

I looked visibly confused and gave away my lack of literary knowledge, and even my pop-culture movie knowledge. My free time was always spent being groomed or taking voice lessons. I wondered if she already thought I was an idiot.

"Jeffrey Eugenides. Give it a read. It's dark and interesting, and simple in some way. It's a good one. Super fucked up, too. But doesn't that always make it a little better?"

"What?"

"Things that are a little messed up."

"Oh…I—I don't know," I thought of all the time I spent trying to be perfect.

"Just read it. You'll see."

"Will do." I smiled nervously.

"Lux…that means light. So does Eliane. So bizarre," she paused to deliberate, "well this must be fate, then."

"Must be." I shrugged though I believed it hard.

"Oh, I meant to ask you, do you know anything about that notice on the door?"

"What notice?"

"There was like this flyer thing posted on all of the doors when I came in—kind of freaky. It said all females should travel in pairs, not to be alone at night. It said there was a possible predator in the area they'd been made aware of or something. You were here last semester. Has that been like an ongoing thing?"

"First I've heard of it." And it was. "But I don't really watch the news or anything."

"I mean, this is a college campus. Something probably went down between a frat boy and his girlfriend or something. Well, here, more likely a hippie boy out of his mind on shrooms…anyway, I was just curious. The note seemed all official, and I am a whispy little thing—might need to pack the mace. I'm sure it's nothing, though. I'm from here. Nothing ever happens."

"I wouldn't worry. The college is so official about everything. Dear God, don't ever get a parking ticket. The cops love to find cars parked in the wrong place. It's all they're here for; they're so bored. If you get three, they will literally kick you out of school. It's so stupid. And I have two already. The lots they want us to park in are a mile away and always full."

"Well, there's the proof that nothing really ever happens around here." El kicked back under the palm tree again. "Damn, I wish I had a cigar."

CHAPTER 10

After a few weeks of living with Eliane, I finally met him. Jett Jorgenson breezed into my life like the first winds of a hurricane. They're curious, but unassuming at first, foreboding, but not a bit dangerous yet. Some defiant part of the human spirit can't wait to walk right onto the beach, arms stretched out, begging that wind to blow them down. That's how he entered any new space, and I imagine I'd felt it just the same as everyone else. I could feel the strange zephyr that flowed with him, and the little hairs at my temples moved and tickled me, causing the goosebumps to show up next. Eliane used to use that word, *zephyr*, when she wrote. I could make word-of-the-day toilet paper off all the ones she taught me.

Before I met him in person, El had mentioned going off to see him here or there, usually at places too cool for me where I'd need a fake I.D. to get in. I had one. A bunch of girlfriends and I all got one from a skeezy guy older than our dads after our high school graduation—in case we wanted to hit up the clubs on "senior week" at Myrtle Beach—which is where every freshly commenced teenager in either of the Carolinas flocked to immediately after walking the stage, smiling innocently for their grandparents. I was too chicken to ever use the I.D. I only ever tried it once, but that was much later.

I first laid eyes on Jett on a warm spring evening in late March. He'd just helped the bulldogs tip the scales for a losing record. I assumed he'd come by to sulk like all the jocks do after a loss. I'd dated two football players and a basketball player in high school, and they were all the same. After a loss, I wasn't to say a word. I was to watch them drink cheap beer and brood in the corner while I mourned with them. I imagined Jett would be the same, that he wouldn't want to be spoken to and would also scowl and drink beer on the outskirts of the room to show everyone how serious he was. But he didn't. That night I realized quickly that I'd never met anyone like Jett.

"El...El...Ellllllllll." He burst through the door without knocking.

I poked my head out of suite A into the small living area to say in my even smaller voice, "Oh, um, I think she's in the shower."

He smiled with half his lightly stubbled mouth. He didn't say anything. He didn't acknowledge that he'd entered without knocking. He walked over to the burgundy standard-issue couch that looked like it belonged in a dentist's office and plopped down, pulling his hat down over his light eyes.

"I'm out." Eliane called as she opened the bathroom door and stepped into the common area. "What the fuck, Jett?" She wrapped the towel tighter. "I told you I'd text you after I got out of the shower."

"What? You're not naked. I'm bored. Hurry up, and let's go do something."

"Don't *you* want a shower? You look like you'd smell like a jock strap." She took a step back from him.

"I'll take one here, I guess. I threw some clothes in my bat bag."

"What's wrong with your dorm?"

"It's fucking disgusting. I don't want to get athlete's foot. And everybody's pissed, anyway. We lost. I just don't want to pretend to mope around like the world's turned to shit or something over it. I don't have the energy for it."

"I get that. The pouting is so stupid. Well, let me get out of this wet towel, and we'll go somewhere and not pout, alright?" That's when I first heard it.

Eliane wanted him. She spoke so coolly, more coolly than I ever could, but she wanted him. She'd given him just enough hell. She mentioned the towel just barely, strategically, hoping he'd reply. And he gave her nothing. It was the air she sucked into the only cavity she'd ever had. He was her weak spot in that hard enamel. I'd smelled it as easily as I'd heard it. Jett Jorgenson was Eliane's kryptonite, her blind spot, her F. Scott. (I looked him up).

"Hurry up. It's getting late and everywhere with the good bands will be crowded as hell."

And she hurried up. It was the first time I'd ever seen her follow directions of any kind.

"You're coming with, Lux. Jett, did you meet Lux?" She called while she rushed around.

"I met Lux." He said dryly then looked at me. "You like good music, Lux?"

"I—umm—"

"You listen to the radio. I can tell," he said before I could respond, walking toward me where he'd throw one arm around my shoulders. "The only song you can even think of right now is Pharrell Williams' Happy, because it's all they play. It's OK; it isn't your fault. The "man" wants you to like that song right now. No one ever taught you. You were probably busy learning to waltz for cotillion or some weak shit. We'll fix it."

"Stop being sanctimonious about music, Jett. It's pretentious as fuck." She cursed more around him. "But he *is* right. He knows good music, and we will fix it." She adjusted her black crop top— she also dressed differently around him.

"I'm not gonna shower," Jett announced.

"I'm sure you're not. I imagine it's impossible that you think your sweat stinks, since your shit doesn't." She winked at him.

"Precisely." He replied, his arm still around me. "Come on, Lux. Let's go get you an education."

He smelled like fresh laundry.

CHAPTER 11

Asheville, NC
Now

I watched Eliane bebop into the U-Haul rental office—still in tights and a ballerina bun from practice—and fill out the paperwork to rent a massive vehicle that she would attempt to drive about 900 miles. And I had doubts. It wasn't because she was a woman or because she was a wannabe ballerina, or even because she looked so small. It was that she was Eliane. She wasn't the best at driving her little four-cylinder sedan and had only recently began driving again at all. I'd made the mistake of going for a "little cruise" over the Blue Ridge Parkway with her before. We almost took a little Thelma-and-Louise-style cruise over the edge of a hair-pin curve more than once. The memory flashed through my mind as happy somehow...one of those Eliane happies I couldn't ever quite put a finger on. And she was as confident now as she had been then. She walked up to the counter and presented her move to the staff just like she had to everyone else.

"I'm moving to Paris," she blurted.

"OK..." answered the heavy man with the greasy brown combover.

"I'll probably need the truck for at least three days. I need the smallest one you have. It's not because I'm small. But you know that...um, I don't have all that much stuff. It's just me—wait, I shouldn't tell you that, should I? I've pointed out that I'm small and travelling alone to a stranger. All the serial killer shows start with the girl skipping in and announcing she's travelling by herself, and then the guy—and then there's the actual one they're looking for, but I don't think—"

He waived her quiet with his dingey hand. "Umm, Ma'am, I'm a little bit confused."

"Oh, I'm sorry. I don't think you're a serial killer, I mean, I doubt it. I had this experience; well, I can't go into all of that. It's really heavy for polite conversation. I'm trying to put it behind me. I'm sorry, I—" Eliane eyed him for a second. His glasses did look like they came from a serial killer starter kit. Then she looked at her feet, more solemn suddenly. I couldn't tell if she felt bad for joking about something she'd gotten so close to in real life, or if she was finally self-aware enough to feel embarrassed. I didn't have that much experience watching her get embarrassed, and, until now, I wasn't sure that she could.

"No, it isn't that—"

"What? You don't think a little woman in a ballerina get-up can drive a 'big ol' truck? I can't very well haul all my crap in my Honda Accord. I'm having the car shipped to me later, but I can drive that truck, sir." She shot venom with her cat-like eyes even though I think she *was* a little bit afraid that she couldn't drive that "big ol' truck." She was madder and more nervous than she was joking. But she was always cute. I think it was her size. Pixi like. Fun size. Everyone loved that about her, and she had no idea.

"Umm, no. I don't understand why you're here. I don't think you can drive a truck to Paris, Ma'am." His tone was half haughty and half concerned.

"Oh, no...not Paris, France. I'm moving to Paris, Texas. It's about an hour from Dallas. They have their own Eiffel Tower, though. I have dreams that you can also purchase fresh baguettes on any corner. I kind of see it as barbecue and boulangeries, but who knows? It's probably all barbecue and no baguettes. A girl can dream, though, right?"

I think she'd been leaving the Texas part out on purpose. She wanted people to think it was France, that she was pirouetting off to Paris to dance at the Moulin Rouge. She'd never admit that. She'd act like it was unintended, just an oversight, but everyone, even Eliane Pangolin, projected an image sometimes. Everyone had an inauthenticity of some kind. This was hers. When something wasn't as artsy and weird and outside of the lay man's grasp as much as she hoped, she made it seem that it was. She wouldn't lie, but she would shape things like a potter shaped mud on a spinning disc. She'd wield clay into something prettier than just mud. She needed people to strive to be her, to be amused by her. She needed it as much as she hated it...the muse's curse.

"Well, that makes a little more sense. Here, fill this out, then," he handed her a clipboard and pen. "Why are you moving to the Lone Star State?"

"Well, my writing career is currently in the toilet...and I've been dealing with some things that suck, like the big life things—love, hate, life, death, and the likes. You know how it is. I've been living at home with my emotionally unavailable mother and am just realizing there's nothing here for me. I just want to try somewhere new and better, get some inspiration along the way. Plus, this town is just fresh out of any suitable man to sleep with." She spoke so fast that it seemed like her tone would bounce like a lowrider car speeding down a straight stretch of road, but it didn't. It was casual and forthcoming, careless even. I wished I could tell my little open book that the man across the counter didn't want to hear about *any* of it. I wished I could pick his chin up off the dirty tile floor. But she carried on, and I cringed. Oversharing was another one of her therapies, and I also think, one of her amusements. And right then, she was a cat with an unassuming mouse.

"When I was bored at night during the worst of it, when I was dealing with my head, I'd binge watched Dallas Cowboys Cheerleaders: Making the Team as a guilty pleasure. Honestly, I thought I'd laugh at it. I mean, it's adult cheerleaders on CMT, but man, I really dug it. Those girls work so hard, and they're so... fabulous, I guess is the word. So, I thought 'I used to dance and cheer. I could totally do that.' So, I'm going to move to Texas and be one now. Sounds a little bizarre for a writer, I know. But, why? Why can't I be both? I won't be young forever, so go for it, right? Can you imagine the rush of all eyes on you? The pressure? The unmatchable, delicious anxiety? The things I'll learn about myself? About the other girls, all struggling, all from somewhere not as shiny as where they want to be? That'll give me something to write about—that and living in the redneck Paris. It has to, right? I'll have a little weird journey and bestseller in no time." *Didn't. Even. Flinch.*

The man's mustache twitched, and he looked physically terrified. He tried not to make any sudden movements.

"You asked." She folded her arms.

"I did." He stared blankly.

Eliane then softened her voice a bit and added, for the pure sake of her own fun, "I'm a little bit crazy," in a whispered tone. Then she winked at him. She always winked when she was pleased with herself. Making another human squirm probably pleased her more than anything.

"Well, umm, enjoy Texas." The man jerked the clipboard back. "You've got a good driver's license and you're old enough, so, safe travels I suppose." The statement sounded more like a question.

Eliane snatched up the keys, blew the man a kiss, and did chaine turns out of the building just to screw with the dude one more time.

CHAPTER 12

The University of North Carolina Asheville
Back Then

"Are you watching *Twlight*?" Eliane appeared in my doorway chomping on popcorn. "Dear God, you are actually watching *Twlight*. You are. And on purpose, too."

"I can't help it. I was a Twi-hard. It's embarrassing, I know." I slapped my laptop shut.

"I wasn't judging—well, maybe a little bit. I know it was this pop culture phenomenon when we were tweens, but I kind of get it. People like that kind of love, especially when it's all twisted up. Everyone wants to be the muse for the brooding bad boy. Everyone wants to be the one reason on earth he'll change, his little bright spot. It's fine for escapism, but damn, just remember it's fiction. None of us are really anyone's Bella Swan. No one will smell us in the air one day, then like dedicate their whole existence to us. No one admires anyone that much, no healthy person, anyway."

"Yeah, I know it's fiction. Vampires, werewolves, true love." I grinned. "But all that's pretty cynical of you. I thought you were an optimist. You're always so, I don't know, preachy about the way you look at life." I didn't mean that as a bad thing. I wished I could have spread my own gospel like that, but Eliane was the evangelist in the relationship, an evangelist for the doctrines of El.

"Do you hate me?' She blurted, still chomping the popcorn.

"What? Of course, I don't hate you." I fidgeted at my clothes. I didn't want her to think I hated her, but I also didn't want to reveal that I was desperately intrigued and intimidated by her. "Why do you think that? If I said something—"

"I have this thing that I think shy people or natural introverts hate my guts. You've always been quiet till now. I thought maybe I annoyed you with my anti-Twilight sentiments. I kind of like that you called me preachy, but then I thought, maybe she can't stand my ass…I'm chatty for a writer; maybe it's why I am one. I make up people to talk to. I want the real people to talk to me and they don't…not even my own parents. Well, I don't know why I said "parents." I never met my father. My mom is an introvert. She doesn't do feelings either. She's more about paying the bills and making sure there's dinner. She was never much for conversation, though. I also spent my childhood wondering if *she* hated me. The only people I don't want to talk to are people *I* hate."

I wanted to speak, but instead I nodded. I didn't know what to say, so I gave her nothing, just like everyone else had apparently.

"Tell me how you grew up." She sat Indian-style on the edge of my bed. She might have been as desperate to be my friend as I was to be hers.

"Umm—my parents didn't talk either. I mean, not about anything real. My mother always looks perfect. She was better at pageants than I was. She never said that, but she makes it obvious with constant little tips and sighs. My Dad—he's a guy's guy. He makes good money and likes sports. He owns a chain of carpet and flooring stores he started out at as a teenager. That's kind of all he does. He says, 'hey there, princess' when I walk into the room, but not much else." I shrugged.

"It's all so traditional. I think that would have been nice, though, having a dad to pat you on the head on the way to his man cave. How in the hell did you end up at a school like UNCA? I bet he hates it, too. I bet he wanted you to dance at Clemson or some party school with pretty people who will look like leather from the tanning beds by this time next decade—you know, the kind that are so beautiful now."

"I don't know," I bit the side of my lip just like Kristen Stewart. "To be something different...I think. I've always been told who I am, what I should do. I just wanted to be somewhere that didn't match that, I guess. It was all so boring and stuffy and empty. My life was just a routine...go to voice lessons, dress conservatively, pick a tried-and-true career, be pleasant and pretty. But I didn't go to tanning salons; I always got spray."

"Was that a joke?" She exclaimed, "Welcome, Lux. There you are."

"And now I won't make another one for a year."

Eliane smiled at me, the look on her face saying she'd finally met me. "In all seriousness, I get that—why you came here. You don't want to be what you were molded to be. You're new at nonconformance though. You always followed the rules other people gave you."

"I followed all of them. Always." I spoke quietly. "I hate disappointing people."

"I disappoint everyone. I literally don't fit anywhere. I was a cheerleader who went to metal concerts. I wear sundresses with leather boots. I believe in Jesus, but I say the f word all the time. I'm too liberal for the Podunk town I was raised in, but too conservative for anyone I've met here. I drink gin and read and write, but I would listen to Britney Spears and watch reruns of The O.C. any day of the week. I don't make sense to anyone."

"You make sense to Jett. What's that all about?" I pried.

"He...is...my best friend—I think, most days."

"What does that mean? You *think*?"

"Jett is complicated. I mean, nobody gets me more. And I get him. But I don't know if we make each other better or if I can count on him all the way. Sometimes he surprises me, though. Jett and I are the same in some way that I can't understand and I'm not sure is healthy. We're both halfway enlightened, and smarter than the average bear…we can keep up with one another. But we compete. We don't complement one another at all. We were cut from the same cloth, but not to be worn together at once, you know? That's way too much monochrome. We were the most natural friends ever. I don't even remember exactly how that came to be. We just always ended up chatting in groups or at parties. We found ourselves in the same hideouts, smelling rain or looking at a painting on the wall. We've known one another since kindergarten. I honestly don't know why Jett doesn't treat me like the other girls. He's such a savage slut. I'm not like that," she said quickly, "I've been with one dude, so far; it was a guy too nice for me that I was a co-counselor with at a writing camp. He was way too nice, but the first should be nice."

"Wait, so you and Jett never…"

"God, no. I don't need that too "un-nice."' She threw her head back and laughed.

"But you've thought about it? I mean, there's energy there, right?"

"I don't know. There's energy everywhere, isn't there? The parts fit and we all know it. That automatically creates some kind of tension. Nature tricks us all sometimes. I don't think I'm his type, though." She shrugged.

"But is he yours?" I looked up at her, still clutching my movie-watching pillow, which was a Sponge Bob whom my mother had hated.

"I think he'd be my type maybe the way heroin is an addict's type, so it's best not to try it to begin with."

"Do you write like you speak?" I looked into her eyes like the answer would be there.

"I do everything like I write, I think. I'm just me." She shrugged again; it was her favorite gesture, I think. She had no idea what she could be. She also had no idea that she wanted Jett so badly she could almost taste him, his post-gig, post-baseball-game sweat right on her tongue. And she was terrified that if she did taste it, that she'd like it. That's what all the shrugging was about; it was meant to dismiss. It was meant to slough it off of her, that desire to let him inside to turn her veins black.

Eliane bounced up onto her tiny Tinkerbell-like feet. "Do you want to get drunk and have a dance party? I have tequila. I hate it, but it was all that was at the house when I went home last weekend. After my second Marg, I won't care anymore. I'll pretend it's The Botanist."

"The Botanish?"

"Expensive sipping gin, very dry, but, oooh..." she closed her eyes for a moment.

"I like Margaritas." I got up and followed her to the Wal-Mart mini bar in the common area.

"We'll fix that," she replied.

"OK, Jett. Can we do that the same day we fix my musical taste?"

"Oh gah...no! I sounded just like the bastard. I'm sorry!" She laughed.

"I'll give you a pass this time." I handed her a bunch of ice from the top of the mini-fridge and dumped it into the top of the blender. "Who doesn't like Margaritas, anyway? Maybe you're the alien."

"Grab a solo cup off that shelf over there." She instructed, shouting over the grinding noise.

She poured the icy light green concoction into the cup and then gave me a nod that meant I should taste it.

"It's good." I licked the salt from my lips, then took a bigger gulp.

"Then cheers." She tapped my plastic cup with hers. "Are you ready for Mariah and Whitney? Hell, I might even let Taylor join since it's a dance party. I completely abandon all musical snobbery if—and only if—it's to get wasted and shake my ass in my pajamas. Oh, and it was a given that Britney is coming, too. She always comes to the party."

"You know that's my kind of music," I joked, the alcohol already loosening me up a little bit.

She cranked up the blue tooth speaker and the music started, followed by Whitney Houston's famous "wooo." Eliane was already on her feet, the red solo cup in the air. She took my hand and dragged me to the center of the tiny living room. "Come onnnn…"

"I'm gonna need a little more liquid courage before I start dancing," I said pulling the cup to my mouth again.

"Oh, to hell with that. It's just us. Who cares?" She shouted over the lyrics, bouncing up and down on her bright blue toes.

I threw the rest of my drink down the hatch and took her hand, mostly because I knew I didn't have a choice. By the time Whitney belted, "I wanna dance with somebody. I wanna feel the heat with somebody," I was already twirling underneath Eliane's fairy-like arm. Then I let myself go. I shut my eyes and swung my long strawberry blonde hair around and even allowed a few laughs to come out. I eyed the opened curtains by the window, turning around to face it. For once I hoped somehow someone was seeing me, so sexy and free in that moment. I hoped someone was watching me instead of me looking in from the outside. This wasn't like being paraded out as a pageant queen, following the rules, exposing my only-revealing-enough bathing suit when I hit my mark. This was my body moving like liquid in water. I looked out into the night at the few people passing by our building. I swore one paused and admired me for a moment, hoped at least. But it could have been Eliane they were enamored by if they'd even stopped at all. That made me want to stop, but then I shook the thoughts out of my head.

"See what happens when you breathe? You laugh!" She yelled, her arms reaching over her head, her fingertips reaching toward the ceiling like she was searching for a hand to grasp onto. When she didn't find them, she took my hands instead, like we were four-year-olds playing Ring Around the Rosy.

"Well, well, well. What do we have here?" A voice broke into the place that I'd lost myself, shocking me back to reality.

"Come join us!" Eliane shouted out, still dancing while I stood frozen.

"Y'all are fucking dorks," Jett laughed, but threw down his bat bag and took one of each of our hands. I hesitated to move, but then he said, "But, don't stop on my account."

He let go of Eliane's hand to dip me to the floor and back up. I caught my breath at the top and looked into his multi-colored eyes for a minute.

"Margs are on the counter. It's all we've got, but help yourself," El motioned.

He went over and took a quick double shot of straight tequila, then offered each of us the same. We threw them back. I got chills all over my whole body and shook my head like a spaniel coming out of the ocean. Eliane didn't flinch. My guess is that she'd wanted to, but then, that was just Eliane. She knew better. She'd never have shown the weakness. If she'd agreed to take a shot then she was taking it without a tell, just like she had a good hand in poker.

Jett took one more, then loosened the buttons on his shirt, already starting to sweat a little bit. He danced up behind Eliane, letting his hands fall down her body like he'd met it before. It was like he'd memorized her slight curves and had touched her a million times. Then he turned, facing me, grinning like a wolf at the moon and pulled my hips to his, grinding against me a little while Eliane spun around in her own bubble. The thought that he had bigger plans than I was ready for floated through my mind for an instant. They even excited me for that instant. But I never should have worried. He stayed over at our place that night. We were all up until 4 a.m., then awoke around noon together, piled into the same bed, exhausted, thighs burning...because all we had done all night was dance. It was the best night I ever had.

CHAPTER 13

Somewhere between North Carolina and Texas
Now

It should have been a twelve-hour ride from the west side of Asheville, North Carolina to the heart of Paris, Texas, but it was fourteen—not including the impromptu overnight stay in the middle of Alabama. It's better to take the northern route and pass through Birmingham, but Eliane had to stop in Montgomery to see Zelda. I had a feeling she would when she rejected the first option the GPS lady had offered her. I don't know why I was even mildly surprised. We were passing right through the middle of Zelda country. Of course, she'd stop, out of the way or not. I suppose I'm glad for her that she did. It also broke up the drive through the non-eventful parts of the South.

The southern United States offers everything from majestic mountains with blue ridges to marshes and bayous wearing Spanish moss like an antique cloak. It has sandy beaches and mysterious swamps full of cypress knees and secrets that date pre-Civil War. Most of it, we travelled through at one point or another throughout our journey. However, the mountains began disappearing with the brightest part of the sun somewhere in northern Alabama, and we hadn't made it to alligator country just yet. And Eliane once said that everything most beautiful in the southern US came with a side of alligators. Well, she didn't really say it to me. She said it in an essay she'd left lying on her desk at the dorms. It was the most beautiful writing I'd ever read, but she'd gotten a B minus on the paper with a note that said GRAMMAR in all caps. Ironic. But she had done well at describing the best parts of the South, the parts that we were certainly not in. We were driving along the interstate in the in-between, which looked similarly to where I grew up in the Piedmont of North Carolina, except with more dead armadillos. It was green enough, nice enough, populated enough. But it just wasn't all that special. My apologies to Greensboro, and Central Alabama. The point is, I think Zelda decorated this place all by herself, and I was happy to see it with Eliane. No one better. In that moment, I almost wished she knew I was here. But that couldn't work. Our arrangement is our arrangement. We tail one another, and it's best she doesn't know about it. However, I'm sure it's harder for her because she, unlike me, doesn't understand why it has to be like this.

It was late afternoon by the time she made it to Montgomery. I knew she was already exhausted, but when Eliane Pangolin had a plan in her head, it was strictly followed. And she had more than a plan; she had a mission to connect with her favorite ghost, probably her best friend. I no longer held the title, and God knows Jett had squandered his chance at it years ago now. Really, it had always been Zelda, anyway—at least since she first watched that special on her sick day I mentioned before, after which she demanded her mother take her to see the burn spot for the first time. It took about a month, but she finally got to go after promising her mother she'd load the dish washer after every meal. Then, of course, the letter-writing began. She'd told me about it one night back at Mills Hall—the tale about the first time she'd nestled down into that grassy area that she'd declared holy and got to know her ghost. The rest is history. Jett, nor I, ever really stood a chance of dethroning Zelda.

It was late in the afternoon when we pulled up to 919 Felder Avenue. The jazz-age home in Zelda's hometown is where she and F. Scott lived while she wrote *The Last Waltz* and he wrote *Tender is the Night* (Eliane's favorite—and don't claim F. Scott wrote it by himself around her). Eliane threw the U-haul into park and gazed up at the tall multi-chimneyed structure.

"Huh." She shrugged looking at it. It was charming, but not as truly Southern as she'd hoped. She hated that it was brown. She'd hoped for white and bright with enormous porches. I think she somehow hoped Zelda might even be there, smoking on the porch with a smirk on her face. Things were often a let-down to Eliane because no matter how great something was, it was never greater than her own imagination. It would have been hard to live in Eliane's mind, such a fantastically better place than the real world.

She looked down at her phone and checked the time. Then she glanced at her email app. She watched the unread messages pile up, the little red number growing every day, now at a number with a comma in it. She refused to check it anymore, but she couldn't delete it either. The last time she'd checked that old account was right after her release from the hospital, and it was still happening, the unwanted emails she was receiving from brr6@brrco.com. She probably thought she didn't open them because she didn't know what to do with them but didn't delete them in case one day, suddenly, she did. But I know the thing it really is; she's afraid of the details, of possibly finding a description of what he did, of the terrible thing Eliane had put into motion with a few words she'd written on a piece of paper she thought would never be read. She's afraid to learn what it was that she really did to end someone's life. But she's also afraid of never knowing at all. Therefore, the messages remain exactly where they are in purgatory.

She threw her phone into her purse and pulled out a bottle of overpriced gin that she'd stuffed into the glove box, along with a pack of cigarettes and a long vintage cigarette holder she'd won on eBay months before. She opened the gin, raised it toward the home, then took a big swig of it without flinching, just like always. Then she took the American Spirit cigarette (certainly not what Zelda would have smoked—but it is the 2020s, not the 1920s) and placed it into the holder. She lit it without cracking a window and took in a dainty but strong drawl, careful not to ruin it by coughing everywhere like a little girl. She took another one until she'd sat there and smoked the whole thing, which meant I'd probably get to watch her vomit later because she doesn't smoke. After she finished it, I expected she'd say something, mumble a few words in honor of the queen of her kind or something, but she didn't. She opened the door and ground the cigarette out on the pavement, leaving it there, holder and all, like some sort of weird offering. Then she dusted off her dainty hands and inhaled deeply.

"At least it smells like magnolias. That helps," she said to herself before she walked inside.

After she marveled at the grand winding staircase that *did* impress her, she ignored the flagging tour guide and beelined straight for an oil painting, Zelda's once lost "White Roses." She stood in front of it and stared for a moment. I thought she might cry, but she didn't.

Instead, she placed her hand on the painting she was in no way allowed to touch and spoke out loud to it, or maybe Zelda, or maybe the girl who had been dumped in the hollow back in Asheville and said, "Flowers are never really lost. They're beautiful forever, and they always exist somewhere. I don't believe in lost flowers, or dead ones, either. They're just flowers, whatever the state."

Her voice wasn't even strange. She'd talked to the painting like it were as flesh as she was, then turned back toward the foyer, skipping over a hundred other historical items. She'd seen what she'd wanted to.

"Ma'am," the tour guide finally got her attention. "Can I show you some other highlights of the property? The painting is just the tip of the iceberg. Are you a fan of The Fitzgeralds?"

"I get your newsletter. I saw that the painting would be on temporary display about the time I'd be travelling to Texas. I came to see it. That's about all I really care about." Eliane didn't respond to the woman as much as she just said what she wanted to say.

"Well, we're glad you stopped to see us. This is the last surviving property of the four homes the Fitzgerald's resided at over the course of their travels. Practically everything left is here."

"Oh, I'm OK. I really just wanted to see the painting. I would have preferred to have had my gin by it, but no food or drink, you know." Eliane motioned to the standard-issue sign by the entrance. "Other than that, I'm as satisfied as I could be. I just wanted to feel the vibe, you know? I think I'm a fan of the feeling more than the people."

"OK, if you're sure you don't want to look around some more..." The woman tried to keep smiling politely.

"No, I'm content. I don't need to see all the artifacts mostly about F. Scott, though I'm sure I would have fallen for him too, had I met him. He probably had that effect on people. It just oozes out of some people, and nobody is immune. But he doesn't need any more fans. The painting; that's about *her*. That's what I needed to do, respect her work." She started to walk away but paused and turned back toward the awkwardly grinning woman. "But do you know of a decent place to stay around here. I'm on my way to Paris, umm, outside of Dallas. It's getting late in the day, and I don't think I can stand to drive anymore." She stretched her arms behind her back to sell it.

"Well, there's a good hotel a couple blocks away that will be your cheaper option. But we just had a cancellation on our Zelda Fitzgerald suite here in the home that we Air B & B if you're interested in the bed and breakfast feel—with a little dash of culture in the—"

"I'll take it," Eliane cut her off, her eyes glowing. "Can I check-in right now?"

"Certainly, you may." The older lady with the small voice and stature to match responded.

"Amazing. The Zelda suite. I had no idea."

"You should know though—some people claim Zelda pays them a visit while they're there. I think it's all tall tales, but you might want to sleep with the bedside lamp on." She chuckled.

"Even better. When I get in there, I'm diving straight for the sheets...and I'm praying for ghosts."

CHAPTER 14

The University of North Carolina Asheville
Back Then

The first time I slept with Jett, I knew he didn't like it, because he told me so. I don't know why I say "the first time" like there would be another time. Let me rephrase. That time I slept with Jett in college, he didn't like it because he immediately said that he didn't right to my face.

It was about a month after we first met in the late spring of 2014. That time of year is about the best time anywhere in The South. In Asheville, North Carolina, however, it's just short of magic. The fall colors those mountains are famous for are calm pastels in their infancy. That's not my line. That's Eliane's, too. She preferred the spring, though the area was more famous for autumn, because it was one of the few places in The South that had one. She's the one who spoke about the colors that way. I was never that eloquent, but I appreciated it. It seems like everything is more beautiful when it's young and new, even the leaves on the trees. But apparently, I was not.

"I liked the idea of you better than really being with you. That happens a lot." He said it out loud like that about ten minutes after we were finished. The nine minutes prior were spent drying in our own sweat, stuck to faux silk sheets in complete silence.

I thought before I answered. I'd waited the standard three dates to seal the deal—if you could call one group outing, one session to educate me on music, and one intense make out session after a lot of beer and a ballgame of his, dates.

I'd acted coy at first, then played the submissive like I thought he wanted. I let him choke me only a little bit before I got on top and took charge, which I thought would be much to his surprise. But he could tell I'd planned it out. He could see who I was...never actually free. He could see the girl who'd come up in the *Twilight* era, who'd read *Fifty Shades of Grey,* who'd always done best when mimicking someone else. He saw it all. Worse. He'd felt it moving against him. He'd experienced it, and that confirmed it. He saw all of me, and we both knew what it looked like.

"I—I...OK. What didn't you like?" *Pathetic.* I should have kicked his ass out then and there. I should have remarked on his manhood, like it wasn't perfection, like it was small and useless, then sat him out on his ass. But instead, after he still got perfectly fine sex, I asked for *notes.*

"I thought I'd be able to feel your red hair like it would really be on fire or something. I think I thought underneath your shyness that you'd be more...bold. I mean...it's not like you don't have a clue how to fuck or anything. It wasn't that. Most guys would really dig it. It was that I just thought you were something else. I thought you had this shiny façade but that I'd get to see behind it. But you're a lot of girls. You're all of them I've ever met. It's probably not your fault—just like the radio you listen to and someone else choosing your music. Someone chose your personality. I bet you had a critical mother. I bet you lie when you break the rules because getting in trouble is worse than the truth. You'd never want to displease anyone, so you never try anything spectacular...not anywhere."

I sighed, a slight crack in my breath that I hoped like hell he couldn't hear. He'd nailed me.

"You can't help it, and in a few years from now you'll make the nicest wife for someone and probably even like it some days.

And he won't be the kind of a guy searching for things like me. He'll be just fine, too. You'll live in a good neighborhood, and you'll like your house because you got a prettier color than your neighbor, even though the floorplan is the same. And that'll please you. Because you'd worry anything different is wrong all together. You might have the balls to upgrade the marble countertops to something slightly bolder, too, maybe a waterfall countertop. Your husband will make good money just under the boss, the job he really wants, and he'll have the best insurance. But that dude won't be able to fuck for anything..." He stood up and I rolled over as casually as I could—like I didn't care about anything he'd just said. But I did. And I even still wanted the best house in the cookie-cutter subdivision, even as he made fun of it. He forgot the white picket fence, though.

Still, I hoped he thought my silence was to freeze him out, and not to hide the tears. I hated that he'd made me cry...again. I think I might have cried in my room the first night I met him. I don't even know why. He had that effect on people. It couldn't just have been me. I bet a lot of girls never knew why they were crying over Jett Jorgenson.

The worst part is that he was right. I'd planned a certain amount of "no inhibitions" for him. I have *all* the inhibitions, but I'd forced myself out of my comfort zone just enough. I thought it was enough that he'd buy it, that I was capable of giving myself freely and wildly. But he'd seen it up close, the diamond too pretty to be real, the cubic zirconia I was. Jett was an asshole, but he wasn't stupid. That was the problem. He would have been much better stupid. It wasn't fair for him to look like that, play baseball like that, play guitar like that, and be a friggin' genius. But he was, and he knew that he was all of it. Hence, the asshole. I wish I could have told him all of that right then, owned his ass like Eliane always did. But I didn't even own myself, not then.

It made sense that she would be his best friend. She'd always seen it all, but it cast no spell on her. I'm not saying it never shook her for a second, but she could always resist it. She could drink his potion and feel all its effects yet still not succumb to it. She was like a honey badger bitten by a cobra. She might take a little nap, but then she'd shake off the venom, wake up and eat him for dinner. But it's also probably why they'd never slept together. He had her considering it might be that she was never good enough for him, but it's that she's the only one he'd ever met who was too good, and everyone knew it but her. She was too good because she was beautiful without trying and because she understood him without a manual. My guess is that he wanted her from the second he'd laid eyes on her. I'm sure she wanted him too; it wasn't obvious by just looking, but I knew that first day after seeing them in the same space. Not that it mattered; she didn't give into it, and she wouldn't. She'd never forgive herself for letting him have the pleasure. She was stronger than I was. And then, of course, there's Jett who was terrified Eliane would see all of him and not like it, just like he saw me.

"Hey, I'm just gonna crash here tonight. I'm still kind of buzzed." Jett came back into the room chomping on Cap'n Crunch, milk sloshing out of the bowl and into the floor.

"Yeah, whatever you want," I answered as though I were half asleep. "Don't feel obligated or anything."

"Don't worry, I never feel obligated. I'm just still half-drunk. Is El in her room?"

"I have no idea." I yawned.

"Well, was she here when you got in this afternoon? I didn't see her when I rolled in with you earlier."

"She was here. She was working on her piece to get into the creative writing program. I heard her pitching a fit in her room, yelling about how it was all shit."

"She does that when she writes. It's never really shit though. She's written some songs for the band a few times. It's always so damn good. I hate her ass for it. I wish I could write like I can play, because I can play like she writes—don't tell her how good she is though, or that I said it. She needs to feel like the underdog to do anything. Our little victim, El."

"Mmm..." I pretended to be barely hanging on to consciousness. I loved Eliane, but I didn't want to hear him compliment her after he'd just expressed his bitter disappointment in literally everything about me, and so casually I'd almost thought I was the unreasonable one for a second.

"I'll let you go to sleep. I'm wound up as hell. I'm gonna go see if she's in there." He threw the bowl down on my nightstand and moved his elbows in and out like he was stretching before an at-bat.

"Just sleep in there or on the couch. I get too hot at night. I don't do well with another warm body in my bed." I lied, my attempt at recovering some level of control.

"I'm sure you do, Luxy." He taunted. The bastard should have gone into psychology. "But as you wish. I've had a lot of sleepovers with El through the years. She won't care if I crash with her tonight."

"Perfect." I mumbled. "Just perfect."

CHAPTER 15

I listened like I was panning for military secrets as Jett burst through Eliane's door. I wish I'd gone to sleep, having not cared like I'd pretended for him, but I was never built that way. I always cared. I still care. And it's exactly why I'm here now. I care about all of it.

"What are you doing in here?" Eliane almost snapped, though she wasn't really annoyed at all. That's just how she spoke to Jett. "And, in your boxer briefs?" She added slower, her head probably cocked sideways like a curious little hummingbird.

"What are you up to?" He ignored the obvious. "You look unwashen and you're in your smart-girl glasses. You're wearing the ratty flannel pajamas instead of those little silk sorts you break out if you're expecting company."

"I do not wear those shorts when I'm expecting company. What are you talking about?"

"Yeah, you do. It started summer before senior year when you banged Jared Prestnell at the senior lock-in. You'd been running around the bonfire looking all sassy in your short jammies. I'm pretty sure that's the night you lost it. Now you break 'em out whenever a dude who you like is around. You like yourself in those shorts better than lingerie. And I get it. You're cute as hell in those shorts."

"I did not *lose it* to Jared Prestnell...I only let him get to third base. I didn't lose-it-lose-it until the next summer."

"I bet you were wearing those shorts though."

"I think you've *lost* it." She tried to ignore him.

"A long time ago. I was like fourteen; it was summer; we were visiting my cousin in Florida..." I pictured him kicked back and smiling into the sun that was somehow on him indoors and at night.

"Shut up, Jett. What do you want? Wait—wait. Your first time was with your cousin?"

"You're disgusting, El. It was her friend who was staying over. She was a year older than me, cutest little birthmark right by her —"

"Shut up again."

"You been holed up in here writing all day?"

I'm guessing she pointed to Jett then at her nose.

"See, I was right. I know my El." He would have winked.

"I wrote a short story. I tried my hand at irony. It was about a technology that could store people's consciousnesses until AI was developed enough to house it, and what goes wrong with all that shit."

"Sounds interesting and disturbing."

"It wasn't. The idea is the whole thing. It takes like two paragraphs to explain why that sucks. It's so 21st century. It's typical. People write about it all the time. I have to do better than that. Plot isn't enough. I need characters, not concept. I don't know. I deleted it all, and now I have nothing."

"Then what are those mountains of words on your screen?" He kicked back onto Eliane's bed, the springs in the outdated extralong twin mattress squeaking.

"Ugh...I hate that I wrote that. That was what I wrote when I should have been writing something meaningful that I could submit for the writing program. It's just you and Lux are always around, and they say you write what you know, so..."

"What the fuck, is all that about me?" He sounded almost manic-level excited. Of course, he did.

"No, no. Don't—" El raised her voice while he undoubtedly snatched the laptop from her. "Give it back, Jett. It's just observations…it's just some stupid—"

He wrenched it out of her hands. "These are fucking songs, El. You're still writing songs for me. Aww. You swore you'd never write another one for me after I played that one you wrote back in tenth grade in the battle of the bands without telling you. Look at you, comin' around. I should pinch your cute little cheek." He held the laptop above El's reach. I might have added that part…but I can picture her little pixie self jumping up and down, swiping the air for it, glasses slipping down her nose.

"OK, first off, I didn't write that song for you back in high school. It was a deeply personal poem for myself, and you turned it into a song about a girl who hates herself far more than I ever did. Secondly, I didn't write this one for you either. They're just…they're about people in my life. They're just thoughts. When I have thoughts, I'm compelled to make them sound pretty and write them down."

"Then why don't you submit the songs to your writing program? Songs are just poetry set to sound, anyway."

"It has to be longer than that, at least like a short story. They'll think the song thing is a cop out."

"Well, you said you needed characters. It sounds to me like you found some. Use me or whoever else you're in here writing songs about in between writing complete bullshit."

"I need both. I need characters and plot. That there is just…it's nothing. Seriously. Put it down."

"You can call it whatever you want, but this is clearly a song. I'm reading it."

"Fine, but I'm starving. I haven't eaten all day. Let's go to the dining hall. They have a late night café. You can read it when we get back." She tried another tactic but made her voice sound far too casual.

"Nice try. Why don't you want me to read it so bad, huh? Is it sexy?" He gasped like a little old lady. "Oh my God, did you write a sex song about me?"

"No. God you're so stupid. It's just…it's just really honest. It wasn't written to be read out loud. It's for me is all."

"Honest is good."

"I always thought so, too. But sometimes I guess honesty *should* be private."

"To hell with that, El. You've always been bold. Don't stop on my account. Part of honesty is being brave. And I've never known you to cower. Don't be such a pansy. It's only me."

So Eliane shrugged and shook her head. I think part of her even wanted him to read it. If someone really wants to stop something, they stop it. She made the choice to surrender, and in that moment gave every secret she had away in such simple lines—and those words—when said out loud, changed the courses of all our lives.

CHAPTER 16

Somewhere between Alabama and Texas
Now

Eliane didn't see any ghosts the night she spent in Zelda's suite, but I know there was one there. They're everywhere all the time; at least that's my experience. They walk through walls and skin and locked minds and bolted doors at leisure. They do anything they want, and nobody ever escapes them. But that night, the one ghost Eliane felt could solve the riddle of whatever species of girl she was, never showed up for her. That's when it occurred to me why she loved, or connected, or respected, or whatever it was she did when it came to Zelda Fitzgerald. It's why she wrote her the letters before she started writing them to her mother, to her unknown father, to random people on the street, and, eventually, to me. She was looking to all of us for answers about herself. It was the same thing she'd wanted in the first letter I'd received, though I didn't see that at first. Maybe not even any small part of it was about anything I assumed it to be about. Maybe the most authentic, self-assured, confident girl I'd ever met was looking for herself somewhere in all of us, but especially in the two of us, Zelda and me. Maybe she had been looking at me while I was looking at her all along, before I ever even knew it.

But this particular morning, she had again stumbled upon nothing from either of us, and she had again, risen disappointed. She was let down that Zelda hadn't had the courtesy to so much as come to her smelling like good gin in a dream. And she was disappointed with me for the same reason she was every morning. I wasn't answering back, and she knew deep down that I never would. Too much had happened.

Eliane readied herself by putting on the same clothes she'd shown up in. She then dropped a half-wilted flower (she'd had it in her purse for weeks, but I didn't know why) onto the floral bedspread and left without her complimentary breakfast of biscuits, eggs, and bacon. She did drop an envelope at the front desk—just threw it without ceremony into the pile of the other outgoing mail. As usual, it was addressed to me. Then she left another, addressed to Zelda, on the end table by a stack of tourism brochures. I don't know what either of them said this time. I usually try to look on, but I couldn't do it. Eliane was in her sacred place; it was like her sanctuary, and she practiced her religion there. I felt strange about peeking in this place and gave her a little privacy for the first time in a while. It made me wonder if I should just stop this. There were still the logical reasons to watch, the reasons I'd convinced myself were good enough to keep doing it. There was her safety. She had been connected to a serial murderer, though I've yet to explain that. She'd also possibly been a danger to herself...but not really. She had unraveled, but she was never *that kind* of unstable. Maybe what I was doing was wrong; maybe none of it was for her, just like her letters might not even be for me. Maybe we were all just coping...*maybe*. But, still, I wasn't ready to walk away. Not in that moment, regardless of the guilt. Not yet.

Back in the Uhaul, she started up the enormous truck and trudged on in the direction opposite the sunrise, the biggest event stopping at a Bu-cee's, the Wal-Mart Supercenter of gas stations, to get chicken tenders and use "the cleanest restroom in America." From there she just drove, superstitiously lifting her feet at the state lines (probably OCD) through Mississippi, Louisiana, and finally Texas. However, she didn't stop until she got to the Eiffel Tower—meaning the replica of the actual Eiffel Tower east of Dallas in the middle of Paris, Texas.

She jumped out of the truck, her tight jeans loosened around the waist from sitting and sweating so long in the pleather seat, leaving a little skin showing underneath her loose crop top. She'd worn cowboy boots only because it was Texas. I'd never seen her in them before. But they looked worn. My guess is she bought them for a concert or something ten years before. The look wasn't her norm, but it worked. Eliane was a sucker for a good theme, and Texas had a theme. And a motif. God, I wish she could hear me making all these literary references. She'd be speechless.

Out of the truck, she prepared for the spins she was about to perform with a proper pas de bourrée, then did a double pirouette followed by a series of chaine turns to the base of the structure. There were people around, bizarre types of tourists that reminded me of the Griswalds. But classic Eliane, she didn't care about any of them. She simply ended her turns on an odd number and looked perfectly peaceful. She fell to the ground and put her hands behind her head and gazed up at the tower as if it were the real thing and she had spun straight into the art and culture of the real Paris of her dreams. She'd have been no less excited.

"That's a first." I heard a middle-aged woman mumble just loudly enough for Eliane to hear.

"Next show's at 4 o'clock. I'm here all afternoon," Eliane shouted back with the big lady balls I never had.

Then she rolled over and pulled her pen out of her back pocket, a wad of napkins from Bu-cee's out of the other, and she began to write again. Out of Zelda territory, this time, I did look on.

Dear Lux,

I realized what I owe you is a better song than the first one I wrote you. Maybe it'll come to me here. Something tells me that it will. But for this afternoon, I'm going to lie here beneath the fake Eiffel Tower and re-read a handful of F. Scott and Zelda's book of love letters to one another. The

only place better to read them would be in the real Paris. Maybe this will inspire me, and I'll write something good the next time, and maybe I'll one day make it there, eating a baguette by the Seine.
Love,
El

I just wished she knew she didn't haven't to atone. That was never what this was about. I'm not watching for revenge. I'm not watching to catch her in a weak moment. Most of all, even more than her physical safety, I'm watching to see if she ever heals. It's not an apology that I need, nor revenge, it's just for Eliane to survive this, to survive what happened to her when she knew me.

CHAPTER 17

The University of North Carolina Asheville
Then
Jett read aloud, almost ironically at first, verbose and with the slightest English accent. The whole thing was very Shakespearian.

I want what I can't have
Like to know what the sky tastes like
I'm scared she's my other half
But you wish I'd sing to you in this mike
You taste like bread and water and same
You laugh instead of poking back
Your looks really could bring you fame
But being her is what you lack

His face turned more serious, and he read the lines earnestly the next time, an emotion Jett rarely made known. Everything he did always had to seem in gest. He almost never revealed himself, especially if that revelation made him vulnerable.

(chorus)
Her face could make me move, make move
I claimed I'd done it to her, but I lied
Just a glance and it was proof, it was proof
But you, you couldn't even give me a ride

I have fear because I have pride and pain
I'm with you because I'm on a bland fucking diet
You'd never dance in the rain
You won't try to incite any riots
But she makes me squirm
Which is all I ever really want
Her face while I hold you firm
It'll always always haunt

Her face could make me move, make move
I claimed I'd done it to her, but I lied
Just a glance and it was proof, it was proof
But you, you couldn't even give me a ride

Her face could make me move, make me move
I claimed I'd done it to her, but I lied
Just a glance and it was proof, it was proof
But you, you couldn't even give me a ride
You couldn't even give me a ride.

"Oh God." Eliane breathed, her head between her knees.

"Umm—"Jett paused. "You, uh—you heard us in there, I'm guessing. You heard us talking after we—

"Uh, yeah. I mean, these walls are pretty cheap and thin—a state-funded university you know."

Jett nodded. "Then you wrote this from my perspective? So, is this like, me talking...my voice?"

"Look, I'm really sorry to write about your business. I shouldn't have. I could just hear it in my head, and I remembered that thing you said to me in the library a hundred years ago about how you could have written a song from the expression on my face, that you liked to see me move. I just flipped it and considered what might make Jett Jorgensen move? It's not Lux. It's not any beautiful average girl you've fucked without pause since we were freshmen in high school. I just saw a snapshot of that, and I was bored—"

"But there's another girl in the song that you're talking about, the one who can make me move. Who is it, then? Who did you have in mind there?" I imagined him staring into her perfectly murky eyes, his dark brows arched, as I listened on the other side of the wall. I knew I could be listening to *the moment* for them, the moment where he started realizing there was Eliane and then that there was everyone else, everyone like me.

"It's just a girl. Some girl, somewhere, someday, I guess. I mean, I based that one line on what you said to me, because you would say that to anyone." Eliane rarely lied. "It was a good line."

"I wouldn't say it to anyone..." Jett said without any tone to help Eliane read him for once, opening a gate he would probably only leave ajar for a few seconds, a portal to him that if missed, might not open again for years—if ever. And I'm sure it would also never open the same way twice. She'd navigated to the back of that wardrobe and was stepping onto the snow like a kid discovering Narnia. The gate was weak because he'd just been with me. He invited something else, something that he hoped *would* make him move.

"It's just about whatever girl will wrangle you one day. Like your Zelda. You're F. Scott, the tortured artist. One day you'll find your muse and she'll do a number on you. I hope I'm there to see it, too." She ribbed.

"Some girl, somewhere? No one specific, El? You have no clue who you think my Zelda is if in this scenario I'm your dead dude you're always reading—that I still can't figure out if you love or hate..."

"No. I—I guess the universe has yet to spit her out into your world. So, uh...be careful out there." She must have made a weird smirk, sure of her own awkwardness.

Surprisingly he relented. He let her have her face. He wouldn't have for anyone else. Then, the portal closed.

"Can I keep this, El? I won't do anything with it. I just want it."

"Uh, yeah, you can have it." El's voice grew softer. "It's your voice anyway. I guess it's sort of yours."

Then silence. They were hugging, an eyes-closed-unspoken-bond-hug that I could feel through the wall. I stared up at the basic white girl glow-in-the-dark stars on my ceiling, and I cried. I tried to be quiet. I held it in until it hurt, but then a gasp came out just loudly enough. Then a second one when I tried to catch my breath.

Footsteps pitter-pattered down the hall. "Lux? Lux, you OK in there?" El asked. Then she whispered. "Oh, shit, she heard us. She must think we're the worst."

"Nah, she's probably like snoring or something." Jett whispered before opening the door.

I was already on my feet and into my skinny jeans.

"Lux." Eliane said, humility in her voice, not faking it this time.

"Hey. I just need to get out of here for a minute. I'm going to go grab a drink or something. I just can't sleep." I tried but was too upbeat while still fighting the tears to really knock it home for them.

"Lux, I know you heard us—the stupid song. I was exaggerating. It was more about how Jett is, not how you are. I didn't mean to—"

"Oh, no it's fine. It was just truth, you know?" I scrambled to put my hair into a messy bun. "I'm nothing special. I get it."

"It was a shit thing to do. I adore you, and it was so wrong. I love having you as my roommate. I love the notes you leave me on the mirror in the shower steam. I love that you always leave me a piece of toast in the morning because you know I'm too lazy to cook anything. You are special, Lux. It's just Jett—he's—"

"I think I know everything, El. Really. I know what kind of girl Jett's kryptonite is, and I know what kind he fucks out of boredom. I honestly knew it all along. I don't know why I'm so pissed off now about it."

"Just don't leave mad, please. I mean, you have every right to be mad, but please, let me somehow—" I pushed past her. "Jett, can you please say *something?*"

"I mean, if she wants to go, you should just let her go." He bit into an apple he found on the counter.

Eliane rolled her eyes and grasped me by the arm.

"Let me go." I dropped the nice routine and pushed the words through my perfectly straight, snow white teeth.

Eliane loosened her grasp and sighed to signal surrender. She didn't know that I realized it was to give me my dignity, but I knew. Still, I showed no forgiveness on my face. I stalked out of the threshold of the dorm to get a drink. And I got the drink, and then I never came back.

CHAPTER 18

Mostly Paris, Texas and a little bit of Dallas
Now

The apartment was in a red brick building in "downtown" Paris. The side of the building had an old ad painted on it that read "Topic Cigar Mild Havana." I kind of liked the ad. It had that warm-on-the-soul effect like drinking a coke out of an old glass bottle. It was from another time, some time when kids watched Lassie on a black-and-white television set that sat on olive green carpet, a time I never knew. I think that would have been a simpler era, though, and there's a reason people look back at simplicity and long for it. People never value simple enough until things are already complicated.

The general area looked like it was, for the most part, on the upside of "up and coming," and the building itself had just enough charm to suit someone like Eliane. It was the kind of place where a calm little yoga studio would sit right next door to a liquor store that got robbed a lot. There was probably one of those gas stations nearby that sold drug paraphernalia masked as little trinkets, but also a cute organic fruit stand that offered goat's milk soap by the register.

The apartment unit was fine. It had polished cement floors and exposed brick in the hallways. The stove and heater were gas, and the lights were a series of sconces, none overhead. The place had been revived like old buildings are in the 2020s, with an artsy, industrial theme. But it also held onto the past in certain ways.

I'm not sure apartment was the right word; it was more like a studio with a little divider in the middle to break up the space but had no doors except for the one to the tiny bathroom. The afternoon sun sliced through the living area, and I was sure Eliane would find something to do with all that light soon enough. She'd likely continue to write, because that's just who she was at the core, but she might also temporarily take up something weird like raising an herb garden because she thinks it'll be cute. Then she'll discover she doesn't have a green thumb and hates the smell just like she hates the pachouli in health food stores. At that point, she'll use the space to write like she should have to begin with. Just hide and watch.

The first thing she unpacked was the dry erase wall calendar. When she hung it by the refrigerator, I could see that she'd raced into town with only hours to spare. It was April 26th, and on the 27th she had her first day working for Skyla Free. It was circled enormously on the calendar, and it was in about 12 hours. She also had her dance workshops notated, and then nothing else. It didn't mean there was nothing else to do, but those were priority, and most importantly, they came in a set of three on that perfect seven-day week. Her calendar always remained odd and prime, to her, perfectly imperfect just the way she liked.

Eliane picked up her cell phone and hit *Mommy Dearest*. "Hey. I told you I'd call once I was in. I'm in." She put the phone on speaker and threw it on the counter to grab a box.

"Well, thanks for letting me know." Her mother said as if she were already exacerbated.

"I can't talk long. I start work with Skyla tomorrow. Then I have dance workshops in Frisco on Tuesday and Thursday. That's where the DCC training facility it. It's a little trot from here."

"How far?"

"Close to an hour probably."

"Then why didn't you find somewhere closer?" It was an accusation, not a question.

"I wanted to live in Paris."

"It isn't *Paris,* Eliane. It's a small town with a big drive ahead of it, and in Dallas traffic. You shouldn't have picked it just because of the name." Her classic half-sigh-half-huff followed.

"It's *my* Paris."

Another sigh. "It's weird that you say it like that, too. You want people to think you mean *the* Paris."

"For me, now, it is *the* Paris. It's the only Paris I have today." She stopped shuffling boxes for a moment, "Mom, do you have a Paris?"

"El—for the life of me, I never know what you're talkin' about. I know you think I'm some small thinker with no dreams, and that's why you ask me crap like that. You want to catch me bein' normal and make me feel bad about it. But feedin' you was my dream. And I did that. You'd think you could appreciate me for that at least. You have no idea what it was like bein' a single mom, tryin' to get through some schoolin' while potty trainin' a toddler and worryin' about leavin' you with a babysitter I barely knew. I had to study and work and feed us and try to keep you safe. We had no family around. The sperm donor was no help. I just wish sometimes you had a little gratitude."

"I do. And I love you for that and not just because you're my mom. I really do, even though you and I are so different. I just—I never thought to ask you before. You deserve for someone to ask you. So, tell me, what's your Paris?"

"Oh, I don't have time for this, El." She coughed into the receiver.

"I want to know." She pressed. "This is me trying to talk to you. You always say I don't talk to you. And you're the one who gave me this French name that means light. That's pretty out there for you. You must have at least had dreams when you picked my name."

"I saw your name in a book of baby names. But I did like that it meant "light." I'd had enough dark. I'd just gotten out of a relationship with a drug addict who I barely knew anyway. My own parents had gotten killed in a car wreck together a couple years before. It had been a bad time. I needed light, and I wanted that light to be you. So, there's that; the dark was why I picked the name that meant light."

"Sorry to disappoint."

"That's not what I meant. I meant, you were my hope. I wanted you to be my opposite, and, girl, you are. But I had to be the logical one. I dreamed for you, but I forgot a lot of mine along the way. Mine never mattered to anybody, anyhow. And now they don't matter to me, either. You let go of silly shit as you age, Eliane."

"I know you remember." El pushed again, "Mom, what is your Paris? Don't let go of it."

The raspy sigh again. "We don't all have the luxury to dream, El. And it hurts too much to try. Don't you care how I feel at all? This stuff isn't good for me, and it might not be for you either. My Paris might just be makin' it through another day or puttin' food on the table. And I'm sorry that's not good enough. Not everybody is born thinkin' like you. Most people just live. But try to care enough to stop makin' me feel bad about myself. Just let me live. Can that be my Paris? A little peace?"

"I do care." Eliane said sternly. "I called, didn't I?"

"Yes, yes you did..." More sighing. That woman huffed, puffed, coughed, scoffed, or just released air made up of some kind of stress more than anyone I'd ever seen. She could have been in the middle of Disney World after winning the lottery and it wouldn't have changed it.

"I just wish you had something that was your Paris. I wish you felt things like I felt them, just so you'd understand it. That might be a little selfish, but not all the way. The good is worth the bad. And everyone has the right to dream. It isn't a luxury. You should let yourself feel that hope."

"You feel too hard, El. It's why you make the little rules to ward off the bad stuff. You feel that as much as the good. You think it's worth it, but I've watched it since you were little. I'm not so sure you're right about that. I should have gotten you help when you were six and found the dead bird in the driveway."

"What are you talking about? What dead bird?" Eliane doubted any such story.

"I ran over a bird in the driveway. He was gnawin' on a piece of sub sandwich you'd dropped the night before. It probably was already injured, or it would have just flown off when it saw the car comin'. But you panicked when I flattened it. You jumped out of the car and tried to scoop the diseased thing up and save it. You couldn't sleep over it for days and days. You cried and pitched a fit over that thing, goin' on and on about it bein' all your fault for droppin' the bread."

"Wait...I'm vaguely remembering this now. Then I made you buy birdseed so I could spread it in the grass to lure the birds away from the driveway. I remember the bird now. It was beautiful, a little bright yellow tuft right on top of its head." Her eyes bulged, almost ready to cry for the bird all over again.

"Yeah, but you didn't just throw the seed. You started puttin' it farther and farther from the road, addin' on another pile for every bird you claimed to be new in the yard. You were out there makin' little piles constantly, before school, after school, before bed. You even got Grandma to buy you a set of binoculars so you could see better. You'd watch from your window at night. This went on pretty much that whole school year. You finally counted thirteen birds and made thirteen piles every mornin'. Then you'd count obsessively until all thirteen were accounted for each evenin', always so scared you'd lost one. Sometimes they weren't all there and you'd melt the hell down. That's when I should have said somethin'. It might have made a difference for you."

"Thirteen? There were thirteen birds to save?" She asked quietly.

"Yeah...isn't that your favorite number now? You like thirteen, don't ya?"

"Yeah. I like it the most of all."

CHAPTER 19

Skyla's office was in her house in a historic section of town near downtown Dallas. It was a miniature version of the typical Texas mansion, full of all the charm, but less of the size. The porch, however, was enormous and the façade sort of Victorian-like. The whole thing was white, except for the blue-grey porch. But the rocking chairs on it were all white. None of them looked like they'd ever been sat in either. They didn't have a scuff on them and were adorned with the plush pillows that had never had a sweaty back pressed up against it in late July. They were for looks. I considered the possibility that the whole thing might be some kind of life-sized doll house.

The inside was decorated in the insta-famous "grand-millennial" style mixed with a little mid-century mod, not southern like the outside—not traditionally anyway. Everything was too intentionally placed, even things meant to seem whimsical, and the whole place smelled like coconut and vanilla. Nothing was out of place, but to a weird level. This woman clearly had no pets, no roommates. I had a feeling her refrigerator would be nearly empty, except for the perfect rows of Fiji Water that weren't really meant for drinking.

Eliane had been waved in frantically by the petite blonde (not Eliane blonde, *blonde* blonde), who was talking at warp speed on her cell phone and now waited in the office to the right of the front door. She sat in a random pink velvet chair across the room from an enormous solid black, but otherwise, traditional desk. A floral mural was painted onto the wall behind the desk in muted bright yellows and oranges. At the top, the words "Skyla is the limit," were painted into the clouds. Eliane gazed up at it...and I couldn't read her. She was either fan-girling this person or disgusted it had come to this. I think maybe it was both, and both were highly unusual for her. Thinking about it, everything Eliane did lately was off her normal track a bit.

"I'm sorry about that. I've been dealing with promoting this enormous event down in Austin. I had to take that. Fewww." She threw herself into the oversized white velvet chair behind the desk that was clearly used when getting down to business. She changed from a blogger appeasing someone in charge to the person *in* charge when she sat in that chair. Maybe everyone should have a boss chair. "So, tell me, how were your travels, hon?"

Eliane eyed her, cocking her head sideways like a curious long-eared dog, taking in her airbrushed makeup and hair extensions. Then she answered, "It was good. I stopped in Montgomery at the Fitzgerald Museum, then at a Bu-cees, which is both a terrifying and exciting place, then I drove through some weird swampy farm areas full of weird-looking trees, then I came here. I'm renting a place in downtown Paris. It's a little bit down the road from here, but I get to see the Eiffel Tower every morning, so that's exciting." Eliane laughed.

Skyla grinned and spoke in strong country twang that might have been put on a little, "You're gonna be a quirky little thing aren't ya? That's why you can write like that though. Your samples are the only ones that reached out and just grabbed me, you know? Everything else was just Plain Jane, and that's just not the Skyla Free brand. I need somebody who kind of sings what they say."

"Aww, thank you for saying that." Eliane knew how good she was, but earnestly tried to reach for humility. Hence the aww.

"It's the truth. You put into words what I can't. I love what I do. I build brands. I promote. I make things pretty, but people want those words from the heart, even in a simple top ten or list-style article. Hell, they want heart in a simple caption. I can't just be some blogger from 2015 posting cute outfits. I have to be a master at everything these days to stay relevant. I have to be out living the good life, but to convert that to dollars means having my shit together. You're a missin' piece of the pie. Happy to have you."

"I'm excited, too. I love to write. I'm thrilled to get paid to do what I love, but I'm also happy to be a part of something so—" she searched the air with her hands, "alive. I can't wait to experience the people and places alongside you. I'm tired of the shadows, and it's where writer's land a lot of times."

"Not with me. This is Texas. This is Skyla Free. Everything is bigger and it's 95 degrees in the shadows. The pressure is on. I just hope you can keep up the pace. I'll need you at events writing in real time, and captioning my posts, stories, and videos as I spit them out. It'll go quick. I hope you can think, or write, I guess, on your feet."

"Good. I need a busy mind right now. And, yes, I can write on my feet." Eliane seemed almost annoyed to have to clarify it. She wasn't so much cocky as she just wasn't used to answering to anyone.

"So, our first event is in Austin. It's a music and arts festival. It's brand new, and the idea is to bring starving artist types and Indie bands on the verge of making it to the mainstream. Our headliner, though, is a band that's already pretty huge. So, that's the draw. It's a mix of pop culture chaos and true art. I'm promoting it with a few other people. I'm the pop culture piece of that marketing puzzle. So, we have to make this look fabulous. We have to bring the bodies. We need it to seem exclusive but somehow available. We need Gen Z to be so jealous of everyone able to get in. Can you bring words to that? This part is where you're a marketing writer. I'll figure out who to invite first."

"I can do that easily. We just need to appeal to desire. I'm a young millennial, but I can get inside the Gen Z head. It just starts with asking one question: What does Gen Z desire? Ease. Comfort. Veering from the norm. Glam won't cut it. It has to be about defying the norm, and it should be ironically casual...but not overly available. And we have to sell it in one concise graphic, perfectly captioned. They'll be annoyed by too much information. They're annoyed by everything, so we present it, make them salivate, then back away."

"You've got it." She winked, then pointed to a turning frosé machine in the corner of the office. "Wanna celebrate?"

"Why not? It is...10 a.m..." she glanced at her phone.

"Perfect. I'll pour you one." Skyla skipped over to the machine full of pink ice and blush wine.

"I was surprised it's a music festival. I pictured you as more high fashion and trips to the Caribbean."

"Well, I'm that too. I'm more about that, honestly. I love to worship the sun and drink rum...and frosé." She handed Eliane the drink and slurped a sip off the top of her own. "Mmm. So good. But, anyway, this guy I'm seeing is headlining it. His band is really taking off. We met in L.A. at a launch party for some new fashion line I can't even remember now. I was there to promote this boutique hotel in the South Bay and wound up meeting people and then more people and was at this event half-lit, no clue how I even got there. This band was playing live as the music for the runway show. It was so hot, so L.A., edgy offbeat rock n' roll and models of all different shapes and sizes—all friggin' fabulous. Anyway, I had a drink after with the adorable guitar player. And that was three months ago. I can't even believe it. Musicians, right? They get me every time, and I never understand any more about 'em by the time it's over." She sipped the froth off the top of her glass.

"They can have that effect on people, I hear. I've known a few myself. I think their pheromones mutate when they learn guitar. I don't know." Eliane chuckled.

"Right? So, that's how I got all tangled up in the music fest. My man and his band will be in town for about a week before the event doing all kinds of press and pre-events, so anything you can drum up there would be great. I'd start by writing a press release and sending it to all the local publications to draw some attention. I can't write a press release to save my life. We are promoting it, but we want the media to cover it too. I'm sure you can do that, easy."

"Got it." El took notes.

Skyla paused. "I can tell you're a good writer just chatting with you. You said something a second ago I've been trying to put my finger on for weeks. The pheromone thing. That's it. That's what made me like feral or something. When he got close enough to inhale, he had me, but I'm telling you, I could smell the sex on Jett Jorgenson before he even left the stage."

"I bet you could." Eliane's lips curled into a simper.

I was shocked, like gasping-for-air-level-floored, but Eliane didn't flinch. She hadn't seen him in years, and she didn't even breathe funny. She didn't raise her eyebrows. She didn't react in the slightest to the mention of that infamous name. She *fucking* knew. I thought I watched all the time, but clearly, I'd missed something.

CHAPTER 20

The University of North Carolina Asheville
Back Then

This is the bad part. Things didn't...go so well...when I ran out the night Jett and I slept together. My running out started a shit storm for all of us, the lengths of which, I'm not sure we've all seen yet. This is part one of two of the "thing" that happened to Eliane. Yeah, she's OCD and anxious. That wasn't my fault and had set in long before me. But my story is the thing that agitated hers, woke up the beast she'd been tiptoeing around since childhood. What happened to me became the gasoline thrown on her fire. I am her accelerant.

I was upset, naturally, at Jett's complete...whatever nonchalant crap he'd handed me, but I was more devastated at Eliane's words, because they were what *she* thought about me. They were honest opinions, and I knew that because she assumed I'd never see them. Words that were written to be kept private were the truest ones ever written. That's how I knew she meant what she said about me. It was just like that time back in eighth grade when Katie Miller passed a note to Megan Cobb that said, "Lux has too cool of a name to be the most boring person I know." Megan dropped it on the floor leaving class, so I picked it up and read it. I knew that was true just like this. The worst insults were always the ones I was never meant to hear. I'd much rather had someone just make something up to say to my face for spite. At least I could dismiss that. This was far too real.

I knew what bland, unbuttered oatmeal I always served up to people. I had just wanted Eliane to see past it, and I thought that she had. I thought she saw that little spark in me, maybe the night we danced with Jett till 4 a.m. I thought she saw the girl who chose the liberal arts college, knowing damn well that she wouldn't fit in. I thought she saw the girl who hoped for more. But when it was my turn to be her muse, she wrote about a lukewarm bath of a girl who could never shine as brightly as she did. She wrote about someone God himself spits out of his mouth. And it killed me. She was the girl in sunglasses under the palm tree. She was my connection to color, to light, to art...and of any color she could have chosen, she painted me bright beige.

I started watching her the next day. I don't why I began when I did. I don't know if I wanted to watch her squirm, or if I wanted to see her fail, or if I wanted to see if she'd give into her feelings for Jett. I don't really think it was any of that though, not for more than a moment. It was never that cruel. I think I just wanted to watch my best friend, the last place I ever felt safe.

"Jett, she still isn't back. It's been over half a day. It's almost dinner time. I figured she'd come back by morning. I'm getting really worried." Eliane paced back and forth in the dorm, hands on her hips, holding her cell phone with her face and shoulder. "God, she still won't pick up."

"Maybe she went home to Greensboro. You really pissed her off." Jett was kicked back on the couch in workout clothes picking at his guitar a little bit.

"*I* pissed her off? You have a hell of a lot of nerve sometimes, Jett."

"Chill, El. She'll be back. She's being a girl, trying to make us sweat. Just live your life and let her do her thing. You're such a control freak. I've seen this shit a million times. You're biting the hook."

"She didn't go home. I called her parents' house right before I called you. I've checked all around campus. I even drove down Broadway looking at some of her favorite hangouts. I checked the clothing stores down on Lexington. This isn't like her. I'm really freaked out, here. You're so cavalier, but something really could have happened. Things happen to people. Haven't you ever been on social media? Haven't you seen those posters about that creeper they've been putting on our doors?"

"Don't be dramatic, El. Girls like Lux are a dime a dozen. She had her feelings hurt, so she's pitching a fit. I bet you a million dollars that she'll show up by tomorrow morning acting like everything is fine. She won't miss my gig tomorrow night."

"You're the most arrogant human I've ever met. You're damn near sociopathic. I hope you'd do better by me if I were ever MIA."

"El, if it were you, I'd already have organized a search party. You're on a different planet than everyone else in my mind. You damn well know it, too, and I'm not ever going to powder your ass by telling you again. So, just remember this time, alright?" He peaked his dark eyebrows, a hint of seriousness that rarely showed. Then he returned to the strumming.

"Ugh. Now I feel like the asshole. This isn't about me and I'm making it about me. That's what started this whole thing to begin with."

"We're all assholes, El. I just wear it where everybody can see it."

"That's for damn sure." She continued pacing, her bare feet starting to ache from it.

"Look, if she hasn't turned up by morning, call her parents and let them deal with it. You have a big writing project to finish. Don't get caught up in other people's bullshit, you know? You always screw yourself over. You have a huge savior complex for someone so self-absorbed."

"That may be so, but I sort of helped cause this bullshit, Jett."

"All you did was write a song, El."

"That isn't all I did. I hurt her. My words hurt another human, Jett. That matters." Tears formed in her already glassy eyes, and I saw another genuine truth. She was sorry. People were rarely truly sorry for anything.

"The good songs are always painful for somebody. I think it would be an honor to be the casualty of a song. It's like sacrificing yourself to the gods of art. Being the artist is never as good as being the subject. The subject is why the art fucking exists; it gives birth to something that just wasn't there. She finally did something that means something and gave us a song. I'm not crying like a little girl over it, and neither should you."

"I gotta go, Jett. This is exhausting me. I'm gonna go out and look again. I'll catch up with you later."

"Peace." He said too casually for her liking.

"What? Are you just going to sit there on *my* couch while I do everything?"

"No, I'm gonna lay down here and maybe eat the rest of your Cap'n Crunch after you leave."

"There's no hope for you. At least clean up the fucking crumbs, OK?" Eliane tapped on my name again, and again was sent to straight to voicemail. "Dammit." She shoved the phone into her pocket and grabbed her keys.

I watched her look all evening for me to no avail. And I didn't enjoy it at all. It was terrible. She was frantic and scared and riddled with guilt. She looked like a mother bird flying around before a storm, trying to gather bits of food and find proper shelter for herself and the babies. She spun in circles until she was dizzy and sweaty, but there was no trace of me.

She finally called my parents again around midnight when the dorm was eerily quiet, and she had that gut check moment when everything became so clear. She stopped ignoring the pit in her stomach and faced the reality that something was terribly wrong.

I don't want to recount that phone call because it was too sad. My mother sobbed and Eliane did too. My mother, however, was so pitiful when she had to acknowledge that I was missing that I can't bear to relive it. So, I won't. And that's why I never watch her, not for a moment.

My family filed the missing person's report in the middle of the longest night of their lives. Then they waited, but not long. Jett was right about one thing. I did turn up by morning.

CHAPTER 21

Frisco and Paris, Texas
Now

The evening after Eliane met with Skyla Free, she headed due west to Frisco. The town just north of Dallas probably wouldn't even be on the map if "the Star"—which is the pet name for the Dallas Cowboys training facility—wasn't there. Other than that, it was rather unremarkable, except maybe to weekend antiquers. A lot of the old charm the town had once boasted had started to get traded in for typical suburban haunts easily built in the flat lands. It wasn't ugly, nor was it beautiful in the way that mattered to El. It was perfectly acceptable in all the ways. But I was glad she chose Paris, despite the drive.

I was still curious to find out how El knew that Skyla had attached herself to Jett, but that would have wait. I couldn't break off into my own research; I was still too compelled to follow her. I had to. Was this sort of what her OCD felt like, having no choice but to live a certain way? I had a feeling the forces that pulled her were even bigger than the ones that pulled me, though it was hard to see how. I *had* to keep watching.

I was fine to table the Jett thing for a minute, anyway. I needed a little bit of entertainment, a little bit of calm. I was about to watch El in my favorite way to watch her, Eliane just being Eliane—whimsical and random, yet focused and serious about the whimsical random thing she was doing. Maybe she would be the one to sprinkle a little bit of magic onto that average American town. I just wish I had popcorn.

Like all the other girls, Eliane was dressed in toast-colored tights that looked like the kind Hooter's waitresses wear. The dance outfit they were paired with looked like a bathing suit had gotten into a fight with a bedazzle machine. Like the town of Frisco, none of that looked like Eliane, either. However, the fact that she was doing this at all was so *very* Eliane.

The veteran cheerleaders were dressed in blue spandex and served as the instructors. Four of them spread out across the head of the room in front of the mirrors, though the one in the center was clearly in charge. She was tall and tan, her hair strategically balyaged into a light brown that had been sun kissed just barely blonde. Her legs seemed as long as Eliane's body. She was intimidatingly beautiful, but normal beautiful. She was beautiful in the way I had been beautiful. I wouldn't have been surprised if she hadn't been a pageant queen herself. Eliane, however, was striking in a different way, maybe more striking than anyone there, though I wasn't sure it's what they'd want. Her eyes glowed differently, and her hair fell a little more unkempt than the rest. Her body was fit and gorgeous, but her legs were short, and it would show in a high kick line. She wasn't particularly tan compared to the others, but personally, I liked the lack of orange tint. If someone were to hug one of the other girls, I think they'd wear the color of her skin the rest of the day. It was a color that resembled red clay mud full of mica. I don't know why they were all so damned shiny. I didn't even get *that* shiny for the pageants I used to do. Eliane didn't have glitter on her like the rest though; she was probably afraid she'd get it in her eye. She had a weird thing about glitter cutting her eye. She had a weird thing about everything.

At the lead cheerleader's request, all the prospective dancers lined up on one side of the room. "OK, ladies, we're going to start off with a dance-class-style warm-up across the floor."

Line by line, they kicked with pointed toes, then turned, then turned some more in a squatted position. Just that much looked confusing enough. My talent was certainly never dancing. I could sing better than average but was average for people who could sing. Dancing had always escaped me, and I think I'm still amazed by people who can move like that.

After all the turning and kicking, the Dallas Cowboy cheerleader hopefuls went back to face the mirrors and started learning the dance of the evening.

"Pay close attention, because parts of this dance will be used at auditions if you make it past the first round. You'll have a leg up for coming to the clinic. We move very fast, so try to get where you can see and follow along." The tall, tanned girl spoke like she was demonstrating heart surgery, her face so serious.

Eliane hadn't been able to elbow her way to the front of the crowd of girls, and I could see her tiny neck straining from one of the back rows to watch the instruction. The teachers moved as quickly as they'd promised, and I wondered how the best girls up front retained it all at such a fast pace. I watched Eliane amble through it.

Eliane could dance, especially to a beat she could really feel, but some of the more complex turns and technical footwork tripped her up. She'd been a cheerleader and had liked hip-hop. She made up a lot of Eliane originals, but she'd come to ballet and jazz late, past the time many dancers would have already retired. With a better view and a little more time, she could have picked it up. She could pick anything up. But there was no time to clarify moves, ask questions, or revisit a count of eight that had already passed. She just had to try to keep up; but she couldn't. She was stumbling, like she'd fallen down a steep hill and struggled for her footing. If she could have just stood up, she might have been OK, but instead, she kept rolling. Eliane's face grew splotchy, then her chest. This was her give away anytime her nerves were getting the best of her. The splotches were the only tell she ever had, and in that outfit, they were out for all to see.

"OK, let's try it in small groups," the instructor with the six-pack abs called out.

Eliane's face dropped, but she moved to the outer edge of the dance space to be assigned a group anyway. The instructor numbered everyone off, and Eliane learned that her group would be the third to perform. I could see her face lose expression. She was in over her head and trying like hell to just go through the motions and blend in. Eliane never aimed to blend. She was so far out of her element. She tapped her fake nails on her teeth. I knew she wished the real ones were available to bite, but she'd gotten a mani to look more the part—along with teeth bleaching and her first spray tan (that still wasn't tan enough).

The first group was called up, four girls with long legs standing in a perfect row. The music started, and they all performed the routine they'd freshly learned moments before. I don't think anyone missed a move. They had smiles on their faces, and their bodies worked effortlessly to execute the jazzy steps. They could have run out of the tunnel on game day. No one was a novice.

The second group got up and one of the girls was slightly thicker than all the others. I felt sorry for her. She was perfectly healthy and an above average dancer, but she didn't have a prayer. The uniform wasn't made for her. But I thought maybe her lack of perfection would encourage Eliane. Maybe she'd show her that not everyone was showroom ready. I was suddenly rooting for her; I usually just watch. But in this moment, I wished I could help her in some way. I wished I could intervene and save her face.

When the third group, Eliane's group, was called up, she took a deep breath and put a big smile on her face. She executed the first few moves with confidence and even a healthy level of cockiness. She tossed her hair and rolled her body like it was what she was born to do. It was impressive, even. But then came a series of turns. She focused so hard to get them right that she lost the choreography when she came out of them. She tried to jump back in, but she was a good four counts behind everyone else, who were moving in perfect unison, two on one side of her, and two on the other. She was rushing moves and stumbling over herself. By the final moves she was standing in place, frozen.

When the music stopped, the other girls clapped while Eliane attempted a slight laugh and skipped off to the side like a child through their own backyard. Then, the fourth group was called up and all eyes were on another set of girls. That's when Eliane quietly walked backward away from the group, then all the way into the parking lot where she sat in her car and cried for the first time in a long time. And she cried big. She wailed and beat the steering wheel with her tiny fist. Then she screamed bloody murder for a few seconds. The harder I watched, the less I think the tears were about screwing up the routine. The tears were for a lot of things, perhaps for all the things. Maybe screwing up that routine had shaken them loose and cast them out of her.

"Get it together." She spoke out loud to herself before wiping the mascara away and checking her phone for the time, hoping for an odd number, so she could start the car and leave.

"Oh God, who's texting me? Don't be my mother." She clicked on the message icon at the bottom of the screen and then on the phone number she didn't recognize.

I hope you don't mind that I texted, and please forgive the length. I don't think you've been getting my emails. I don't want you to feel you have to ignore me. You looked nice tonight, Eliane. Good for you. Don't worry, though. You're still not what I'm after in the sense that frightens you. I know who you really are underneath the spray tan, and you're not the homecoming queen you wish you were. I hated the homecoming queen at my school. So pretty. So empty. She kept everything from me. I tried to show her who I was, but she didn't want to know. She didn't care that I could paint like Van Gogh, or that I could have gotten into Harvard with my SAT scores. She was a couple grades older than I was, embarrassed by the brief time we spent together. She just knew I didn't play football, just like my pretty mother who thought I was so weak because my asthma prevented me the jock life. And the cost of the inhalers made her pick up extra shifts at the Waffle House. Life can't be breathed into that type. You though, you're very much alive. And you've inspired me to see what Texas has to offer. I hope one day we can be friends. It was never my intention to hurt you. And, by the way, you kind of remind me of Zelda, so talented and so lost, lol. You were lost tonight in that sea of more experienced girls that are all my type. So, let's keep our communication between the two of us. I'd hate to see your story end like Zelda's or like your friend's—so tragic, that one.

She threw her phone down and beat the steering wheel once again before she remembered herself and started the engine to get the hell out of there.

Me, I froze for a moment. Had I been watching her so closely that I had missed him watching us...*again*? He said she looked nice tonight, that he'd seen her lost in the other girls. The Blue Ridge Ripper had followed us to Texas.

CHAPTER 22

I thought she'd go to the police immediately, but she didn't. I'd thought the same thing years before when she first realized he knew her. She didn't do it then, either. She was afraid. And the feral cat she's always been, she's prone to flee. She didn't consider the many lives she was putting in danger at that moment. She didn't consider it at all. However, she did buy extra dead bolt locks and alarms for all her doors and windows. But there was also something else. She knew it and I did too. For whatever reason, he was not going to hurt her. So, Eliane spent most of the next few days locked inside her apartment in downtown Paris. She'd lived in Asheville with a serial killer at large for years, so how was Texas any different? She didn't flee this time, not physically. Her mind? I wasn't sure.

She worked on some blog posts as teasers for the upcoming music festival for Skyla and laid out captions for her next 25 posts. I watched her tap at her keyboard and drink green tea for the most part—like everything in the world was fucking brilliant. I hadn't been this pissed off at her in a very long time. She had information on this freak. His mother had worked at an Asheville-area Waffle House. He was now in Texas. That was something. It might even be everything in the right hands. And she was sitting there blogging for an airhead with a strong following.

I had no choice but to look behind Skyla's curtain while Eliane worked. I had to keep occupied because I was growing more resentful by the minute. And in that moment, a rare one, I had no desire to look at El's face.

Skyla had shot most of the pictures Eliane was working on in one or two days, just changing up the outfits and locations. She'd even staged an "underground" party at a speakeasy to make herself look more in the know. The amount of bullshit was shocking, but Eliane captioned everything beautifully, and it all seemed so in-the-moment, full of exclamations and heartfelt daydreams for others to chase, never knowing that none of it even existed to begin with. I was learning that maybe everyone lived in the shadows, only showing whatever pieces they chose to throw out of them and into the light. For Skyla it's only what's beautiful, so different than the man taunting Eliane with all that's dark. It's strange how different people long to show different things, but all wanting the same thing in the end: admiration.

"If I had to do this for the rest of my life, I'd go ahead and open a vein right now," Eliane buried her face into her hands. It reminded me that this job was never about the work, but about making a little cash while she dealt with Jett. And I'd yet to figure out how she planned to do that. I'd missed more than I thought. Even now, I'd not learned to check my surroundings. I still was only able to see what I wanted to see.

•   •   •

In between the work for Skyla, which was like child's play for a writer like El, she focused on the things which did not come to her as naturally, like her double pirouettes and pique turns—that is when she wasn't sitting in front of her laptop watching Netflix in a split for what had to be thirty minutes at a time. I thought, for a moment, that she'd forgotten all about me until she finally stood up, groaning and moaning, out of the split and reached for the stationary and felt tipped pen for the first time in days.

Dear Lux,

I've had such grand plans for months, but now I'm starting to wonder what the hell I'm even doing anymore. I wish so much that I could talk to you face-to-face about it. You always looked at me this way, like you were in awe or something, and it made me believe it too. Did you ever know that? I need one of those looks now, but this will have to do. This is my way to you now, even if it ends up getting me in trouble. I need to talk. I've tried all my usual distractions from you and all that's happened, but it isn't working. The thing is, none of this is over. I wanted it to be, but it isn't, not with Jett or you or him—whoever he is, B.R.R. I have some decisions to make.

I came to Texas to dance. That's the honest-to-God reason. But, along the way, I found other plans. At first, I thought it was fate. I'd already decided to move to Texas to audition for the team...to forget about you...and maybe who I'd been in another life, too. I needed a goal, something big to look forward to when I was in the hospital. I'd sit there in my sweats and greasy hair after a hand-holding group therapy session feeling so pathetic. All the "help" made me feel more like a loser every second I was there. The obsessive thoughts were worse than ever at the beginning. My nails were bloodied, having been chewed down to the nubs. The CBT (that stands for Cognitive Behavioral Therapy by the way) steps they were teaching me took up most of my time. It's basically allowing yourself to have the thoughts that disturb you most come into the mind on purpose, then doing nothing about them. You just think of them until they don't "offend" you anymore, so basically, until you're numb. You sit through the panic, holding onto them instead of trying to make them go away, which eventually teaches your body that the thoughts aren't dangerous at all. Therefore, they will stop being triggers at some point. And I was getting there. It worked, but then I just felt nothing at all. Sometimes I feel so numb, I don't know when to act, when there is danger...and I think I might be in some now. I'm starting to feel again, and it isn't OK.

But I don't want to talk about that. I want to talk about how I got here, now. And that started when I was still in the hospital with nothing to do but think. I just flipped the television on one day and mindlessly started watching these girls trying to make an NFL cheerleading team on CMT or something. It seems so ridiculous. But, you know, I'd danced and cheered in school. I'm drawn to performing but am way too old to try to break into dancing in a company or musical theater. That ship sailed early on. I never knew where or how to train for something like that and had a mother who would have rolled her eyes at it had I wanted to. I mean, I grew up in a double-wide in Appalachia. We didn't "do" the arts. So, I wrote stories about grander things, and I danced the way it was available to me.

We both know my writing had already gotten me into enough trouble at this point, so I just decided to do it. I was going to be an NFL cheerleader who was secretly really bookish and delight over myself on a daily basis about it. I was going to be the quirky main character in my own life, and it was going to take a lot of training and focus on something almost completely foreign to me. It was going to be the best therapy I'd ever had.

So, I started researching Dallas and stumbled across Skyla almost immediately. She's so present in North Texas; she was just in the middle of every tourist spot, major event and activity I looked up. That was all innocent; she was honestly just there. But then, right in the middle of one of her Instagram stories, I saw him. It was Jett, sweat dripping down his face at an after party post-show. And in the next pic, he was kissing Skyla Free.

I dug a little deeper, because we both know, Jett is a little bit like sucking air into a cavity. I just couldn't not. With that, came more Skyla, and I was in a rabbit hole where I eventually saw that she needed a content writer. And I needed a job. I swear at first, I didn't cognitively think about infiltrating Jett's world. It wasn't that maniacal. Until it was. You and I both got screwed and all he got was fame and success. I started to imagine popping up in his world, just appearing like a ghost and fucking it all up for him, and I liked that. I could almost get high off imagining the look on his face when I exposed everything he did to me, exposed what a fraud and user he is. And now I'm here doing all of this, and for the first time, I feel a little bit crazy, like I know everyone thinks I am.

What the actual hell am I doing? I have auditions this weekend and the music festival the next. Am I really going to do all this? I mean both the dancing and confronting Jett. Did I really move halfway across the country for this? To prove some points? To finally rid myself of the shit I'm still hanging onto? I'd convinced myself there was this deeper meaning to all of it. But I'm starting to realize it's all pretty damned shallow. And I think I'm going to do it all anyway. I think I'm about to give in to some part of myself I always try to keep at bay with all my rules about life. I'm going to dance in pretty much my underwear to try to be some adult cheerleader, and I'm going to expose Jett Jorgenson for everything he did to us, and at a festival in front of thousands of people. Yeah, I think I'm doing all of that. And, you know what else? I'm not going to make this guy trying to screw with my head my problem. I don't have to do the "right" thing about anything. I'm going to do what I want, whatever that means as the consequences. And shit—I also better start applying for other jobs; this one will be gone soon enough, I'm guessing.

El

Well, that's one mystery solved. She stumbled upon Jett while conducting some light cyber stalking on Skyla. I don't know how I missed it. I thought I was the best stalker here, but evidentally, there are a lot of us.

Nevermind that. The thing was, El was losing control. Her letter this time was so frantic. Usually, the letters explain how in control she believes she really is. I don't know, though. I think maybe she needs to let go, drop the rituals that make her feel governed. Maybe she should scream at Jett in front of a crowd. Maybe she should make an ass of herself at the auditions, and either be alright or not, just take the journey. Maybe all the therapy she'd ever had led her to this final moment, the most intensive therapy yet...action. And then, maybe after all of that, she'd be able to finally do the right thing and go to the police about the information she sees as pebbles that are really entire mountains. Maybe if she saves herself, she can finally rescue all those little birds so confidently pecking at the ground, so unaware that any danger lurks, the perfect thirteen she's been trying to save her entire life.

CHAPTER 23

Asheville, NC
Back then

They found me about 36 hours after I stormed out that night, just trying to pitch a fit like Jett had said. I can talk about that. I just can't talk about how I got to the place they finally found me, not all of the way. There are certain things that happen to people that are too heavy to ever sit on the tongue. And that line isn't Eliane. That one is all me because I'm the one who experienced something that bad. So, I'll say the parts I can say. The short version is that I was a pretty girl crying at midnight at a college bar off Broadway Street in downtown Asheville, North Carolina. And it never goes well for that girl.

"Let me guess, some guy?" The voice next to me stepped inside my world. It was a voice that belonged to a decent looking man in his late thirties. His face was definitely aged more than mine, but he had a nice smile and pretty eyes. I didn't recognize him, but looking back, it was as if he'd seen me a million times. He wasn't just comfortable around me; he knew *exactly* how to talk to me.

So, I answered, "It always is, isn't it? But it's also my best friend. I don't know which one I'm more upset with. Or maybe I'm just mad at myself. I should know better than to trust anyone."

"They had an affair behind your back?" He asked, speaking in his native tongue of North Carolina good ol' boy, which could fool anybody.

"No, no. Not yet anyway. And he's not even my boyfriend, so I'm not sure how I can really be mad. He's not hers, either. That's all probably on purpose. Just, never mind. It's all stupid. I almost said *complicated*, but it's not. It's just young college drama, and I think I'm ready to grow out of that." I wanted him to think I was a grown-up, not some silly little girl.

"Well, you finished your drink. How about I buy you another one? You don't have to talk. We'll just sit. I'm good at listening to the silence. No drama."

"Sure." It sounded like such a good offer in that moment, and just the idea of someone sitting at a bar and buying me a drink felt so adult like I craved. I hadn't even turned 19 yet. It was all so new. And he'd smelled it. He felt what I needed, and lured me with the bait he knew I would bite.

"What would you like?" He asked as if I'd *actually* know the answer.

I thought of all the fruity concoctions I knew about. They were mostly just words I'd heard my mother say in hushed tones on a cruise. I didn't know what was in any of them, a Bahama Mama, a Bay Breeze. I had a feeling none of those were acceptable, either. So, I said what I thought Eliane would have said, "Gin. Neat." I had not a clue what that was.

"You *have* had a rough night. Gin neat it is." He laughed, then instructed the bartender. I didn't realize then why he'd laughed, but now I do. Of course, he knew what I'd choose.

I should have sipped it, but I threw the gin back all at once, careful not to grimace about it. I didn't remember to appreciate it slower like Eliane did, but it didn't matter by the next one. It seemed easier to get down with ease no matter how quickly I drank it. And especially the third.

I remember slow dancing on a sticky floor. I remember that he smelled like cheap cologne and some kind of metal. I remember that his arms were big and muscular and that I kept falling into them and onto his blue plaid shirt. I remember his voice and the way it started to sound like it was talking to me from inside of a tunnel.

"Easy there," he'd said when I stumbled the first time.

"I'm fine, I'm fine," I kept dancing, freely, awkwardly, my eyes closed like I was letting ocean waves lull me back and forth. Then I was on the floor.

"Whoa, let me help you up," he laughed and pulled me by the arms, almost protective, like a dad scooping up his shaky toddler. "Let's get you some fresh air. It always helps."

I chose to get into his car and let him drive me away; I remember that part, too. It wasn't a sober choice, but I remember making it all the same. He drove me to the Blue Ridge Parkway to an overlook that should have been beautiful and was for the briefest moment. The sound of the river was so calming. I can still hear it. I can feel the stillness of the night and the strength of the mountains around me, and also their somberness. That's my last happy memory, the moments before even the mountains had to look away for a moment. I felt sick in my stomach the second he spoke again.

In a brand-new voice he said, "Get out of the car, Homecoming Queen."

I froze. I looked at him almost wondering if I'd gotten into a car with some other person, not the nice guy I'd been dancing with, not the guy who ordered me good gin. That guy had the voice of a man who would chop wood for your grandma's fireplace when it got cold in the winter months. This one had the voice of something inhuman, something like a machine that had gone off course, defying the laws of robotics.

"Homecoming queen?" I laughed. "I was never the homecoming queen."

"You could have been, easily. Let me guess, too busy with pageants? Get out of the car."

"I'd rather stay here. It's getting really chilly out there." I mumbled.

"There isn't room in here, Homecoming Queen."

"Room for what?" The goosebumps popped up all over my alabaster arms.

He didn't answer, and I didn't get out of the car, but somehow, I ended up on that cold, dewy ground by the river, anyway. I looked up at the stars, begging the sky to change it all. I could feel the sharp rocks digging into my flesh as the cold air of the night touched more and more of my exposed skin.

We all know what he did to me, so suddenly, so violently, before he put his hands around my neck and squeezed until he drained the life from my body. We've all seen the specials on 20/20 or some streaming service documentary. I'm one of those girls, and that's as much detail as I care give about that. That's all I have to give.

I didn't watch what the man who I would later learn was the Blue Ridge Ripper did to me once I took my last breath. That part is just numbness and looking out at a big black sky. They found some of the body that I had lived in for nearly nineteen years in that cold river at the far edge of the muddy hollow the next day, but by then *I* was already living somewhere else. I don't exactly understand where it is. I move about freely. I don't think I have a form anymore. It's just my consciousness. I have no real power, and no one knows that I'm still lingering here-ish. For lack of a better term, I'm a ghost, and I've chosen to belong to Eliane.

I didn't watch my parents after I left at all. It was too painful. I saw them at my funeral because I followed Eliane there, but I tried to look away. The services were almost a month after they first found me. I imagine the cops had all kinds of evidence to collect. I didn't watch that either. Why would I? I know they questioned both Jett and Eliane. A lot of people looked at Jett funny after that for a while, but of course I knew he was no part of it. Not even Jett was *this*.

I heard at some point that I was the third victim, and that I confirmed what they'd feared, that they had a serial on their hands. Shortly after, I saw that they arrested a man who'd been at the bar I'd been at that night. Apparently, I'd danced with more than one of them. He also happened to have connections to the first two girls, one who'd worked in the registrar at UNCA and another who'd graduated the year prior. It made a lot of sense that they would arrest him. I found out later that my guy had even stolen his wallet and dropped it near the dump site. Naturally, I knew they had the wrong guy when I saw his face while Eliane watched the news of his arrest, so relieved. It was sad.

Still, I had no interest in tailing the real perpetrator. I never wanted to see *his* face again. And following him couldn't help bring him to justice. I didn't know where to go, nor did I know how I'd landed wherever I was. I knew there was a destiny, some place I'd eventually get to, but I certainly wasn't there yet. So, I had to decide where it was that I wanted to be in the interim.

I think I went to the place I last felt safe and like I was myself, back to where I was last alive, back to my best friend. That's why I chose her. I wasn't even mad at her anymore. She'd just used the gifts God gave her (and I'm sure there is God, I feel him here, but I just haven't met him yet). However, it didn't matter that I'd forgiven her. I couldn't tell her, and she had no intention of forgiving herself. So, until then, I decided to observe, to cheer her on, to live through her. I decided to do the only thing I could. I decided to stay, and to watch. I never thought until *he* texted her in Texas that *he* would do the very same thing.

CHAPTER 24

Eliane rode with Jett to my funeral about three hours away from Asheville in Greensboro, but she refused to speak to him the entire way there. He didn't press her either. He sat in silence as well, happy to have it. I'm not sure it was out of reverence, probably more like indifference. He didn't want to feel as deeply as Eliane did. The problem was that he *was* capable of it. He wasn't a sociopath like Eliane told him he was; I'd met one of those. But he wished he were one...he wanted to be numb because anything that made him feel alive was too much, like being tickled too hard. He didn't want to laugh or cry. He just wanted to make music about it so at least whatever was inside him could get out. But make no mistake, Jett Jorgenson wasn't beautifully tortured. He'd endured very little pain ever. Any torture he felt was his own pride rebelling against a soul that could have been so good in another life. He could have chosen to feed that soul the day of my funeral and grieve for me, but he didn't. He chose to turn to stone. He didn't so much as send flowers, though Eliane bailed him out by putting his name on the gorgeous display of lilies of the valley she'd sent. I'm sure she chose them because of their incredible beauty, but they're also one of the most fragile flowers found on the planet. They aren't destined for long lives.

My parents asked Eliane to say a few words after the pastor delivered his sermon on how we are to find greater purpose in tragedies which we cannot understand. After he'd done his best considering the situation he was given, Eliane stepped up to the microphone. She looked out at the crowd and then back down at her notes. I could *almost* see the lump in her throat but could *definitely* see the tears forming in the corners of her wide eyes.

"Lux means light," she began, swallowing hard. "That's the first thing we ever bonded over. Both our names mean light. I—I um...." She trailed off and I watched the crowd get nervous for her, everyone draped in black, trying not to squirm in the pews.

"Just keep going." Jett mouthed to her with a hand motion that showed he was more eager for her to spit it out than he was encouraging her.

"Look, um, I was going to give this cliché speech about how bright Lux's light was and how it will continue to burn. I even wrote a poem to go with it. It really is a beautiful poem, and I was proud to read it to you all, but I can't do it." The hard swallow again. "Lux did have a light, but she held it inside because she wanted to please people. She didn't want to be the wrong thing or say the wrong thing. She didn't want to be vulnerable, which ended up making her vulnerable. Those of us that can be so open aren't the braver ones; we just can't help it because we're basket cases. And she admired that about me," Eliane choked up hard. "She admired me for so many reasons, God knows why, and then the one time I saw her vulnerability, I exploited it. I wrote the worst thing about her, and she heard it read out loud. Can you imagine what that does to your soul? Especially to someone who doesn't open up all that much to begin with? I ruined her. Jett and I ruined her together. That's why she left upset that night and wound up at that bar. I put her in the wrong place at the wrong time, and she deserved more. So, her light isn't shining. I put it out with that pen I'm always so damned proud of mastering. I could say all the nice things in the world, because she *was* all the nice things in the world. But what I owe her is her life back, and I can't put together enough pretty words to make that happen." She looked at my parents, who were now on their feet ready to stop this trainwreck. "I am so very sorry. I can't ever change this for you, but I just want you to know that your daughter was amazing. She was better than anyone. She was far better than I am."

She stepped down from the pulpit and paused to gaze at the flowers she'd sent me, the ones she'd been gazing at when she packed her things in Asheville before leaving for Texas. She awkwardly lifted the large arrangement, easel and all, and hurriedly moved toward the back of the church with them.

"What are you doing with those?" My mother asked through sobs and confusion.

"I can't keep these alive, but I can admire them forever. They'll always mean something, and I don't want them to end up lost or buried with her. I promise I'll take better care of them than I did my friend."

Jett stood up and kind of nodded with his hands in prayer and then rushed out behind Eliane. He didn't say anything until they got to the car. Eliane expected he would find the humanity to console her. She had made a horrible scene, but she was clearly drowning. She'd literally stolen the funeral flowers she had sent in front of a room full of my mourning friends and family members.

"What the fuck was that, El? Everything is already bad enough, then you go and pull that dramatic shit?" He punched the steering wheel. "Grow up!"

"What do you mean? I didn't pull anything. I was just honest." She gnashed her teeth.

"And why'd you have to pull me into it? You said my fucking name up there, El. You know the police questioned me. That might make people think I had something to do with it—it involves me at the very least, and you know I don't do messy." He shook his head. "I shouldn't have even driven you here. Funerals are pointless anyway. They don't undo anything. I don't want to be a part of this anymore."

"Oh, that explains why you give a shit. I said your name because you treated her like trash that night, Jett. And then I had the audacity to write about it because I was so smitten with all this shit you spew. I wrote that for myself, to make *me* feel better." She screamed, spit and mascara flying. "I wrote that to prove to my pathetic self that I'm the one that shines and to bring her down a notch because you were in her bed and not mine. That wasn't art; it was just fucking mean. And now she's dead, Jett. She's dead because you're an idiot, and I'm a bigger one."

"What are you talking about? What do you mean you wanted me in your bed and not hers?"

"Give it a rest. You read the lyrics. You've read me like a book for years. I don't know what this relationship is, but it isn't fucking *friendship*. You're a drug, and I took it. I wanted to believe I was yours, but year after year, you just kept choosing everyone around me. I don't know if I was or if I am or if it's all in my head. I don't know your game, and it's not fun trying to figure it out anymore. I'm finished. I built you up in my head, but you're toxic, and I'll die too if I stay near you."

"El, I—it wasn't a game. It was...you're complicated. You make my head work differently. I didn't think you even wanted—"

Eliane looked in his eyes, giving him the opportunity to say it to her, to explain it, to answer the questions she didn't know she had.

Jett stared at her, his breathing hard. His jaw was clenched but his eyes had finally softened. He started to speak and instead he reached and grabbed her face, pulling it in toward his. Eliane let the tears rush out of her eyes when she felt his breath on her lips. Then she almost let them touch her. She almost lost that tiny thread that had been hanging on, but she jerked away from him.

"No, Jett. No."

"I thought—"

"This? Now? Are you kidding me? No." She got out of the car. "I'll call an Uber. Don't contact me. Erase my name from your phone. Erase my face from your memory. You never knew me. I never want to see you again, Jett. You ruined us before we could be us. You ruined Lux. You ruined it all."

CHAPTER 25

Paris, Texas
Now

Eliane practiced her freestyle routine on the roof of her building. Her apartment wasn't big enough, and besides dodging the occasional broken beer bottle, the roof offered her the perfect studio space. She ran through the routine ten times full out, turns, floor moves, and all. Then she added an eleventh run-through even though she was exhausted, because of course, numbers.

She finally laid back and looked into the late afternoon sun, letting the sweat stream down her temples. I'd always liked the feeling of sweat. It meant I'd worked hard; it proved it. I wondered if she felt the same. But my guess is that she wasn't focused enough to appreciate the sweat. She was thinking about everything all at once. That's the only way Eliane thought about anything. There were no compartments, no filing systems. There was just a junk drawer with everything tossed into it. She worried about her auditions while she plotted her confrontation with Jett, and probably also, oddly thought about how to bring quality to Skyla's next blog post. It was all in there tumbling around together like unsorted laundry in the dryer, towels mixed with nice blouses. That's also how Eliane had done her laundry. None of her obsessions made her any less of a slob. She was probably the least neat OCD person on the planet. Order just wasn't her brand of gin. However, numbers were, which is why she had to practice that routine an odd number of times. That would ensure that all the things in her head would take their marching orders. And she'd done it, danced that eleventh dance. So now she could breathe. She laid there, wishing it was Zelda's spot on the lawn of Dr.Vitale's practice, rummaging through that drawer, no doubt wondering what to do next. And she started to itch.

Thoughts of Jett had been too close lately in working with Skyla. Even though she'd planned to confront him about the thing I've yet to explain that's far worse than the funeral debacle, she hadn't thought of him taking up space in her brain. I don't think she'd considered the cold draft that she'd feel in opening up that door again. But she'd opened it, and he infiltrated her mind once again, stomping through it with his guitar thrown over his back and Gestapo boots on his feet. Eliane paused the dance music that was still playing and scrolled to the search bar on Spotify. She gingerly typed in the words Letters to Lux, which, by the way, was the name of Jett's band.

She hadn't tortured herself in this way in a long time. The last time she'd listened to the song that had gotten him those first tastes of fame, she was still in the hospital. But now, in this moment, she chose to listen again. I think it might have been a test to prove her own strength to herself, but I couldn't be sure. It might have just been a weak moment. It might have been for the fun of torture. It was hard to be sure.

The words she knew so well, the words that she'd written that led to the end of my life were set to a melody that she hated to love. It was a damn good song. The words were magic, and Jett made the guitar cry the tears he never shed. Their collaboration was transcendent; it was as if they'd dropped some kind of acid together that only the two of them knew about and chased the journey it took them on into another world where something above a human taught them the genius of what that song became. Because once those lyrics took a different form inside the tune, something was born that can only be felt when that song is heard. She knew it as well as anyone, which is why it shook her more than it pissed her off. She couldn't help but adore it. That sound imprinted on her the second she heard it for the first time, despite her anger. I wondered—and—I'm sure that she did too— if Jett felt it, or if he just enjoyed all the spoils of winning the musicians war with the odds of "making it:" girls, fame, money, admiration. And he got it all. Eliane got nothing but chills down her spine and an irregularity in her heartbeat, not yet anyway.

CHAPTER 26

The River Arts District, West Asheville
Not Quite as Far Back Then

Three years passed in about thirty seconds for me. Literally. Time doesn't seem to matter so much here. I'm not sure how it felt for Jett or Eliane, probably like it did for me when I was there. Three years in your late teens or early twenties might as well have been a hundred. I always heard it would fly as I got older, but I never really got that chance. I don't know if that felt like it does here or like something else. All I know, is that time is irrelevant, and I now see how weird it was that everyone governed their lives around it. I don't know how time felt for the two of them, if it was long or short, but I'm sure it either felt like they'd never known each other at all, or like they'd been together only a moment ago.

They had gone their separate ways after my funeral. Jett stayed in school—probably because it was free with his baseball scholarship. Jett had hated school, and though it's bad advice for most people, he probably should have just pursued music the whole time. He had what the others wished they did. He graduated on time, without any kind of honors, and really for no reason. I didn't know much about what he did, though. It was Eliane I stayed with. So, I found out about what Jett had been up to during those lost years exactly the same time she did. Had I looked in on him and discovered it first, it wouldn't have mattered anyway. I couldn't have changed the outcome. I think I have less effect on destiny here than I did when I was there.

El dropped out of school after that one semester, which I was oddly happy to see. That meant I didn't have to linger around our dorm anymore watching her sob in my doorway. It was too much to bear, and she did it almost every day. Maybe it was selfish for me to want her to quit, but Eliane wasn't built for that kind of normalcy anyway. It got better for us both when she left...for a while, anyway.

She got a job waiting tables at a place called Seeds that smelled like the spice aisle at Whole Foods to pay for an even weirder apartment than the one she lives in now. It was in the River Arts District, a place full of galleries, breweries and random weirdness in renovated brick warehouses on the outskirts of downtown Asheville. She shared half of an artist's studio with an eighteen-year-old painter who called himself Zen Zee, her side of the room separated by a homemade partition he painted something really bizarre on that I never did decipher. Whatever it was, the design was colorful and whimsical, but somehow a little bit scary to look at. It fit that era for Eliane perfectly in looking back on it now.

She started writing the minute she moved in. She was hungrier than ever and tapped away at a vintage typewriter for the first week. She began her novel that way. It was about a group of people who called themselves the "bathroom artists" and started this post-apocalyptic revolution through graffiti left in abandoned restaurant bathrooms all over the country. About a week in she shouted, "to hell with it," then got out her laptop to continue on. Again, El always romanticized things. She still has that old typewriter, but now only as a decoration.

However, she did keep working on the piece. It's all she did in between shifts at the restaurant. She only let herself drink gin when she was writing at night. During the day it was water with slices of cucumber thrown in it, which she would pull out and place on her eyes by the evening. But she wrote a lot more nights than she did days.

The premise of her new project was great, and the first three chapters were good. But it wasn't what she knew, so it fizzled, though she never realized it. She should have written about Jett and me and her endless issues. She should have dug down deep and written what she was afraid to the most while it was fresh, but she didn't, and so the plot she attempted just didn't come off. I watched her revise everything except for the beginning over and over again. And the more she revised it, the more she twisted it into things she couldn't understand. She'd stare at the screen, eyes red, her first signs of a number eleven showing up in between her brows. She thought she'd eventually get it right. But then I saw her give up. It was a Sunday night. She rolled her eyes after changing the same sentence for the ninth time. Then she shot the rest of her gin and started frantically emailing agents, hoping that one would take a bite. She'd cooked a big meal for them, had chosen none of her native cuisine, had burnt some of it, then served it all anyway because it had been so much effort to make. All she had to pitch was a plot; she hadn't poured an ounce of soul into that recipe, and the agents smelled it right away. It wasn't that the story was bad, it just couldn't beat without the heart, and Eliane was still protecting hers. She didn't yet know that the manuscript she'd spent so much time on would get horribly rejected for another year before she'd stop trying. But that's what was in store.

All the writing failures aside, she was actually getting along OK during the period by the river. At least she was on the journey she wanted to be on. She was trying and failing and trying again and that was good for her. She believed she'd eventually hit the nail on the head, and she wasn't sad as much as she was before and would be after. But then, *he* showed up three years, two months and four days after she'd told him to never contact her again.

It was spring and Eliane was writing with the door open, a new project, just stream-of-consciousness about strangers' intertwined lives in the arts district at the moment—that one *might* have eventually been something, but her work on that one was cut short, and whatever she'd started was left unfinished.

It had been a good day when Jett showed up. The river smelled like mountain trout, cheap beer and sunscreen when it wafted into the room, and the faint laughter of hippies and college kids tubing the French Broad followed closely behind. But then a Jett-shaped cloud came in and cooled the warmth of that pretty day. I felt the chill, at least.

In true Jett Jorgenson fashion, he saw that the big metal door was opened and he walked straight through it without a knock or a word of warning. Eliane didn't see him swallow hard first, nor did she see him pause to watch her write in her crop top and overalls for a good thirty seconds before walking up behind her big industrial desk to scare the hell out of her. But he had. Despite his apparent boldness, the sight of her had given him pause. She would have so loved to have known that.

"Boo." He said quietly, and Eliane's notes flew into the air, as she drew her arm instinctively.

"Oh my God." She shouted, lowering her arm to her side. "I almost hit you in the face. What in God's name are you doing in here?"

"I was in the area. I heard you were living here. I mean, the door was open. I thought it was like a free, hippie, arts district thing you were doing. I figured it would be crass to knock." He flashed his charming smile.

"You were in the area?" She furrowed her brows and moved her hands to her hips.

"Yeah, I was. And I just thought it had been long enough. Or, are you not finished pouting yet?"

"What do you want, Jett? You always want something. You don't appear like a ghost after three years and pretend you just thought "what the hell? I'll check on Eliane today.""

"OK, fine. I have a small motive, but I did want to see you. I missed you, El."

"What's the 'small motive,' Jett?" She flashed air quotes before crossing her arms.

"I want to help you before something gets way out of hand." He reached in his pocket, pulled out a stack of letters addressed to me, and threw them down on her desk.

"How the hell did you get those?" Eliane stated rather than asked. It was almost like she was saying "of course, you have those."

"Lux's parents tracked me down and wanted to know if I was still in touch with you. They said that you've been writing letters addressed to her and mailing them to their house in Greensboro ever since she died. It's really upsetting for them, El. They said they've done everything to reach you and you won't respond. So, they reached out to me."

"It's just—yeah, I write them. I'm not, like, trying to hurt them or something. That would be so twisted. I haven't thought about what her parents must think, honestly…which I now realize is so stupid. I wasn't thinking at all, I guess. I just needed a process to get through. I had things to say to her, to you even, that I could have only said to her. It was just something I did, I —"

"Well, you have to stop it. You always "do" instead of think. It's keeping the wound open for them and they think you're batshit. The fact that they think you need help is the only thing that's stopped them from going to the police already. But they will, El. I told them I would talk to you. I know you think I'm the biggest asshole on the planet, but I don't want to see you in trouble. You were my oldest friend. You've got to get a hold of yourself. They don't know this is just how you deal with shit. They weren't there when it was cute when you wrote letters to

Zelda Fitzgerald when you were twelve. They just see the girl who had a meltdown at the funeral, took responsibility for the death, then stole her own flowers back. It doesn't look good, El."

Eliane bit her lip hard, like doing so would keep her from crying. But it didn't.

"Hey, come here—" Jett reached out.

"Don't." Eliane flinched. "God, I don't want to do this with you here, of all people."

Jett rolled his eyes and pulled her close to him anyway. And it was earnest in that moment, even if not much else ever was, and even if that moment was meant to have a short life.

"I know this has been hard. And with the police realizing that they have the wrong guy, you've probably needed an outlet."

"Wait, what?" Eliane pulled away quickly. "What are you talking about?"

"I—I assumed that you knew. It's all over the news, social media, everything. They got the wrong guy. The actual killer struck again. And he left a note, like taunting the police about it. They had to release the guy they thought it was, but he's still out there. I thought maybe that was why you were writing so much more."

"No, no I had no idea." El's heart started pounding, but of course, I wasn't surprised at all. "I need a minute." She lowered herself to the couch.

"That's why her parents are freaking out even worse now. They've even asked me if I think there could be any way you could have been involved."

"Are you joking? How could I have been involved? This has nothing to do with me. I would never—"

"El, I know. I know none of this is your fault. But they think you're insane. They're spinning with questions. They think maybe it could be someone connected to your life somehow. You're making them think that by going on like you are."

"Oh my God. I feel like I could throw up." She held her stomach.

"I think I have another way this can be an outlet for you, though. You still need to work a lot of shit out with this. I mean, especially now. I really didn't know that you hadn't heard about that though. I'm sorry to come and dump it on you like that."

"What do you mean?" El looked up at him, tears still in her eyes. "What kind of outlet?"

"There's some good stuff in those letters. You're a poet even when you're trying not to be. Maybe that's why you can't ever write a novel to save your life. There's nothing prose about you, El."

"Prosaic," she corrected.

"Whatever." He rolled his eyes. "The point is, I think you're a song writer. The band has had this producer chasing us. He loves the melodies we're coming up, thinks the words could be a little stronger. He hates the name of the band. He says it's too high school and won't sell."

"He's right. I think you were thirteen when you came up with the name *The Wannabe Rejects*. It sucks. I told you it sucked then. And now it's too outdated, too bubblegum punk. It sounds like Avril Lavigne's boyfriend's band," she rambled. "But wait a second. How do you know you liked stuff in my letters to Lux? Did you read them?"

"Yeah, I read 'em all," he answered quickly and shrugged.

El flared her nostrils and swallowed hard before she spoke. "OK, huge violation. I'm not at all surprised, but that's so screwed up that you read them." She paused, "But, um, there was some ugly stuff about you in those...really ugly. How'd you enjoy that?"

"So, let's use it. That's how I feel about it. It was the realest shit there is."

"Unbelievable..." Eliane said almost to herself.

Jett trudged on. "I want to rename the band *Letters to Lux* and base the songs in the first album off what we went through losing her. You can travel with us and write. I'll hammer out the tunes. It'll be amazing. It'll make you a real writer, out on the road, living this huge life."

"Jett—I mean, part of that sounds like my *Almost Famous* moment, and it would be incredible. But, if you were worried about secret letters rubbing salt in the wounds of the people who love Lux, what would this do to them? The songs could be everywhere, and we'd literally be exploiting her death for our gain. We'd be profiting off of something we caused. Not to mention, the killer was never caught, apparently? This is like...glorifying him. It might even encourage him, draw him out. And the other girl's families—"

"We didn't cause anything, El. We were just there. Life happens. This is what we have to work with. These are the cards in our hand. How is that our fault?"

"No, life is a series of choices, Jett. You have one to make right now." El put her hand to her furrowed brow. "Were you even worried about me at all? Or did you read my letters and get an idea. Did you come here out of thin air to help me, or to help yourself? Am I charity or opportunity in this scenario?"

"Why can't it be both?" He answered easily. "And I mean that I was helping, not that you're charity or something."

"Because, Jett, you can't do anything for anyone without just a little something in it for you. Even if there's some realness, and some decent intent, you have to go and amend it to serve your own interests. I should have known when you darkened the door. You are just the same Jett I've always known."

"You're so sanctimonious, El. You're always telling me what I am, but you never scrutinize yourself like this. When are you gonna face all the things that you are? They aren't all pretty, El. A lot of it is completely fucked to be honest."

"Oh my God, Jett. All I do is analyze every move I make. All I have done is take responsibility for my actions. I just want you to do it, too for once!" She shouted.

"Well, that's not your job. I don't belong to you. I'm not yours to save, El. I never was."

"You know what? You're right." She shook her head. "Three years, and we're still having the same weird argument. We just create some kind of toxic gas the second we're in a room together and then I can't breathe."

"Whatever. You know, if you weren't like this, if you didn't have to wallow in fucking *everything,* you'd be on the edge of success like me. You sabotage yourself, El. You hold back. You don't use your own life in your stuff and that's why it all sucks. Maybe you could learn something from me."

"If I suck so bad, then why do you need me to write your songs?" She clapped back, tears in her eyes this time.

"Because you don't suck. It's only that bullshit you try to spit because you feel too guilty to write what's real if you think anyone else plans to read it. You only write the good stuff in secret. It's a damn shame, too."

"Well, maybe one day I can find the right way to write about Lux. But, this isn't it. I can't take those letters, or especially the song that made her storm out, and ultimately got her killed, and use it to make money."

"You don't have to. That's what I wanted. I wanted to be a team, but you can't. Just let me use the song. I have a form with me that you can sign." He pulled the folded paper from his pocket.

"I could literally throw up." She just stopped and held her hands at her sides.

He said nothing, but then tried to hand her a pen anyway.

"I'm not signing that, Jett. You aren't using my words. I cannot believe you came here with that ready to go. You have no shame, do you?"

Jett flared his nostrils and crumpled the paper into his fist. "Whatever, El. What fucking ever. I'm over this. And I'm over you. Don't worry, I won't show up again. You'll hope I will in the darkest corners of your mind, but just know, I won't." He got closer to her face before turning to leave. "Ever."

Eliane stared back at him no more than an inch away,

"Umm, hey…" A voice startled them both into taking a couple of steps back.

"Oh, Jake. Hey. You scared me." Eliane smoothed her hair.

"What's going on here, you OK?" The guy with neatly combed hair, who stood about 6'3 inched a little closer, his eyes on Jett, though he spoke to Eliane.

"Oh fine. This is my old friend, Jett. He was in the area. He was just leaving."

"Jake," The much taller of the two extended his hand like a gentleman.

Jett reluctantly shook the hand, harder than he normally would have while he eyed the large ring that said United States Marine on it.

Eliane stood between them, with her arms folded while they all took turns eyeing one another. Then Jake put his thick arm around her, pulling her close to him and kissing her on top of the head.

"Nice to meet you, Jake." Jett finally said looking him in the eye before turning to El, "So long, Eliane."

CHAPTER 27

I'd only seen Jake a handful of times before that afternoon. I hardly considered him noteworthy until that day. El dated occasionally, but no one ever stuck around. I rarely saw a face twice, but Jake was a man of persistence.

He'd met Eliane by swiping right, like a lot of people meet now. I'm not that sad I missed out on the swiping era. It looked like hell.

Jake wasn't anywhere near her type, and she knew it the second she opened the door for their first date. She knew it because he'd shown up with candies and a flat top haircut. He'd shown up wearing honor and formalities as clearly as the pressed button-up shirt. But I think she kept seeing him for exactly that reason: the normalcy. And he kept seeing her because she wasn't. Honestly, he didn't look like the type that would have even been on the dating app to start with, but he was the type that was always looking to settle down. He was a man who wanted a wife and family to take care of back home while he defended the nation he revered. A buddy probably convinced him he had to start shopping a little harder, and with the life of a military man in the 21st century, that meant learning to swipe. So, he swiped, looking for someone he could protect. And Eliane swiped, looking for the first time ever, for someone to do just that.

After Jett left, Jake so maturely turned to Eliane and said to her, "So, I'm assuming there's some kind of history there."

To which Eliane quietly nodded.

"Do you care to tell me about it?" He asked honestly, his tone gentle while he tucked her wild hair behind her ear.

Eliane put her hands to her temples and rubbed them around in a circular motion. "Does it have to be right now?"

"Of course it doesn't. Just tell me now if I should be worried. Tell me honestly, and if you say no, I'll believe you."

"Absolutely not." Eliane affirmed, and she might have even believed it herself as pissed off as she was in those moments after he'd left.

"Then let's not worry about it. I have to go back down east for maneuvers in two days. I'll be gone for a couple weeks. I want to soak up as much of you as I can, so let's not spend it sorting through messes if they're messes that don't matter. I trust you." He kissed her on the temple that had grown red from her rubbing it.

"Why are you so solid?" Eliane leaned up and kissed his lips gently. "I didn't think they made them like you."

"They made me for girls like you," he answered.

"You do keep me grounded." She smiled. "And what is it I give you in return?"

"Everything that's not on the ground."

"So, you're the ground, and I'm the sky? That's a really good answer, soldier." She kissed him one more time, deeper this time, deeper than most times.

He kissed her back and the muscles in his large arms tightened around her. She was happy to kiss him back and did so eagerly. But she wasn't hungry. She was satisfied enough with it, but she wasn't sweating. Her pulse wasn't racing. She was comfortable and protected. But she hadn't written about him once, not even in letters to me.

She pulled away and looked up at him for a moment, "You have a nice face. It's so symmetrical. Zen says that's what makes people attractive, and that's why he never paints them that way."

"He doesn't want attractive people in his paintings?" Jake raised one sharp eyebrow.

"Apparently not. You'd certainly never make the cut."

"Well, I'll take that as a compliment, then," he said, though I wasn't sure coming from Eliane, that it was a compliment. It was more an observation about how flawless he was, and I knew how Eliane appreciated flawlessness. She didn't at all.

He kissed Eliane some more, then reached and unhooked the straps on her overalls. Then he pulled the white crop top off over her head. Eliane answered by reaching and unbuckling his belt.

"Are you sure? You haven't let me get this far yet?" He leaned down and kissed the tip of her nose.

"I'm sure. I just feel so lucky to have you in my life right now. I want you." She urged him on, running her hands down his perfectly chiseled abs.

So, they continued. I didn't stay for all of it. That would have been obscene and disrespectful. Though, there was part of me that wished I'd seen them make love. It would have answered a lot more questions. It would have told me if she'd had sex with Jake because she was upset with Jett or because she wanted to be with him. It would have told me if she were only passing the time or if she were really starting to fall for him. Plus, I kind of wanted to see how someone like her made love, like art maybe, full of color and happy accidents, something I never experienced myself.

When they first started seeing one another, I thought it was just passing the time. She tried to be interested, but the way she'd send him home early or just stir her meal around her plate made me think otherwise. However, today there seemed to be a spark of excitement that wasn't there before. There was something more alive about the whole thing. But was that because of him, or because of her argument with Jett? Which of them had really brought her back to life that day? I couldn't tell. She had either decided to move on and was experiencing something healthy *finally,* or she had been brought to the point of raw desire by five minutes arguing with Jett Jorgenson again. Truth be told, it probably had shades of both. I just wondered in that moment, which one would win. I supposed time would tell.

CHAPTER 28

Paris in the morning and Dallas in the afternoon
Now

The alarm was set for five a.m., but Eliane had been awake since a little after four. She tossed and turned all night, slipping in and out of dreams of both performing well and failing miserably at her preliminary auditions. For the longest time it was just this fun thing she might excel at, and it was so far into the future. But now, it wasn't the future anymore. It was here, it was audition day.

Eliane rose when the second the alarm rang and marched straight to the shower, her stride stiff and dutiful like a soldier's. She was serious Eliane again; this would be one of those days for plans and precision that she only could bear once or twice per year.

She shaved her armpits in every direction, careful to leave no hint of a little black stub hiding in any crevice. She shaved extra, until her skin hurt, in which she feared redness, and stopped on the next available odd number. I wasn't counting, but it was a high number of swipes across flesh. I'll guess 37. Then she exfoliated her face a bit more carefully, only five swirled scrubs with the washcloth that she counted in a whisper.

When she got out, she dried her hair straight, then strategically curled beach waves into it with a wand that burned her fingertips. She applied makeup primer, foundation, and three or four components from a contouring kit before adding the false eyelashes, eye shadow and liberal amount of lip plumper. She stood back from the mirror to admire herself. And I think she liked what she saw, a classic beauty that looked more like the kind I'd been. I personally hated it. It was El; she should have at least worn her real curls instead of the pseudo ones everyone wears.

She walked back into her bedroom, standing up a little straighter than normal, and pulled the unused sticky boobs that looked like raw chicken cutlets from her top dresser drawer. They pushed up what little she had to offer and gave her an extra cup size, which meant a full B. Then she put on the Hooters tights, hot pink bra top, matching bottoms, and jazz sneakers. She put large fakes studs that matched the rhinestones on the dance getup into her tiny ears, and then took a breath as she gazed in the mirror one more time. She looked the part from head to toe, and she knew it and was satisfied. She threw on her warm-ups over top of it all and doused herself in something that smelled like cheap coconut I'd never seen her use before.

It took her about an hour to get to the stadium, even on a weekend, with no commuter traffic. When she arrived, there were already at least a hundred other girls in line waiting to get in, and others pulling in by the minute. Though there were various hair and outfit colors, they all looked virtually the same. They were nervous, pacing, or hopping in place. Some chatted hysterically with others. Some said nothing to anyone. Eliane was one of those. She rarely found herself without something to say, but her nerves could always get her to shut her mouth.

Men behind cameras interviewed various hopefuls, and they all said the same thing. "I feel the nerves a little bit. I have butterflies," they'd admit, "but I just want to go out there and have fun. I want all the girls to do a great job and have a blast." *Yeah right.*

Once inside, Eliane was given her number, 120, perfectly even, a round number to beat it all.

"It means nothing," she whispered to herself before placing it on the tiny piece of cloth on her hip.

She avoided the groups gathered around the "spruce-up" stations. She'd readied herself. She didn't practice fueté turns in the corner, or chat with other girls about why she was there today. She found a corner to shove her warm-ups and stayed by them stretching. Once she was finished, she just pretended to stretch some more. She was out of her element. She was the least free I'd ever seen her. She looked how I'd looked in every situation I'd ever been in. I just wanted to get her out, but as I've explained, I only exist. I have no form, nor power of any kind.

The veteran cheerleaders began to call groups of five girls in to perform their freestyle dances to a clip of music selected by the judges, which composed of the Dallas Cowboys Cheerleaders' famed coaches, some cowboys staff, an ex-reality TV star, a couple choreographers, and a well-known country music artist. All five girls would perform at once, each doing their own dances, hoping to stand out in a crowd of knockouts. Even though I no longer had a stomach, I felt like I was going to throw up just watching it all.

Eliane picked at the corners of her nails a little bit while she waited. She couldn't bite them because she'd gotten a perfect gel mani the day before. That wasn't that bizarre. She normally kept her nails nice for precisely this reason. She'd always bite if they were available.

It took about an hour for her turn to roll around. The auditions were fast, but Eliane, being number 120, was in the 24th group to perform. When they finally called her, she stood casually and walked to her mark, which was on a small piece of dance floor just on the other side of a rented blue curtain with silver stars all over it. The music that had been available on the audition website for months began. She and her dance teacher had prepared the perfect routine for it, and she'd practiced. Her muscles remembered the opening moves like they remembered how to walk. She looked good, moving like butter through the dance space. Then, when the moment came, she prepared for her double pirouette. She was famous for stepping out of it early, but she didn't show it on her smiling face. She smiled with confidence and rose onto the ball of her left foot. She spun twice to the right and landed with perfect precision. When the music stopped, she was in her final pose, hip thrown out, jazz hands in the air. And she was proud.

CHAPTER 29

The River Arts District, West Asheville
Back then, but not that far from now

Eliane spent another three years in the little breezy studio by the river on the outskirts of Asheville. By this time, she was 25 and her life was on a path that faced a very different direction than where it does now.

She was still rooming with "Zen Zee," and something about his oddly serene paintings strewn about with the sound of the river nearby was good for her. She admired his paintings and his philosophies on life. He wasn't a bit cute to her, weighed about 110 pounds, was five years her junior, and had never shown the least bit of interest in any human, male or female. He was a great man for Eliane to have as a truly platonic friend. His world mixed with her just fine, like oil and vinegar. A lot of people think oil and vinegar are enemies, but it isn't true. They sit in the same pot just fine. They create beautiful meals together that everyone enjoys. They sit together happily on healthy salads and make lunch pleasant. They coexist without mixing. And that's what Eliane needed during that period.

Jake was also still in her life in the only way that could have worked for her. He'd been deployed to a base in Okinawa, Japan for the past year. They'd kept in touch via Facetime and PG-13 sexting. They'd exchanged the I-love-yous before he left and had only fought once or twice during the whole three years. The whole thing was little bit like a Hallmark Christmas special. The relationship had been cute to watch at times, but I'd also often changed the channel. It wasn't enough to keep me watching all that much. There was kissing and decent love-making and hand-holding. There were gifts and chocolates on Valentine's Day — just never flowers. There was a strapping boy who did everything right and a pixie-like girl who made him laugh. It was as calm as the river in a drought, no rough water to speak of, just like El's life had been lately. Some people would comment about how well she was doing considering "everything," which confused Jake if it was said in front of him, due to the fact that she'd told him nothing. Others would pat her on the back and encourage her to keep writing, which she'd honestly done the smallest amount of in her entire life. No one was worried about her, and in secret, her counting habits were worse than ever. She'd never ever let Jake see any of it though; she'd let him see very little of her all together. But maybe that's what he was for. Some people are meant to be easy, even if they don't come packing fireworks. Not every day is the fourth of July.

The evening that quickly changed all of that had started out nicely enough. The spring had come late that year, and the breeze was warm for the very first time. Eliane threw all the windows open and wrote a little for the first time in months (still the bathroom artist novel) for a while in earshot of the rushing water while Zen painted quietly. She'd sat out a bowl of fresh fruit to pick from every few minutes and drank a little white wine only because it was the first real spring day. Otherwise, it would have been gin. She only gave into clichés with specific reason. Having died at nineteen, I'd only tried whatever liquor was left in my parent's cabinet, some cheap beers at high school parties, and Eliane's Margaritas. I wanted to sip from her glass. I think I could have been a white wine drinker. Actually, I'm sure of it. Red stains the teeth.

A Facetime from Jake popped up on her screen and interrupted her writing, but she was in a good mood, so she welcomed the break.

"Hey, sweetie," she answered with a sleepy smile.

"Well, look at you all set up with your wine. Having a nice evening?" His face was clean shaven, his green eyes bright, and he wore his fatigues.

"It's been the best day. It's finally warm, and I felt like writing. I think the weather tempers my moods a lot."

"Huh. Interesting. Well, I'm glad you're writing."

"Thanks. Me too," she winked at him.

"Have you thought anymore about coming to see me. I know you're not thrilled at travelling so far by yourself, but I'll set everything up nicely. I really want to see you. We'll walk the botanical gardens and go to the beach. We'll eat sushi and drink good sake. You'll love it."

"Aww, I know I would. I really, really, would. That flight is just so brutal. And you know I can't afford it. But I'm not letting you pay."

"I want to pay. You're my girlfriend. We've been together a good while now. Why shouldn't our lives be more merged?"

Eliane laughed nervously like she always did when he said things like that to her, which as a lot lately. She hadn't said it, but I knew why she didn't want to go to Japan to see him. She feared that if she did, they'd walk those gardens and drink that wine, then he would get down on one knee and ask her to be his wife.

"Where's that beautiful mind of yours at?" He asked pretending not to feel the vibe, always trying to logic through it and convince himself that she was in it just as much as he was.

"Sorry, I'm just in writing mode. My mind drifts. That's all."

"I miss you."

"I like that you miss me." She winked again. "I'm going to hop off and write a little more while the mood is still on me. I never know when it might get up and leave again."

"You do that. I'll call you tomorrow. I hate this is how I have to be connected to your world, but just as long as I am, then I'm happy. Enjoy your wine."

"Will do."

"I love you."

"I love you, too." And I think she meant it when she said it, but she didn't love him the way she wished she did, which is why she always made the long face once he couldn't see it anymore. It's why she hadn't ended it. She didn't want to hurt someone whom she loved.

She rubbed her eyes and shook her head a little bit like it would reboot her. Then she picked up her phone and put Spotify on a list called "Straight Outta Asheville," which was a list of only artists from the area who'd made it. She had no idea who managed the account, but every now and then there was a new song on there that stirred up some inspiration. It's what Eliane called "good writin' music." It was a total mix of rock n' roll, country, alternative, electronic, and everything in between. Lynyrd Skynyrd was on there because the drummer, and only survivor of the plane crash (I learned this from Jett), lived somewhere local. Then there were the usual suspects, like the dude who sings like Meatloaf that won American Idol, Luke Combs, Warren Haynes, Secret Lives of the Free Masons and a bunch of others. Those are weird artists to mention in the same breath, but if that isn't Asheville, I don't know what is. There was even some dude who sang gospel in a quartet at Dollywood and had a famous country song in Europe on there. He's apparently the deepest voice in all of country music. It was a mix to say the least, which is truest Asheville. It was Eliane.

Eliane was humming along nicely while she worked on her doomed story that she tried too hard to keep writing. One of the country tunes popped up and Zen grimaced from behind his easel, his pale thin face scrunched up into a wadded piece of plastic wrap.

"You want me to change it?" Eliane reached for the phone.

Zen nodded his "Of course, and hurry." Come to think of it, that day, just shortly after this, might have been the first time I ever actually heard Zen speak.

Eliane hit next, and a song she'd never heard started to play. The drums started first, then came the guitar. The song was brand new, but the sound was familiar to her, and dropped a sensation into her stomach that made her feel the same way she would have if I'd suddenly appeared. It impressed her, it moved her, and it absolutely terrified her. Then came the words, not just familiar, but hers.

I want what I can't have
Like to know what the sky tastes like
I'm scared she's my other half
But you wish I'd sing to you in this mike...

"Oh my God. Oh. My. God." El stood up.

Then she looked down at her screen at the name of the band, "Letters to Lux." Her head spun, and her eyes blurred, but she couldn't look away. She saw his name there, Guitarist: Jett Jorgenson. Then the cover art, red hair peeking out from a heap of dirt. Her face got hot, and her hands started to tingle and draw in until she dropped her phone.

"Umm, Eliane," Zen spoke softly. "Umm—why are you being weird?" He continued painting.

"I—I can't. I feel like...I...can't...breathe..."

"Is this, like, a writing exercise?" He adjusted his hipster glasses.

"Zen, help me..." she gasped.

"OK, OK. Calm down. Put your head between your legs." He stood and patted her back. "Don't try to breathe. Hold your breath for four seconds, then let it out slowly. I think you're having a panic attack. I've had like 600. I take pills. Hey, do you have pills?" He asked excitedly.

Eliane shook her head while she tried to hold her breath.

"You're already calming down, see? Your hands aren't drawing in now." He kept patting her the "there-there" way. "It's going to be OK. You'll see. You're not going to die. Just keep controlling your breath."

And that time, she did. She was able to pull herself out. But, as the months went on, and the songs grew in popularity, and she kept hearing bits of her letters to me from *Letters to Lux,* it got harder to control. She tried to block out the memory of my death, of my funeral, and of her role in it all by making more little rules for herself. She'd think something like, *if I close the car door three times, I won't have a panic attack today.* She'd try to Facetime Jake and chat about nice little things, never saying a word about anything she was going through. She could "play normal" with him, but she'd remember who she was the second she closed the screen. As the weeks went on, she was counting cracks she skipped over on sidewalks, pieces of rice left on her plate, and drops of dish soap squirted on each dish. But stop now if you don't want the spoiler, none of it worked.

CHAPTER 30

Dallas in the afternoon, Paris in the evening
Now

After the last group auditioned at the Dallas Cowboys Cheerleaders preliminary auditions, the judges deliberated for about thirty or forty minutes, but to Eliane, who paced the lobby area with her hands holding her bare stomach, it felt like days.

However, I was less concerned with the outcome of the audition and more concerned with the man standing, watching, at the far end of the parking lot. It took some courage to continue to look in his direction, but I had to be sure, although I had been immediately sure. I knew who it was the second I saw his blank eyes. I just didn't want it to be true. He was standing right there, only yards from wherever it is that I am, and from Eliane's very much alive and thriving body. *He* had followed her again.

"Eliane, get someone now. Anyone. Call the police." I shouted into complete silence about the time a jolly security guard with a healthy belly wheeled out at large dry erase board covered by some sort of tarp-like thing.

"Eliane, now. He is here. The man who killed me is outside watching you!" I could feel the racing pulse I didn't have.

The hosts of girls tried to look excited and even cheered loudly when the man came bebopping in, feeling powerful and peppy all at once. However, it was more anxiety and expectation than enthusiasm that ushered them all like a big spray-tanned wave to the board. When the guard counted down and whooshed the covering away, the board revealed about 75 or a hundred numbers written neatly on it. The handwriting looked like the kind the girls who tried too hard in high school had. They were the ones who took an hour to write in the yearbook because they wanted some sort of unspoken superlative for best penmanship. I could have written it myself. The pretty handwriting. The bliss on the girls' faces. The terror on mine that no one could see. It swirled around me.

Eliane was about a quarter of the way back in the crowd of hundreds of hopefuls. She watched as girls squealed with excitement, holding one another and jumping up and down; and she watched while they sobbed silently while trying to keep their heads down. A couple of them just wailed loudly while getting embraced in a group hug. Eliane had decided that no matter what, she wouldn't be the hysterical girl bawling for the crowd to watch with their lips rolled out slightly to signal their feigned empathy for her. My eyes darted between her and the man with nothing behind his eyes.

She didn't rush, but steadily continued to creep forward, then finally made her way to the board full of lucky numbers. She stopped in front of it and eyed them all while processing nothing at first. After readjusting, she quickly ascertained that they were in numerical order. She skimmed down the board, again, taking her time. When she saw numbers in the hundreds, she slowed her gaze even more. She saw the row ending with the numbers 103, 112, 114, 117, then she closed her eyes for a moment before looking at the next line. With a deep breath, she opened them up again. 122. She calmly skimmed the entire board again just be sure there was no mistake. And there wasn't. Her number simply wasn't there. She hadn't made the cut. She hadn't gotten through the first round.

I turned back to the parking lot. I swear he could see into the lobby. It was as if he'd watched for Eliane's reaction, because immediately after he saw it, he got into a white sedan and left. And there was nothing I could do.

I turned back to Eliane who didn't know that she had bigger fish to fry than not finding her number on that board. I wasn't sure how she'd react. I'd seen her experience rejection with her writing before. I'd seen her form letters from literary agents instructing her to keep trying but letting her know they weren't going to be the ones. Sometimes she didn't react at all. Other times she'd scream and fall to the ground, after which she'd normally drink gin and write me a letter. I think the letter writing was less therapy and more her version of cutting her inner thigh with a razor blade in times like that. I think she did it to torture herself, especially when she'd do it sad. Instead of crudely sliding a sharp blade across her skin, she'd wallow with a ghost just to let it haunt her. Then she'd mail it because it was more dangerous. The therapist never did get that one right. Eliane wasn't compelled to mail it the same way she was compelled to lick the envelope exactly five odd times. She wanted to self-destruct by putting herself in harm's way. Part of her wanted the trouble that she thought she deserved. I was about 90 percent sure I—well, my parents—would get a self-loathing letter out of whatever this was.

So far, she hadn't moved a muscle. She just stood staring at the board, her body sort of loose, though her mind must have been rigid. After a few moments more, she readjusted the bag on her shoulder, clenched her jaw, and walked out calmly. She made her way to her the car, tossed the bag into the backseat, and then gently got inside. She looked at herself in the mirror and smiled with half of her mouth. Then she reached up and pulled the false eyelashes off her eyes, then the gel boobs which resembled chicken cutlets out of her bra top. She tossed them into the passenger seat and drove away at a perfectly normal speed. She'd shown me absolutely nothing, her eyes almost as blank as the ones that had been watching us.

CHAPTER 31

I watched Eliane as she made her way home, and I was certain he wasn't following her. I could cover good distances quickly, and I had no idea where he'd gone. I just knew he wasn't with us, and that was enough in that moment. If he wasn't here, she was safe.

It took almost no time for Eliane to begin one of her letters, but instead of starting it, "Dear Lux," she instead wrote, "Dear Lux and Zelda." She hadn't written to Zelda, as far as I knew, since I'd become her ghost of choice nearly a decade ago, minus the tiny card she'd left on her bed at the home place. But apparently, she had something to say to us both this time. I wondered if she'd mail it to my parents' address or to one of Zelda's many. Maybe she'd have to make copies. I didn't know; this was uncharted territory.

The pen was still in her hand, and I couldn't wait to see what she had to say to us both. I kind of wished Zelda were here to see what she was up to with me. That would be an interesting celebrity ghost to meet, but I don't think that's how it works. Wherever I am, I'm the only one. But it made me wonder if somehow Zelda was somewhere watching her too. I don't know though; it seems Zelda would be too cool for such things.

However, I waited with bated breath, or I guess, fantom bated breath—like an amputee that can still feel the missing leg—while El paused to check her phone. She had several missed calls from

Dr. Vitale, along with a few voicemails from both the doctor and her mother.

"No, you guys can wait," she said aloud and more self-assured than she had in a long time. Then she focused her attention back on the felt-like stationary. It was fancier than usual. It confused me for a moment, but then I remembered, Zelda was invited to this party.

Dear Lux and Zelda,

I've realized, just today, why I only write letters to dead people now. And, in particular, why I only write them to the two of you. I write to the dead for one healthy reason and one completely sad reason, though I'm not sure it's particularly unhealthy. The sad reason is that I've chosen to write to ghosts because they never talk back. I've chosen women I admired, that I felt connected to because it made me feel like I was talking to a friend, but then, there was no real chance of getting an opinion that I might not like. I could say whatever I wanted, workout whatever I needed, and never have to listen to anyone disagree. For some reason I couldn't just keep a normal journal or diary like every other girl in America. I think that made it seem pathetic. Writing to the two of you made it seem real, and maybe like an artform even. Hell, maybe it is. The point is, I thought it was delicious instead of depressing, and it got me through. However, it's inherently sad because that puts me only in the two of your companies. But I'm alive. I am alive.

The healthy reason I do it is to keep you two alive in some form. It's similar to the way I keep dead flowers in vases everywhere. They're still beautiful, and once upon a time, they meant something. The flowers were sent to congratulate or console. They were tokens of love or light. They weren't only meaningful while they lived. I think my letters assigned you two meaning after life in my head, which was also to console myself some too, so it wasn't all unselfish. But today, I realized something. You two don't need my letters. They were always for me. Now, the mailing them...not even I fully understand why. Maybe it's the realness factor again. I don't really know, and it doesn't matter anymore. But I've decided to stop. That gives me physical anxiety, and my stomach hurts just writing it. But I have to. To keep myself alive, I have to. The flowers aren't capable of admiring themselves, of seeing their own glory. But we are—while we're here at least. And today, I felt alive and glorious for the first time in a hundred years. I don't know why I say a hundred, but it's how it feels.

I tried something hard today and failed...well, I failed at what I thought the goal was. I didn't even make it through the first round at my auditions. I don't know if I wasn't that great of a dancer, or if they didn't like my hair color, or if my legs were too short, or if the girl next to me just shined a little bit brighter than I did. And I don't care the reason. I thought that I would, but it feels pretty damn good that I don't even in the slightest. I just needed the goal to get me through. I needed to go through with something I'd planned while I figured out the rest of it. Maybe that's why you, Zelda, took up your ballet dancing in your late twenties. I bet you just needed it. Lux, maybe that's why you stormed out that night. You had to commit to showing Jett and I both that you weren't soft, and by doing it, proved to yourself you weren't soft. The cops told your family that you fought like hell. They could tell from the scuffed up dirt and skin under your nails. That bothered me at first. I couldn't get the images out of my head. I pictured the effort and let myself feel your muscles growing weaker, having no choice but to eventually give in from pure exhaustion. It was so ugly to think about, and I won't fully describe it because I don't need to. But now I'm proud that you fought. I hope you know you did, and that wherever you are now, that there is only peace. And I hope you love yourself and realize you had all along, else you wouldn't have battled for your life. I hope you both love yourselves.

When I was cut today, I was relieved. I realized that what I did was never about making a team. It was about taking a journey. It was about doing something hard and coming out on the other side. It was about seeing myself do it—not about watching somebody else. It was about choosing something and seeing it to the end—physically observing it while feeling it...living it. And it was a little bit about feeling like a pretty girl, too, I'm not going to lie about that. I loved the spray tans and glitter...for a minute.

I'm not an NFL cheerleader. I'm a writer, and I'll always be one. I'm ready to write the story someone will publish now. I'm finally brave enough. And to do it right, I have to let this go. I have to stop writing to ghosts. I have to write something that shines life... for the living.

So, this letter is my farewell to you both. You've inspired me more than you'll ever know. I hope one day, a far day from now, that we'll meet in a place that makes sense to all of us. But for now, I'm off to rejoin the living while I'm here. I think I'll go to Paris.

Love and Admiration Always,

El

After she signed the letter, she took a deep breath and placed it in a sealed envelope. She scrawled Lux and Zelda on the front in her pretty chicken scratch, but with no address. Then she dropped the letter into the trash can beside her night table.

If I had a throat, it would have had a lump in it, and I wondered if somewhere Zelda lingered, watching like me, feeling the same. No one was too untouchable for this. El was still making people move, and even the ghosts could feel it. I bet Zelda had known Eliane afterall, in some dimension. And if she had, she was as proud of Eliane now as I was—she was likely both proud and grief-ridden that our El had chosen to live among her own kind and leave us behind.

Eliane stared at the trash where she'd thrown the envelope. I saw her mumbling, counting I think, under her breath. Her OCD was in a fight with her about the envelope, but she was going to win this small battle, and that was something. She left it where it was. Instead of giving in and pulling it out to properly mail, she grabbed her phone again. She tapped the voicemail from her mother and put the phone to her ear.

"Eliane, why can't you answer the damned phone?" Her mother's voice was frantic. "I've tried to reach you a thousand times. Your therapist is on the rampage. First, she looked up that Skyla Free you work for. She said she thinks you wanted her to discover her ties to Jett. Does Skyla even *know* Jett? What the hell is going on, El? She said with your past behaviors of the letter writin' and bein' party to a restrainin' order, that she feels like your move to Texas was an unhealthy attempt to contact Jett, who is now famous or somethin' *apparently*? And I didn't want to leave this on voicemail, but you haven't left me any choice. The police found a girl in Texas, on the outskirts of Dallas yesterday afternoon. She was auditionin' for that team, just like you. They found her near the stadium, with a letter just like in Asheville. They contacted the police up here and Dr. Vitale. They think he followed you there. I think they're suspicious of your involvement with all this now—everyone is at the least of it, worried for you. Vitale said she had no choice but to alert the Texas authorities of a possible threat of someone unwell stalkin' Jett Jorgenson and havin' possible connections to a string of murders. They'll be lookin' for you. There could be a warrant out for you. You need to call me right now."

CHAPTER 32

The River Arts District, West Asheville
Not all that far back then

El took a turn once those songs came out. They washed over her too much, adding the art of sound to all that haunted her, her own version of hell set to a soundtrack. She wasn't sure if she had quit her job waiting tables, or if she'd gotten fired. She called in sick three times because the panic was so bad that she couldn't drive. She was terrified that she wouldn't be able to breathe in the middle of the Billy Graham Freeway and that she wouldn't have anywhere to pull over. She pictured herself passing out in the fast lane while the other vehicles slammed into her like dominos. The last time she'd called out, some manager named Jim with a slight lisp and bad mustache told her that if she did it again, she was done. So, she just didn't call and didn't go back. She didn't blame them for being upset, but she couldn't get it together enough to just show up. It wasn't just the music that had tipped her over the edge. The songs had gotten popular. Everyone was listening to them, but it wasn't just hearing them that sent her past the point of no return. It was that one of the things she'd feared most had now happened.

She had no idea how *he* knew where to reach her. El still used her old student email from UNCA. She only checked it every couple of weeks or so, but shortly after she'd heard her song on that playlist for the first time, she was sifting through a bunch of emails that had been piling up, and it was there right in the middle of them. The subject line said in all caps, IMPORTANT: OPEN IMMEDIATELY. Though she didn't recognize the email address, brr6@brrco.com, she opened it anyway.

Dear Eliane,

It's nice to finally "meet" you. I just wanted to express my deepest gratitude. I've enjoyed the songs you've written about our Lux very much. I stumbled upon them in a chat room I follow where my fans discuss my work. Good stuff. I should have known you'd be a writer. You might have just made my art even more famous. You were given no credit, so it took a little detective work to figure out whom I should thank. I visited your friend, Jett, at a show after I found the songs. We had a cold beer together after, but I'm sure he won't remember me. There were hundreds of people there, and caravans of fans following the band around the after party and bar scene till the sun came up. I blended in perfectly, and damn, it was a great time. Jett was standing on a table making a toast at one point. He said something very bizarre, which got me to researching you. He shouted into the air, his glass raised, "Thank you, Eliane Pangolin. Thanks for all the words that made my dream come true." Then he threw the drink back. Everyone cheered, and no one cared what it meant, no one except me. That's when I put two and two together...I should have known as long as I'd been looking in. Of course, those bright words were yours. You were always interesting to watch. Please don't be alarmed. You aren't the type for my proclivity. I enjoy you in a very different way. I just wish to express my deepest thanks.

> *Yours,*
> *BRR*

That had been the first time. I watched as she slammed the laptop shut and immediately vomited into a trash can. I could feel every heave like I were the one spewing into the bin by the kitchen cupboards. It sickened me just as much as it had her. It made me frantic. I tried so hard to speak, to scream from where I was, but I couldn't.

"Take it to the police, El," I wanted to shout as badly then as I do now. "Maybe they can trace the email address. Maybe Jett remembers his face. Someone at that venue could have seen something. Help them catch the bastard before he kills someone else!"

But she didn't. She couldn't. Instead, she said nothing. She curled into a ball in the corner and cried into her knobby knees. And it's what she was doing when I left her for a while. I expected to find her just like that when I decided to come back. But instead, Zen and I found her lying in my death spot instead of Zelda's where this tale began for me, at Eliane's breaking point. She was lying in it just like she had the knoll on Zillicoa Street— perhaps more morbidly this time—but still the same. She hoped it would be her therapy. Maybe she hoped she'd find me there, or maybe some other answer even. But she didn't. She found a place she can't ever seem to crawl out of again. I'm still watching, waiting for her to climb out.

CHAPTER 33

She tried to act like everything was fine after receiving the email then getting pulled out of my spot by Zen that evening. She tried to pretend that whatever she'd attempted had worked and that life was clean and normal. She tried to make her hot tea in the morning, then do her daily crossword while listening to the river.

"Everything is fine. You are fine." She would say out loud to herself, but the pit would burrow down into her stomach anyway.

Jake still called almost every day, one routine that didn't change that she wished would. He wasn't as easy to avoid like the other things she'd just will her mind to shut away, like the information she had that could have possibly busted my case wide open. But eventually, she was able to. She just stopped caring. She didn't even try to maintain to keep face. She'd hear the phone ring, then the laptop would go off. She'd see his name on the screen, but she just couldn't answer. She tried. She owed him an explanation after three years, but she went quiet instead. She completely cut off a marine on active duty in a foreign country who wanted to marry her. And somehow, she didn't even have time to feel badly about it. Finally, Jake had a buddy come out and check on her. She'd simply told him to tell Jake that she was sorry and that she just couldn't do it, then slammed the door in his face. After that, she crumbled into a heap on the floor to weep, and not just in that moment, but just about every day to follow.

A couple of months like this went by before the money ran out along with her mind, and Zen had to find the nerve to talk to her. She'd rolled out of bed around noon as usual. She tried to sleep as late as possible because the mornings were the worst. She had the pit in her stomach immediately upon waking up, and it reminded her that the whole day would be her battling the obsessions and warding off panic attacks. There didn't even have to be a trigger anymore. Jett had released more of the songs, and the popularity grew. It was everywhere. High school friends would slide into her DMs saying things like, "Wow, aren't you so proud of Jett? Are you guys still close?"

Those things didn't matter. The trigger was the fear of having another attack now. The obsessions were more time consuming than ever before, and she was drowning. Night was a little better because she knew she'd made it through another day, but then morning would come again to remind her that her only purpose was to try and make it through. It wasn't a good enough reason to want to wake up.

"Eliane, could you join me at the breakfast table?" Zen asked in his monotone when she'd finally made it to the couch wrapped in her comforter.

"I'm not hungry." She responded quietly.

"I know you're not. You don't eat. If you try, you get nervous and throw up. What do you weigh now? Like 95 pounds?" He pursed his lips together and made his mouth look as buttoned up as his plain black shirt.

"My nerves, Zen...please don't..." She didn't have the energy to get mad or to finish her sentence that normally would have clapped back at Zen to make fun of his slight frame. She only had the energy to tighten her blanket around her bony body.

"You haven't been able to pay rent in two cycles now. I've had to cover it all myself, and I make art. It wasn't easy. I had to beg my parents for it. And my parents almost hate me; I had to tell them I didn't have the money to eat to make them pity me enough. It was embarrassing."

"Well, I hate it for you, Zen." She mumbled.

"You have stopped going to work, and you don't shower. Your legs are hairy. I mean, this is Asheville, whatever. But they weren't hairy before. They're new-hairy. You've stopped grooming. I believe you're depressed...like clinically." He sipped his cappuccino out of a tiny cup.

Eliane was embarrassed that he noticed her legs and sank further into the blanket. She didn't tell him why she hadn't been shaving, but I knew. I watched her pick up the razor and set it back down over and over again. Then, after a few days, she quickly grabbed it and wrapped it up in a bunch of toilet paper, taped over it, and threw it into the trash can. But that wasn't good enough, either. She took the whole trash bag down to the river and threw it in. Then she googled, "Do OCD people ever get compelled to commit suicide? Do OCD people kill themselves on accident? Do OCD people do things they don't want to on an impulse?" She had no intentions on hurting herself even in her mental state, but her thoughts kept ruminating, and she was scared she would somehow do it involuntarily. That, unlike suicidal thoughts, was classic OCD, and Eliane knew it from googling it 800 times. But it didn't matter. Zen hadn't noticed that the steak knives were gone too.

"Eliane, I'm sorry, but I got in touch with your mother. I'm worried about you. I'm afraid you're going to get much sicker, especially if you don't eat. You need help."

"Why the fuck would you do that, Zen?" Some of her color returned to her gaunt cheeks. "I have some issues I have to work through. I always eventually do. I don't want to move back home. I—I'll make some money. I'll find another job—"

"One you can walk to? You can't even drive, Eliane." He spoke like the guy who played Zuckerberg in the Facebook movie, robotic, smart, unsympathetic. "I should have called after I found you up on the parkway that evening, but I've acted now."

Eliane covered her face and started to weep.

"I'm really sorry you are in this state. I'm not one to hug. But—I am here. I am your friend. You can talk if you like."

"There's nothing to say." She eked out. "I just don't want to live with my mother again. She doesn't help this. It's worse back home. It started there."

"I'm sorry I was so terrible." Her mother's voice sliced in, and Eliane looked up to see her image in the partially opened front door.

Eliane didn't respond.

"Thank you for reaching out, Zane." She looked at the boy? man? at the table.

"It's Zen. You're welcome. I'll leave you two to discuss." He stood and trotted to the tiny back patio, which was really some kind of weird fire escape that no one should trust.

"I can't come back and live with you. Being there...it'll get worse." Eliane shook her head.

"Well, we agree on one thing, then."

"What?" El sniffled.

"You won't get better by coming home. I know you think I'm such a terrible mother, but I still carry you on my insurance, and you're lucky that I do. I've packed a bag with everything you'll need. You're getting some help. Now, get on up."

"What are you talking about? You want me to like go talk to a psychiatrist or something?" Eliane's mouth hung open, her hair still all over her head.

"Yes, I do. But you can't wait weeks to get an appointment. Zig called and said you weren't eating. I can see that. He said you'd quit your job and that you can't get out of bed. He said your little counting quirks and routines are so constant that you don't even try to hide them, and that he's witnessed you have several panic attacks. He said you won't get behind the wheel, not that you should like this. Oh, and he said you hid all of the sharp knives? What the hell is that about? Are you afraid that the man that came for Lux will come for you or something?"

Apparently, he *had* noticed the knives, and El said nothing. Her mother's explanation seemed less crazy than the real one.

"I'll get it together. I can figure this out. I always do. I always reel it back in. Just, let me get a hold of it. Just let me think for a minute." She buried her face into her hands.

"No, when this has flared up before you hadn't lost a roommate to a serial killer."

"I just have to get my head together about it." She whispered, believing it. "Please understand that."

"You will. I'm taking you to the hospital. They have a mental rehabilitation center there. They'll take you immediately. I've already spoken to them."

"Mom! No!" Eliane burst into full blown tears. "I won't go. Whatever, I'll talk to someone. I'll try Lexapro or something. Half the nation is on it. I don't care. Put me on benzos half the day. I'm not going to some nuthouse. You can't make me."

"Eliane, how do you think you would even get those pills? As bad as this is, you're going to need an evaluation. You can't just call your general practitioner and ask her to call it in to CVS because you prescribed yourself. And you do need something. You can't make it like this. You need a reset. This is your whole life. It's been a problem since you were little, probably since even before the dead birds. But now it's everything. You need more than a pill, baby girl."

"I'm an adult. I won't do it. You can't force me."

"Zeb said you threw out all your razors, too. Are you suicidal? That'll easily get you involuntarily committed if I need it."

"No." She answered emphatically.

"Then why'd you throw them out? Did you want to harm yourself? Cut?"

"I was afraid I'd just cut my wrists or something!" She shouted. "I didn't want to. I was just scared I would. It's the same as how I'm scared I'll push twelve on the treadmill or drive my car the wrong way on the interstate. I'm just scared I will for no reason if I don't control everything. And I'm scared I'll kill someone else like I did Lux. I'm not scared someone will kill me at all. I'm scared I'll let down my guard and do it to somebody else again!"

"What are you talking about?" Her mother lowered her voice. "They haven't caught the man who killed Lux, but they know who he is. They have DNA. He'd killed six other women before her."

"I didn't literally kill her, Mom. I killed her by sending her out that night. I wrote something awful about her and she heard Jett reading it out loud. Now he's made it a song. What if I meant to do it? What if I meant to be cruel? What if I *kill* people? What if I'm some kind of psychopath?" She sobbed.

Her mother softened her stance and hesitated for a second. Then she walked over to her daughter and pulled her close to her own body like she should have the moment she saw her. "You won't. I work in healthcare. I've seen this. OCD people are scared of doing the things that are furthest from who they are, then they obsess about it and do whatever they can to prevent it. You didn't kill Lux on purpose or on accident. It wasn't your fault in any way. She crossed paths with a sick person. It was chance. And you won't cause anyone harm...not anyone but yourself if you don't get the help you need."

"I'm scared, Mom. I'm. So. Damned. Scared." She gasped for air.

"Then come with me. Check into the hospital willingly. Walk in there and sign yourself in. I don't always want to use tough love. You're strong, and you require it. But I swear I'm not lying. You're tough and stubborn. You can overcome this, little girl. But you gotta put on big girl panties first."

She kept sobbing into her mother's chest. Even with the strained relationship they'd had, I knew she was comforted by her mother's smell. It's natural. Even if her mother smelled like stale cigarettes and Wal-Mart body splash. It's what she needed.

"So, will you come with me? Can I hear you say it?"

"I—I'll come with you. I'll try." She paused. "Just don't let me die in there like Zelda did. Please."

"I promise, baby girl. You aren't going to die. This is how you live."

CHAPTER 34

The facility creeped me out; and I'm a ghost. However, I don't think my presence could have possibly made the place anymore spooky. Whoever designed it took care of that. When people try to create a serene atmosphere, they get it all wrong. It's always quiet and lifeless. If they really wanted to encourage healing, they could probably ditch the fluorescent lights and beige floors, too. The few couches and potted plants thrown about didn't help it much, either. They should make it look like a home where people feel safe, with real couches and plushy pillows. Maybe have some music going somewhere. They could have at least thrown a fountain in the courtyard just for the sound of running water. But they had what all the "peaceful" places like funeral homes and prayer rooms had: isolation and eerie stillness. It reminded me of reading that short story, "The Yellow Wallpaper," back in high school. They locked some woman—who was clearly battling depression—away in isolation in some room with disgusting yellow wallpaper and it just made everything worse. Evidently, no one had learned a thing from reading that.

That drab atmosphere was probably why after those first seven or so days, which I could barely watch, because it was pretty much crying, despondence, and med adjustment, Eliane spent all her time watching the T.V. in her room. When she wasn't in a one-on-one session with her assigned therapist or being forced into a group handholding session, or to rest — once again, in total silence, she was glued to the tube. She didn't reach for a pen to write to Zelda or to me, though she'd eye one occasionally. She didn't work on her manuscript. She didn't stand to stretch. She'd pick up a hairbrush, shrug her shoulders, then set it back down again. She wasn't brave enough for gen pop in the craft rooms or lounges. And who could blame her? There might have been people in there who even claimed to *see me*. El wasn't to that level. She needed help for sure, but she only half belonged some place like this. As far as she had spiraled, she wasn't ready to make a popsicle stick handbag with a girl who believed she'd lived in an alien colony for the past six months. So, the sound of voices on the screen was the only life there. She chose it. And that gave me hope. She wanted to be near the lifeline. She hadn't given up yet. She ate ice chips and watched girls with bare midriffs dance and cry and blow easy interview questions, and thought it looked glorious. It was her hope.

"Are you still watching that show?" Dr. Vitale giggled when she entered her room during an ice-chomping session a couple weeks in (I'd lost track of exactly how many days — time is weird here anyway).

"It's getting really good now. One of the veterans gained four pounds since last year. She has two weeks to lose it, or one of the rookies will get her spot." Eliane didn't move her eyes from the screen.

"That sounds healthy." Dr. Vitale used sarcasm in an attempt to be more relatable. "I hate to pull you out of it, but it's time for the group session today. I think it's really important that you come and connect with other people who have gone through what you've gone through. It can really help to know you aren't alone."

Eliane sighed and turned the television off.

"Hmm? No protest? You usually protest."

"I've realized that nothing you present me is actually a choice, so let's just get on with it, OK?"

"OK."

•   •   •

The group therapy room must have smelled weird because El always made a face when she entered it, a face like passing a sewer. It looked shockingly clean, so I always imagined it was some sort of industrial cleansers, probably so strong that it would be burned into her memory forever.

"Take a seat everyone. We're ready to start," Dr. Vitale sat down in a circle with Eliane and three other women.

"We're in a much smaller group today because we have broken you all down by diagnosis. It sometimes helps to connect with someone else struggling with the same things that you are. It can normalize it in your mind and help you to accept that you aren't crazy. You have something that other people have and that can be treated, just like any other illness."

"Megan," Dr. Vitale turned to the girl a couple of years older than Eliane. She had a plain face, but pretty chestnut brown hair. "Megan, you have done this before. Would you mind to share with the group?"

"Not at all," Megan smiled like Dr. Vitale's special little helper.

"Megan is actually about to go home, and I thought her experience might help some of you newcomers gain a little bit of hope and perspective." Dr. Vitale clarified. "Go ahead, Megan."

"OK, well, hello all." She waved awkwardly. "Um, I was first diagnosed with OCD when I was in my late teens. I was a hand washer," she nodded, and another girl with red hair did as well. "I washed my hands every chance I got, probably as a response to a trauma I had as a child. It started with the idea that I could scrub what had happened off of me, and then it would just be gone. I thought scrubbing physically could scrub me mentally. I just didn't realize it then. However, it grew beyond just trying to wash off that one very bad experience. It became the method that made me atone for things. It became the thing that could set me free from anything I did wrong, or that was done wrong to me. Just wash it away. Then it became the thing that prevented other bad things, until it didn't. I had to see a doctor for second degree burns on my hands three different times, and I was peeling all the time. I got chemical burns at one point because soap wasn't enough anymore. I used lye solutions and bleach. It ended in inadvertent self-harm. And that's why I finally came here. No one made me. I chose it because I wanted it to stop. I don't know what made me want to stop exactly. I guess I just dug deep and found some value in myself somewhere in there."

"And has it stopped?" The redhead with her hands wrapped in gauze asked.

"Not all the way, but I'm washing less. Dr. Vitale has helped me use my steps to think about the events that trigger the washing. I think about them in a safe space, away from a sink, and use coping tools if I panic. It was bad at first. I would cry. I would hyper-ventilate. I would run to a place that had a sink available. But then it got easier. The method works. It just takes perseverance and commitment. But it works. And when I need to wash my hands after the restroom or something, I set a timer. I must stop when the timer stops. That helps, too."

"Thank you so much for sharing, Megan. I know that was difficult, and I'm so proud of you for your willingness to confide in the group." Dr. Vitale smiled with her mouth closed and made her eyes show sympathy that might have been real.

"Eliane, you're new. Everyone, meet Eliane."

"Hi, Eliane," they all said in unison like she was at AA. She said nothing.

"If you feel safe, please share as much or as little as you like with the group," Dr. Vitale urged.

Eliane looked startled. She hadn't expected to hear her name called out. She thought this time she'd just watch, then maybe she'd tell her big success story in a few weeks.

"Just start with your name. That's where we all started," Megan nodded, not as patronizing as the doctor.

"I–I'm Eliane," she began. "I—I don't really know what I'm supposed to say here. I don't usually think about that. I just talk, but I feel super awkward right now. I feel like there are rules I don't know and wouldn't like if I did." She spoke honestly.

"Respect is the only rule. Just be kind to others and don't judge. But say whatever you like. Maybe start with why you're here," Dr. Vitale spoke softly.

"OK, umm, I was just diagnosed with OCD. I mean, I knew. I've researched it, and I think I've known for a long time. I don't know why I'm a counter, or why I like prime numbers, but those are my poisons. It's gotten bad lately. My, umm, my best friend was murdered because of my negligence, and it just all snowballed from there. With OCD, we all know, everything we do is to prevent the "bad" thing. But I had let my guard down somewhere. Something bad happened because I wasn't careful enough...with someone's feelings. But then the rituals got worse than ever. I got lost in the regimens, then just fear, and now, I don't know what I am..." She trailed off becoming quieter.

"Thank you, Eliane." Dr. Vitale said. "I want the group to know that though Eliane had most definitely done something unkind, as we all do, because we're human, but she was not indeed negligent," she turned to Eliane. "You were not negligent. You were human. You did not make the cognitive choice to harm your friend. However, you felt you lost control. It's often our fear of losing control of a situation that awakens our triggers. That is part of Cognitive Behavior Therapy. We give up control by controlling it in safe and fabricated atmospheres. We practice losing control so we can maintain healthy habits in the event that we actually do at some point. And we will. No one can be in control all the time."

Eliane looked at Dr. Vitale differently. She didn't scoff or roll her eyes. She wasn't sold, but something in her face changed a little bit. She was afraid she was being sold snake oil, but she wanted to try it any way. She wanted out of this place she'd been.

"Will it—" El hesitated, embarrassed to ask the question. "Will it be a painful experience. Will I panic during the therapy? I mean, when that happens, I feel like I can't breathe, and my hands draw in. My chest throbs. I guess what I'm asking is: will it *hurt*?"

"Probably," Dr. Vitale nodded. "But sometimes getting to the other end of that pain removes the fear of it. Then we're set free."

When she said that I thought not of Eliane; I didn't even watch for her reaction. I thought of myself, and I thought of where I was "trapped." I started to wonder if I wasn't trapped at all, but if I'd chosen this for myself, chosen this journey to eventual freedom.

CHAPTER 35

Paris, Texas
Now

El lowered the phone to her lap after listening to her mother's voicemail. She stared into space for a minute, rifling through her thoughts like files in a cabinet drawer. She was searching for what to do next. She knew as well as I did that there would be no explaining away her actions to Dr. Vitale. How would one begin to explain something like this even if they hadn't been under psychiatric care? When looking at it all in black and white, it looked bad. There was no use in calling her and appealing to her in any way. She'd have to cover her bases by hospitalizing El again at the very least. She could be looking at getting arrested for stalking or withholding evidence.

To Vitale, El was a patient going rogue, a liability—and with a connection to a killer she couldn't even explain herself. I couldn't explain it. He'd wanted me. Why was he still following *her,* and being so clear that he didn't want to hurt her? Of course, he could very well be lying. However, that didn't seem to be the case to me. I don't think he could have held back this long. Whatever took him over when he'd been with me came on fast; it wasn't controlled this way.

I also knew El wouldn't call her mother back when stakes were this high. That would just add an antagonist she didn't need to the situation. Her mother would immediately start trying to logic through it, go through the processes. She'd run straight to Vitale, give El another tough love speech, then she'd end up in the exact same place she'd been before.

Eliane stayed in deep thought, sitting up straight as an arrow on the edge of her bed, still wearing the warm-ups from tryouts over the jewel-encrusted get-up. Her eyes gazed into the distance, and she deliberated. She moved her thumb over her phone and landed it on Skyla Free.

"Hellooo?" Skyla's peppy voice answered on the ring right before voicemail, which I was sure was on purpose. Her kind always did this in order to seem less available.

"Skyla, hey, it's Eliane."

"Oh, hey girl! How was that audition today. Good news?"

"Umm, it went well...great news, actually. It was a perfect day. But, um, I'm calling on a work matter. There's so much to do before the music festival. I was just feeling good, so I wanted to work on it over the weekend."

"OMG...love that initiative, girl." Skyla snapped her gum. "And it sounds like somebody will be getting me free Cowboys tickets this year. Yasss, girl!"

Eliane chuckled super awkwardly then continued, "I—uh, I just checked my email and this journalist from *Austin Today* wants to interview you and Jett." She lied, something I'd never seen her blatantly do. "They want to interview you each separately to get the feel that they want. They want to set something up with Jett ASAP. Can you get me his info? I need to know where he's staying in case the writer needs to meet him at his hotel."

"Oh sure, hon. And that's so exciting. Maybe they'll put us on the cover. Can you see it? His long hair in his face, such a delicious bad boy with me on his lap? I'll dress very girl-next-door. Ahh! It'll be a trip. Anyway, his number is 828-555-0141."

"Oh, I have his—I mean, I need the address to the hotel and room number. Journalists don't like to call people on their cells.

Celebrity types usually won't answer numbers they don't know. If she calls the room, it'll seem more pressing, and she'll probably get him."

"Oh, I'll give him the heads up, babe. Don't worry. But he's at the Hyatt 6th Street Hotel in Austin, um, room 4058. Feel free to tell the journalist lady or whoever give him a ring. I'll make sure he's expecting it."

"Thanks, so much. I'll do that."

"Sure, babe, have a good night."

"You, too." Eliane hung up the phone and grabbed her car keys. I guess she'd chosen to get out of town and deal with Jett first, before she lost the chance to do it—the one problem always on the top of her list.

CHAPTER 36

Asheville, NC
Barely back then

"Knock, knock." Dr. Vitale pecked on the door before she peeked around it. Watching your favorite show again? The cheerleaders, is it?"

"Yep. It's a really good episode. They just found out one of the best veterans was fraternizing with a player. Cut her on the spot. But I think that makes room for a rookie that I'm really pulling for."

"Oh, so they can't socialize with the players, huh?" Dr. Vitale looked at the screen while she did a notably poor job of feigning interest.

"She probably just sent him a nude or something." Eliane was getting back to herself, because she only said that hoping for a reaction. She hadn't cared enough to hope for rises out of anyone recently. It was nice to watch her poke at worms with a stick again.

"Well, I hate to crash the party, but do you think you can pull out of it for a few minutes so we can chat about a couple things?"

"Do I have a choice?" El said facetiously, and reached for the remote to mute the program. She'd been generally more compliant lately. She'd been there a while, and could smell the front door.

"I was just going over the notes from our sessions, and I think you've made a lot of progress. You've been able to discuss your triggers and expose yourself to them without signs of panic for the past several days. You haven't even cried in..." she referenced her notes, "three sessions. That's huge."

"It's the meds. They've kicked in." El gave her one of those let's-be-real-faces.

"It's also you, Eliane. You've become receptive to the process. You aren't avoiding the thoughts that upset you. You're allowing them to come and functioning through them. That's how we get long-term success. You've even listened to all the songs and read through the obituary without reacting with compulsions and counting. The meds just relaxed your mind and jacked your serotonin levels back up enough to let *you* do it. They helped you fire properly, but you did the work. Let yourself have that."

"I do enjoy the serotonin. I didn't realize that life without it sucked so much until I got a little taste of the good shit."

Dr. Vitale half smiled.

"It's OK to laugh at jokes. This is still only life, you know."

"Well, I am glad you like it. It helps having a necessary chemical for brain function decide to step up and do its job," the doctor now tried to match El's energy. "I do think you're going to need to practice driving again with a safe person in the car until you get comfortable. And I want to see you in my office weekly at first. And as long as you agree to stay with your mother for a period, I don't see why we can't continue your treatment outside of this setting."

"I'm getting out?"

"You're getting out if you agree to those terms."

"I'm feeling good. I'd rather go back to my studio... if Zen will have me. I'm sure he thinks I'm crazy. I've never had a problem living on my own, well, minus those last few weeks. With the meds, I'm sure I'll be fine there."

"The meds help tremendously, but you still have a lot of work to do. I know your mother is the tough love type. She's gruff. And at times when you were growing up, she was working so much that she was absent. We've talked about this. But I've also talked to her. She knows how to guide you through the steps when the obsessions get too much. She's prepared to help you heal, and I think a family member is your best bet. Your roommate can't create the safe zone you need while you reacclimate. It'll be too isolating. Also, it could trigger you, returning to the setting where things got tough. In a couple of months, that could totally change. You can visit the apartment, acclimate to it, and see how you react—when we agree you're ready. Can you get on the same page as me on this?"

"I just want to get out of here," Eliane rubbed her tired eyes. "And I never want to come back. I'll go home...for a while. But I'm never doing this again. Never."

"I'm glad to hear that. She's here waiting for you. But, before you gather your things, there is someone waiting on the phoneline for you. You're allowed calls, and he knows not to upset you. I think you have the right to take a call though. It's a guy; I'm sorry. I forgot the name. I wrote it down somewhere. I ran it by your mom. She said she knows who it is, and she feels OK about it. It starts with a J, maybe..."

"Oh, umm, yes. I'll take the call, please." El's heart picked up pace a bit.

"Pick up the phone by your bed there. Line one."

El nodded and Dr. Vitale turned to walk out of the room, still searching her charts for the name that had escaped her.

"Hello?" El began slowly.

"El?"

"Yes?"

"How—how are you?"

She recognized the voice and answered, "I'm OK all things considered. I might not have said that a week or two ago, but I think I at least will be alright, now. It's good to hear your voice."

"El, I wasn't sure if I should call after the way things were left between us. But when I heard you were in here, I had to reach out. I—I didn't realize. I tried to call before, but they wouldn't let me through to you."

"That's OK, Jake," she replied, settling down onto the pillow. "It's feels like, normal or something to talk to you. Calm." She paused. "Look, I'm so—"

"No, don't apologize," he stopped her. "I was so mad at you at first. Of course, I was. I thought a woman whom I was in love with had just taken the easy way out and abandoned me while I was on the other side of the world just trying to protect her and everyone else. I was more pissed and hurt than I wanted to be. But I couldn't put it to bed that way. I couldn't get you out of my head, and so I reached out to Zen. I finally got him to tell me what happened...all of it."

"All of it?"

"He told me about your friend that passed and about what your childhood friend, Jett, had done. I knew I didn't like that guy when I met him that day. He just had one of those airs..."

"Yes, yes he does." El nodded.

"But it made sense. You didn't have any more to give. You were cracking, and I had no idea that whole time. I'm not sure why you felt you couldn't share it with me, but it doesn't matter. And I'm afraid I made it worse because you were trying to put on this perfect face for me."

"I did try to put that face on for you, Jake. But it wasn't anything you did wrong. It was a face I wanted to try on for a while. I chose it. You made me feel so normal, and I never felt normal, even before everything. I just didn't want that to go away. You were this soldier from a perfect family and had a jawline like Buzz Lightyear," she laughed. "I didn't want to be that person with you, that girl who went through something. And before you left, it was easier to fake. I just morphed into your world and left mine. But mine will always be there in the background. I can't escape it, and I don't know that I want to. Complicated is somehow easier for me. But you, you are not complicated. And I have never been a good mimicker, but still, I can't really be me when I'm with you, either."

"I would have still loved you," he answered.

"I know you would have. Maybe you still do, but...I can't let you."

"Why not?" He asked quietly. "Did you ever really love me? Or did you just wish that you did?"

"I do love you, Jake. I love you like I always did, but I don't think it was ever the kind of love that goes the distance. It was only love, like the love for a family member. And it isn't that you aren't gorgeous and perfect. Your chemistry and mine just didn't make anything that spilled out of the beaker. It just didn't. We were never parts of the same puzzle needing to connect. We were just parts we tried to make work."

"Maybe for you—"

"Jake..."

"And Jett? I know I'm an asshole for bringing him up in this setting. But I need to know, for me. I guess I'm not perfect after all. I just cruised by that high road, didn't I?"

"Jett and I melt down the laboratory." She just answered his question. "He's the other side. He'll never love me. Not right anyway, and I don't know the word for what he is. But I didn't lie that day I told you he was nothing to worry about. He isn't the reason we can't work. We exist completely separate from that. Please know that. He wasn't a part of what we had."

"I believe you," he said quietly. "Well, I guess there's nothing more to say here."

"I hope someday I run into you with the love of your life on your arm, Jake. You deserve it. And you'll be thankful that it wasn't me when you have her. She'll be beautiful, and she'll adore you. You'll watch her kiss your children goodnight, and you'll be so happy it's her."

He sighed deeply into the receiver. "Go live your best, Eliane Pangolin. I couldn't begin to know what to hope for you, you're still a mystery to me. But still, I hope you get it all."

CHAPTER 37

Austin, Texas
Now

It took Eliane four and a half hours to get from her apartment in downtown Paris to the Hyatt 6th Street hotel in Austin, Texas. She didn't stop to pee. She didn't stop for a bag of the trail mix she loved the most with all the M & M's, and she only barely braked for an armadillo. She drove, her tiny foot almost touching asphalt.

It was about 9:00 p.m. when she arrived, and the streets of Austin had just changed into their nightwear, an outfit that smelled a lot like smoke and heat and good whiskey. It was also far too early for Jett to go out, so she knew she'd find him there, probably napping before hitting the scene on the famous music street.

I could picture him lying there snoozing like he was having an afternoon nap before finding the most underground blues bar he could, but one that was still somehow right in the middle of all the hype. That was Jett, always looking for the rarest part of the mainstream, just going rogue enough to be too cool for the rest of us.

Eliane had ripped out her dry contacts about two hours into the trip and switched them out for her big quirky glasses that she was still wearing with her warm-up suit hanging open, the bedazzled bra gleaming in the city lights. Her hair was piled on top of her head, now in a cascading and completely unintentional messy bun. She trotted with purpose, her legs stiff, keys still jingling in her hand, passing bar after bar, a different flavor of blues coming out of each one. Sometimes it had a country twang, other times, a strong dose of rock n' roll. One gentleman played Radiohead's Creep on an upright bass in the middle of the sidewalk. El stopped to admire that one for only a moment. It was musical alchemy, and it stopped her in her tracks against her will. But I think she liked it; she liked anything that stopped her like that. And now I get it. She and Jett had been right. I had loved terrible music my entire life. I wouldn't have even recognized that song without them, but the way that man played it; that was much more than just a song. He played his instrument like he was massaging the sound out of it, like a man would help a woman give birth to his own child. He had created something with it, and he wanted it to come to life. His voice was full of gravel, but gravel he'd washed with that good whiskey that Austin smelled like. I would never have noticed any of it without either of them, Jett and Eliane as the unit they were.

There was a pulse in this city so strong, it even made me feel like I had one, pumping blood from my heart, rushing my body for a moment. It was 95 degrees at 9:00 at night and everyone was sweating all over everybody else, all those creative juices mixing, the constant being the sorrow in the music, and the variable being the brand of hope in the overtones. This place was built for Eliane. If she was only destined to pass through it for a moment, she was destined to touch the ground here, nevertheless. She was meant to collide with this place and wear it like a coat overtop of all that she already was. In whatever she was about to do, the energy, the vibe, the spit on the sidewalk from a mouth that sang like angels after they fell so crudely to earth—it was all there to help her. I was worried at first, but now I felt differently. Whatever she was here to do, she needed to do. It was going to be OK.

She finally made her way into the lobby of the tall building with shiny glass on the side. The hotel was nice, modern, not as full of the personality as the rest of the street. It was sort of like an iced pumpkin latte (which I used to drink). It was good, appealing to most, but not really unique.

El breezed past the hotel personnel. There was no fire emitting from her nostrils. She was clearly on a mission, but it wasn't as angry as I thought at first. Honestly, I'm not sure what it was, this emotion. I feel like the French would have a word for it; they drink wine a lot and have dinner at 10 p.m. I think that's required to have a word for whatever this was. El used to say "America, God love it, is too prosaic for this" if she couldn't find the right word for something. I never knew what that meant until now.

She rode the elevator to the fourth floor, got out, and looked at a sign that directed her to the right. Her purposeful walk slowed a bit as she made her way down the long hallway that smelled like a mix of bleach and potpourri. She took her time all the sudden, but it still didn't take long for her to find room 4058. She stood outside the door for a minute or two, staring a hole through it. I think she was trying to communicate whatever it was she'd come to say directly through the door. We all do silly things like that from time to time, even though we know it won't work. I used to rewatch *The Lion King* as a kid, truly believing that if I thought on it hard enough, I could save Mufasa. I could just will him right back into existence, draw the scene entirely differently. I think that's what El was doing now. But, as we all do, she came to her senses. She closed her eyes, took a deep breath in, then balled her fist up and knocked twice. Nothing. She waited about thirty seconds and knocked twice more.

Finally, the door swung open. "We didn't order any—Eliane? What in God's name are you doing here?"

"I—I..."

Skyla stood there in an old, oversized shirt of Jett's that I recognized from years ago. It just said "Finch" super small in red letters in the middle. I think they used to be a band a hundred years ago. I'm pretty sure they were one of the ones Jett made me listen to while he stared at me, watching my face for a reaction. I remember one song talking about some girl being the only person besides the songwriter who knew what it felt like to burn. I don't remember the exact lyric, but it was about this girl being the only other person to feel what he felt, the way he felt it. I knew for whatever reason, this made him think of El, not of me. If he could see everything I know now, so jaded and wise; this is how he wished I'd been for him. And now, I am. I only had to give my life for it.

"Skyla, I, um. I thought you were back in Dallas." El could feel how wide her eyes must be.

"I was halfway here when you called me. What is going on Eliane? Are you here for me? Is something wrong? I—"

"This must seem so weird to you. God." Eliane put her hand to her head. "Look, I have a lot to explain to you, like more than I could try to in this awkward and just fucking *horrible* moment." She cringed as she spoke. "And I swear that I will explain it all, but, is Jett—"

"El?" Jett came up behind Skyla. "Is that you?"

"You know her?" Skyla whipped around, her Botoxed brow refusing to let her scowl.

"Just a little bit." El said quickly and dryly. She might as well have thrown her hands into the air. Then she turned to Jett. "We need to talk. You got a minute for an old friend?"

CHAPTER 38

"How are you even here right now? How did you know I was here? What's going on, El?" Jett looked around like the answer would be in the air somewhere. He wasn't showing confusion as much as, *amusement*, maybe?

"I got a job writing for Skyla after I saw a picture of you guys on social media and had a batshit plan to come down here and fuck up your music festival for revenge."

Jett folded his arms, more tattooed than before, and nodded.

"I hadn't decided how exactly I was going to do it." El spoke coolly, just chatting with an old friend, "I thought of rushing the stage, but, you know, security...then I thought of inserting myself as some kind of announcer and then just telling everyone what a piece of shit you are in fraudulently stealing my words...but I changed my mind about that, too. I wasn't like...afraid of getting arrested or anything. I expected that I would. But some shit has gone down...and...I just sort of *evolved* today, literally like five or six hours ago. So, lucky you." Eliane smiled and cocked her head sideways, to which Jett smiled back almost saying *classic El*.

"What in the hell? What are you, some kind of stalker? Holy shit. I—should we call someone? Jett? What's—" I'd almost forgotten Skyla was even there until she spoke. I felt bad for her, even though she'd only annoyed me until now.

El cut her off. "Skyla, I'm so sorry. It was the worst plan. It was impulsive and childish and crazy. Like I said, I have so much explaining to do, but, um, can I have a minute with Jett first? I know that also seems crazy." She paused to see if Skyla's jaw would return from the floor. "Please?"

"What? No. Jett, do something. She's clearly—"

"Babe, umm, can you give us a sec? Maybe go grab a drink or something? I'll come down and get you in a few. Then we'll hit up 6th Street. It'll be fine."

"Are you insane? Is *she* insane?" Skyla had started to sweat a little bit. "How do you even know her? Are you screwing her, too?"

"I guess I'll be obligated to explain some shit, too. I will, whatever. But for now, please just go, OK?" He spoke gently but the room still got colder.

"Whatever. I don't know what this is, but I'm out of here." Skyla grabbed her jeans out of the floor and pulled them up her body quickly. "But I'm not getting a drink. I'm going back to Dallas. I'm not doing this. And little Miss Crazy is fired."

El nodded, smiling slightly, her lips rolled in.

"And I'll decide later if *you* get to explain anything or not." She shot venom toward Jett. "It's looking pretty doubtful." She walked out, slamming the door behind her.

"Well, that went well," Eliane nodded.

"She'll be alright." Jett shrugged. "And if not, I don't really care. She's cute but she makes me look at other influencers on Instagram and tell her all the ways she's better than they are after sex. I was gonna can her after the festival anyway." He grabbed a beer off the end table and popped it open.

"Are you not even fazed by my showing up here?" El put her hands on her hips.

"I know you, El. I knew you'd show up somewhere eventually. So, you stalked my girlfriend for a while and hoped to make a big scene before that good conscience of yours kicked in. It would take more than that to shock me. You're...*you*. And I've always known you climb a different bean stalk."

"I hate that you're not intimidated right now." El chuckled, "But I also feel like I'm home or something for the first time in a long time...I hate that, too."

"So, what did you want to talk about, El? You've come to Texas to do it. So, spit it out." Jett flopped onto his back on the big, disheveled bed, obviously just used.

"To be clear, I came to Texas to be a Dallas Cowboys Cheerleader. Fate just put you here at the right time."

"Are you shitting me, right now?" He almost spit out his beer.

"Look at what I'm wearing. The audition was earlier today."

"That, I didn't expect." He eyed her outfit. "How'd you do?"

"Shitty, but I loved it. Unlike me. I don't think I've ever enjoyed failure so much."

"You didn't pour expensive gin you can't afford into a teacup and drink it in the bathtub with the lights off?"

"No, I reserve that for when my writing gets rejected. This goal was something else. It was like a rebound relationship. It was to get me through. It really wasn't gin-worthy."

"I think all of mine are that."

"What? Your relationships?"

"Yeah."

"All of them I've seen you in, sure."

"Well, nothing's changed. Age hasn't helped me at all." He was half-right. It might not have matured him, but it did look good on him. He had the slightest beard now and just a couple hints of lines appearing at the edges of his eyes. He looked better than ever. I hated it, and I was sure that El did too. He was beautiful, really, hair a mess, shirtless and tattooed, a warm-blooded grown man now. It would have shaken me. But she pulled up her big girl panties. She didn't show it if it moved her, not this time.

They sat in silence for a few moments, locking eyes, deciding if they'd small talk some more. For a second, I thought Eliane would say no more. She was more comfortable than she'd planned, and Jett looked too human. I thought she might realize there was nothing to say and simply walk away. Except, there was stuff to say. It just wasn't the stuff she thought it would be. It wasn't anger, not at all.

"I came here to tell you a few things. Some of them, I don't need to say anymore, but some I still do. First, it's really fucked up that you stole my words and used them to get everything you ever wanted. It's one of the worst things anyone has ever done to me, and it's even worse that it's all based on someone who was special to both of us getting brutally murdered. You're a bastard for that. I don't think I'm mad about it anymore though, just a little sad." I could see that even that was fading. She was getting too tired for sad or mad.

"I know. I figured that was part of it, and you're right."

"And—wait, you *know*? I'm *right?* You're owning up to that?"

"Yeah. I am. It was screwed up. I saw my chance and thought that you'd stand in the way, so I took it anyway. I stole it, and I didn't even feel bad about it at the time. And I'm sorry for that. I can try to make it right. I can call my lawyer and get you the royalties you deserve. I've been thinking of that a lot lately, even before you showed up tonight."

"I don't want royalties from that. I don't want every dime I spend to remind me of it all. I didn't come here to collect. I just came to stand up for myself. I never stood up to you, ever. I'd get mad. I'd blow my top, but that was just reaction. I never just calmly told you how I felt. I could come to blows with anyone. I just couldn't with you."

"Are you joking? You might be the only person who ever did."

"No. I'm just me, and I seem sassy. People think I'm this little spitfire. But I was just good at stringing words together. I still let you into every area of my life that I knew I shouldn't have. I chose you over and over again. And that's the second thing I came to admit, because I need to. I kept choosing you because I was either in love with you or addicted to you, and I have no idea which it was. But you never deserved to be my love or my habit. It killed me that you were such a slut and never tried to nail me. How pathetic is that? It was bad for my self-esteem, but I've also decided to release you of that. You spared me, really. And my worth isn't about you at all. You don't get to assign that to me, or to Lux, or to anybody."

"El—"

"You don't have to say anything to try and build me up. This is my closure with you. I don't need you to participate in it out of pity, especially out of pity." She took a step backward, inching a little closer to the door.

"No, I have something to say now. It's your turn to listen. You barged in here and I let you say your piece. So let me say mine."

"Then do it." She folded her arms.

"I know you think I'm such a piece of shit, and I probably am. But you played games too. You constantly reminded me that I wasn't good enough to be in your presence. I just wanted so much not to care. I liked being cool. I liked being a little strange. I liked people wanting me so bad they could taste it. I am a dickhead. I know that. But it still killed me that I couldn't get to you. I had a feeling I did a little sometimes, and apparently, I was right. But, still, I couldn't have been with you. One, you would have rejected me out of pure defiance." He counted on his fingers. "Two, I would have had to be a dick to you after because I just can't help it. And three, I was most scared that—well, you know what? It doesn't matter. None of this stuff matters. What's the end game?" He leaned back to swig the beer again.

"What's three, Jett? You owe me. Give me whatever real thing you just hid away. I think I deserve it."

Jett sighed and rubbed his eyes. "My tongue is like literally rejecting the words right now. God El." He paused and she waited. "I—I was terrified I would try to nail you but...but, that I'd end up making love to you. I was afraid I would meet your soul face-to-face and then love you forever. That's the worst thing I could have ever done. Neither of us were stable enough for that, to have had to get over the other one day. We wouldn't have been able to, but we wouldn't have lasted either. So, I just didn't with you, didn't even take a little bite just for taste. Even I have a limit."

El swallowed hard. Her crossed arms unfolded. She was half scared she'd melt, but mostly vindicated. Maybe that's what she really came to hear. Maybe that's all she'd ever wanted to hear.

She waited a few moments before she spoke, "Jett—if we had ever crossed *that* line, it would have been the best poetry. It would have been passion and sweat and surrender and uncomfortable eye contact. I would have probably cried, and you would have liked it and licked the tears off my face. We would have been in mad love for a fleeting second, laughing and arguing, and sliding down slamming doors to fuck or to fight." She lowered herself to the chair by the bed. "Then, you're right, one of us would have ruined it because of whatever flaws we each have that turn to fire when they're together. Some of the best poetry ends in tragedy. And that's what we would have written together. And the art of us, the story, the legend; that would be better than the real us. People would love to read about it, to whisper about, to watch and see how it would all end. But I know that ending. We would end up undoing one another. We'd be Zelda and F. Scott. We would have been destroyed."

"You and your dead dude..." Jett laughed quietly, his gaze toward the ground.

"You can't ever have me. And that's what I get to enjoy. But the fact that I'll think of you in a certain way forever, and you will always get to be the guy who is kind of a problem for me—that's yours to keep. I think that's all we can ever hope to give one another. I think as sick as we are, maybe those are the perfect parting gifts."

"I would have loved you, El, if I could have."

"I would have loved you, too." She said without the smallest crack in her voice.

"I'm sorry for anything I ever did. I'm sorry for using you. And I'm sorry for being a shit to Lux. And I'm sorry I'll never change my band's name, and I'll ride it till the end like the bastard I am." He meant it in that moment. He might return to never caring again by the next morning, probably would. But that moment was what mattered to El. She would get to keep it, always.

"I know you are." She nodded. "I—I'm actually not sorry for anything anymore. I'm finished with sorry. I'm grateful. I'm grateful I came here like this, in more control than I thought I could ever be. I'm grateful that I know I'll really never see you again this time. I'm grateful I knew you, though. It's all just part of the ride. I can't make you not part of my story, so I won't try." She smiled. "But, no, Jett, I'm not sorry for anything anymore."

"You know what I'm not sorry for, El? It's only one thing."

"What's that?"

"I'm not sorry I saw you out of my car window that day when I was six or seven. It's what made me go up to you at school and start being your friend."

"What are you talking about? You never told me this."

"We were riding down the road, and we stopped at a redlight. I could see you in your front yard up on the hill. You'd made little tiny piles of birdseed everywhere, and the birds had come right up to you. They felt so safe to be near you, kind of like I always did. You had a little notebook, making checkmarks like you were taking attendance or something. It was weird as hell. I'm still not sure what you were doing. But you were so adorable, and you seemed so smart. That's when I couldn't tear my eyes away. That's when you became the bright little girl I just had to watch. I'm not sorry for seeing you that day. And the next day, I pulled your pigtails and started teaching you all the wrong things about little boys. But I'm still not sorry. I think of it often, maybe more than I think about anything else."

"Thank you for telling me that," El couldn't hide the break in her quiet voice this time, nor the sniffle that followed.

"Now get on out of here." He stood up, walking her toward the door. "Go write a million stories. Write about me or don't. If you do, it'll really stroke my ego, though." He grinned.

"I doubt I'll be able to help it, Jett. You can have that, too."

"But also write about you, El. Write from that voice everyone craves to hear. Your words were my muse. But they belong to you. Go do that thing you were meant to do. Be your own muse; you don't need anybody else. So, go move on."

"I think I finally am." She nodded. "I'm think I'll go to Paris, to the *real* Paris in France."

He scrunched his nose in confusion.

"I decided today. I'm moving there to write, and wander, and eat bread, and drink wine, and to venture to the south in the warm months. It'll be my best chapter yet."

"I hope it is."

"One last thing, though. I promised Lux in a letter that I would write her a song better than the first one I wrote for her. I wasn't going to ever let it see the light of day, but she deserves for it to. We owe her that. So, in my moment of clarity, I grabbed it. I want you to perform it if it's the last favor you ever do for me."

Jett said nothing. He just took the paper from her, then stroked her cheek with his hand."

"Hopefully I'll hear it on a pretty afternoon in Paris."

"I'm sure you will." He paused, "Hey, I promise if I'm ever there, I won't look you up."

"You better not," she winked. "Goodbye Jett Jorgenson."

"Goodbye, El."

CHAPTER 38

I hadn't left Eliane to look in on Jett very often, maybe a handful of times in all these years. I don't think I'd ever looked in on him when he'd been alone. He'd usually been with a leggy girl built oddly similar to me, or at a gig, or with just a throng of people clamoring around him for no good reason. However, after Eliane walked out of that hotel room that night, I didn't follow her. I lingered behind to watch him read the song. I had to see him experience it; I was compelled, though I was half sure I should have just stuck to my regular activities.

I hadn't read it myself. I wasn't positive on when she'd written it, maybe alone in the dark one night when I thought everything was still. I found that, on occasion, she was still able to allude me. But I suppose everyone has the right to a little bit of life in the shadows.

When the door shut behind her, Jett stood staring at it for a solid five or ten minutes. I don't think he thought on any level that she'd be back. He didn't expect the door to swing open and for her to rush into his arms. He knew it was goodbye this time, but I just don't think he had the strength to move right away. He didn't know how to move, or why for a moment. I think he'd come the closest to loving Eliane that he could have come to loving anyone, and now nothing made sense. He only thought nothing ever had before.

Finally, he walked back to the disheveled bed and flopped back onto it. He opened another beer and chugged it all at once, his Adam's apple bulging with his neck stubble decorating it. He got strangled on it a little bit at the very end and a couple drops spewed out of his nostrils and onto the bed. But he hardly reacted.

Still clutching the folded piece of paper in one hand, he crushed the can with the other and chucked it across the room. Then Jett Jorgenson did something I'd never seen him do before. He wept.

Jett buried his face into his pillow, snot running from his red nostrils, fists clenched into a ball, and he cried out everything he'd ever wanted to in all his life. Most of it was for losing Eliane, once and for all. But I believe there were even a few tears for me in there. His sounds were a melting pot of grief, loss, love, and nostalgia. Those are the only ingredients that made the sounds coming out of him, and for what it was worth, which was very little at this point, I finally decided that Jett was a human after all.

He finally stifled back the sobs enough to take his face off the pillow. He carefully opened the hand that was clutching the song that Eliane had given to him. He unfolded it slowly with his guitar-callused hands and started to read.

Eliane had scribbled a small message at the top that said:

You title it. I couldn't find the right words. But then, that will make it part yours, for real this time. -El.

Then the song she'd written for me followed.

We did this to you
Reduced you to dust and bones and songs
We gave birth to what you are now
But I'm here trying to right those wrongs
So many wrongs

But we can't carry the shovels forever
To set you free, we have to lay them down
If we stay bound it puts your legacy in the ground
But, Lux, our light, you're the only freedom we've found

Nothing can change what's been done
But I believe forgiveness makes us free
I'm not asking you for it
That job is for him and for me
For him and for me

But we can't carry the shovels forever
To set you free, we have to lay them down
If we stay bound it puts your legacy in the ground
But, Lux, our light, you're the only freedom we've found

In forgiving us, I let you rest
In removing my chains, you can fly
I'm sorry it took us this long
But now you can shine way up high
Way up high

But we can't carry the shovels forever
To set you free, we have to lay them down
If we stay bound it puts your legacy in the ground
But, Lux, our light, you're the only freedom we've found

Jett sat quietly, sobbing more reverently now. Then he got up and walked to the desk on the other side of the suite. He took an ink pen from the top drawer and went back to the bed where he'd left the crumpled sheet El had written the perfect song for me on. It was perfect because she'd finally gotten it. I'd already forgiven her, and all she had left was to forgive Jett and, more importantly, to forgive herself. Finally, she had.

Jett scribbled with the black pen on top of the page, the words "The Last Letter to Lux." For Eliane's sake, I believed that it would be, the last letter, the last song, the last of any of me in their worlds. And that was my perfect parting gift. That's when I believe I said goodbye to Jett Jorgenson.

CHAPTER 40

Paris, Texas
Now

She was almost back to her apartment when she picked up the phone to face the music.

"Hello?" Dr. Vitale's even voice answered.

"Hi, Dr. Vitale, it's Eliane."

"It's good to hear from you Eliane. You've been difficult to reach." Her voice changed and slowed. She was *afraid*.

"Look, I know what you think. I know you think I stalked Jett and Skyla, and maybe I did a little, but that's over. I've spoken to Jett, and Skyla knows everything now. I obviously will not be going back to work for her. That was bizarre, I know, and I'm sorry for that part. It wasn't smart of me. But that's not what I want to talk about."

"OK, what would you like to talk about, Eliane?" She kept her voice as even as possible.

"I want to talk about the Blue Ridge Ripper. I know you know he's here. He did follow me to Texas. He's been emailing me for years. He texted me the other day. I don't know what he wants with me, and I swear I don't know who he is. But I'm ready to share his emails, do whatever I can to make sure he's caught. If I get in trouble, I get in trouble. I don't know that I was running, but I know now that I was hiding. I was hiding behind almost everything I was doing. But I can't anymore. I've worked on myself through *all* of this. I can't believe how selfish I am. I don't want any more girls to die. I want him caught. I've been telling myself that this has nothing to do with me, but it has everything to do with me, even if I don't know why."

Eliane walked up the stairs to her apartment building and stuck her key in the door.

"That's good to hear, Eliane. I think we have a lot to get to the bottom of, here. Where are you now? I will call someone to come to where you are."

"I just got back to my apartment in Paris. I can—"

"Eliane?"

"Oh my God." Eliane breathed.

"Eliane, what is it?" Dr. Vitale said louder.

Eliane started to cry.

"I'm about to call the police. What is —" Her voice trailed.

"Give me the phone. We need to have a chat. Hand it to me, now, and don't try anything stupid." My killer was sitting casually, legs crossed, a gun held like a whimsical little dandelion on her floral couch.

CHAPTER 41

"Nice and easy. Just throw the phone over to me," his voice was sweet like it had been at the bar before he changed, despite the now aimed gun.

Eliane tossed it onto the couch where he hit "end call."

"Now, sit down, in that chair there. Easy does it." He motioned with the pistol.

She lowered herself to it as instructed and said nothing.

"Good girl."

Eliane was still frozen, the most speechless she'd ever been.

"How I've wanted to meet you for so long. You're so very beautiful, Eliane." He smiled with his mouth closed. He looked to be in his mid-forties by now, but his features were the same, still *inviting* almost.

Her eyes darted about, breath quickening.

"You can say thank you. That was a compliment."

"Thank you." She eked out.

"I've been watching you to some degree since I found out about you. I didn't know how or when to do this. Then things got really complicated in Asheville. I'm sorry for that. And I mean it. I don't feel sorrow very often, but I'm sorry for how it *affected* you. And I'm sorry about the gun, too. I just didn't think you'd see me otherwise."

"What are you talking about?" She sniffled. "I don't recognize you."

"You know who I am," he urged.

"You're...*him*...right? You've been emailing and texting me. But you said you wouldn't—"

"Oh, honey. I won't. I would never. As I said, I'm sorry that the thing with Lux hurt you so much. But that isn't even why I'm here."

The thing with Lux? Really?

"I—I" Eliane scrambled until he cut her off.

"I just couldn't help it. I saw her while I was watching you grow into the beautiful girl you are. And I couldn't resist. My issues started long before her. Most of the girls in your world, even the little cheerleaders, didn't fit my requirements anyway. They weren't problems while I looked on, and your only real friend for a long time was that boy. I don't lean that way at all. But then you got that beauty queen roommate. She was difficult for me. But I'd like to get past it if we can."

"What are you talking about? I'm so confused. You're talking to me like you *know* me." The tears and snot stuck against her conflicted face. I looked at her closely, wanting to reach out and grab her, to help in some small way, but I couldn't. I just bounced my eyes back and forth between the two of them. But that is exactly when I saw it. It's why her eyes reminded me of his so much when she went blank after the failed audition. The eyes *were* his.

"Your mother and I had a brief romance. Puppy love. She was so beautiful then, so popular. She thought I was...alluring...at first, reading in dark corners where her jock boyfriends who always cheated couldn't find her. Oh, and I love that you're a reader, too. You're so much like me, but I was more a Hemingway buff when it came to the Lost Generation." He paused to stare at her, so different than the way he'd stared at me. It was still scary, but it wasn't the same kind of scary. Not at all. "I was only 16 when it happened. And by then she was done with me, said I frightened her, that I was too clingy, that I had too many...oddities. She didn't like that I parked too long outside her house, that I watched her always. But I was just protective. I could have protected her forever, but she wouldn't let me. Then she was graduated and gone. I didn't know *everything* until I got the stirrings to look her up again. I wanted her to be the first one...in my collection. Then I saw you, you with my eyes, and I left her be so you could have a mother. It would have been too much for you then. They say people like me don't have hearts, but that was heart, my dear. Maybe you'll see that." His face turned up into a longing, sad smile. Then he reached out his hand toward El.

She wanted to dart away, but she let him stroke her face fearing the gun in his hand.

"Are you going to hurt me?" She asked in a small whisper.

"No, no. Haven't you been listening? I am so very proud of you. You're the best parts of me and her. You have the face of the homecoming queen, but you aren't empty. You have my art inside of you. I meant it when I said I hoped we could be friends. I want to know you, Eliane."

"But those girls, the things you do —"

"No!" He raised his voice. "I don't want to talk about that. That's another part of me, maybe not even me at all. That's just something I have to do to teach them, that certain kind. We can exist completely separately. We can be father and daughter. I know we can. Your mother didn't understand you the way she didn't understand me. I saw it. But I can understand you. We *can* have that."

"How long?"

"How long what, darling?" She cringed when he called her that.

"How long were you watching me?"

"Since you were a toddler. I could see that you were such a bright little girl, even then. You played differently, methodically, and thoughtfully. It was so clear that you were mine, even before I noticed your eyes. So unique."

Eliane didn't respond to him. She was distracted by the officer who had scaled the tiny balcony on the outside of her building. He put his finger to his lips to tell her to be quiet. Dr. Vitale had gotten the call out. The police were there. She knew then that she was surrounded.

Then she spoke, "I am unique. And you're right. My mother never understood me. Not at all. I —I understand the things that you've done. Girls like Lux. They ruined everything for me. They just used their looks and their batting eyelashes to get what they wanted and then they'd discard everyone."

"It's so true. Even your own mother. You see how they turn out if they aren't dealt with."

"I know. I lived it," El responded.

"Can I ask you something?"

"Absolutely, Eliane."

"Would you take me to dinner? Will you take me like a wonderful father takes his daughter? I want us to be friends too, if somehow, some way, we can. I would like to try. I never had anyone. The only man that was ever in my life long-term was Jett, and that's over now. I just need someone to love me." Eliane reached her hand toward him.

He eyed her for a good thirty seconds, and she just gazed back at him, pleading with him. Then he put the gun into his waistband. "Let's go get something to eat. Then maybe ice cream after. I always imagined getting you mint chocolate chip."

"That would be so nice. Ice cream with my dad, my real dad," she responded. "I can't believe it." She leaned in gingerly, then embraced him, his arms wrapping around her. He released her, and she reached for the doorknob.

"Oh, my coat. It's spring but it gets chilly at night," she said, allowing him to pass in front of her, urging him to go out first, knowing what would be waiting just on the other side of the door. He put his hand on the knob, but then turned to look at her, getting a glimpse of the cop on the balcony when he did it.

He paused and shook his head. "You almost had me."

"What? I —"

"I guess getting all dolled up like a whore for your dancing turned you into one of them, Homecoming Queen." There was the demeanor I knew.

"What are you—" she backed away.

"I see the cop outside, there. I guess that means they're everywhere now."

She said nothing.

"How'd they know?" He paused. "You were on the phone. The person you were talking to must have heard something."

"Look, I don't know if the person on the phone heard me get upset or what. I don't know, but let's just reason through this. It wasn't me who called them. I would never. Let's—"

"Shut up. Let me think."

Eliane froze in place.

He walked over to the gas range stove and turned it on high, not letting it quite catch, but letting it tick, releasing the most amount of gas he could.

"What are you doing?" Eliane backed away.

"I'm not sitting on death row for twenty years all for them to stick a needle in my arm after my third failed appeal. This way it'll be poetic. Literary, like us. We'll go down in history together. And you'll get to parish in the fire just like Zelda did. They'll publish you posthumously. It's the most elegant gift I could ever give you." He was grinning like a hyena, sweat pouring down his temples.

"Stop, stop. You don't have to do this!" The cop on the balcony screamed, unable to take a shot due to the gas. "Where's the damn negotiator?" He called.

Then the Blue Ridge Ripper aimed his gun at the stove in time with Eliane beelining out the front door and diving as far as she could away from the building. And *he* pulled the trigger. I stood watching in the middle of the fiery explosion, feeling nothing of course. I watched Eliane collapse outside, the flame's long fingers reaching out to her. And then I watched *him* draw his last ragged breath as his body turned to black stone.

CHAPTER 42

It took Eliane's mother three days to get to Texas because she refused to fly, even with the situation at hand, but Eliane needed the time by herself to think about what she would say when she finally saw her. She thought of how to ask her mother about the man she came to learn was named Larry Matthew Demyun. How would she ask another question about her father like this? I don't think she thought of a thing.

"Hi honey," Her mother spoke as nicely as she ever had when she entered the hospital room.

A middle-aged police officer sat in the corner sipping a coffee and playing some juvenile game on his phone. One had been there since she arrived by ambulance after the blast. She was told that she'd be guarded around the clock until her release. Even though Demyun was now dead, they were taking every precaution with her just in case. In case of what, she didn't know, but she appreciated it all the same. They'd interviewed her off and on in pieces but handled her with gloves at Dr. Vitale's urging. She still kept the emails and texts private. What did they matter now? She'd been through more than she ever thought possible, and at that point had given all she had to give.

"Hi Mom," Eliane responded loudly. She wanted to appear strong despite all the bandages, mostly on the right side of her body, ranging from the shoulder down to her thigh.

"Baby, oh, I am so sorry," her mother leaned in and kissed her on her untouched face.

"It's just a few burns," Eliane replied. "It could have been much worse."

"Oh my God. I'm—I'm just so sorry about all of this. I don't know what to say, but I know you're expecting me to say a lot."

Eliane paused, looking into space for a moment. "Why did you tell me my father was some drug addict who left you? That man was many things. I don't even want to think about it all. But he isn't who you said he was. Did you *know*?"

Her mother sighed deeply and thought for a few seconds before she spoke. "Larry Demyun was obsessed with me in school. He followed me everywhere. He was strange, so strange." She made a face to let Eliane know it was far beyond her kind of weird. "Of course, I didn't know he was *this*, or that he even existed anymore for that matter." She took a deep breath. "But he is not your father, Eliane. That was some loser jock with a habit, but nothing more. Demyun wasn't right in the head. I never even spoke to him. We didn't sleep together. He just liked me. He somehow convinced himself he was your father, I'm assuming. He clearly wasn't well. I am so sorry that I never noticed him there, lurking. I had no idea."

Eliane furrowed her brow. "But his eyes. They look just like mine. I could see it. And he's an avid reader. He told me. It seemed like he was honest about that."

"When something is suggested to us, sometimes we just see what we want to in that moment. Not that you *wanted* to see him in you, but when he so confidently wanted you to believe it, you went lookin' for it. When we look, we find, Eliane. It's why we should always look for the good."

"So, he wasn't my father?" Eliane started to cry. "He isn't why I'm...like this?"

"No, baby. You are nothing like him. You are just perfect. He is no part of you at all."

"Well, that saves me writing him letters every day for the next ten years, trying to figure out who I am now."

"Oh, God Eliane, do not —"

"I'm kidding, Mom." Eliane put her head back on the pillow, exhausted. "But what a relief. I feel like I can breathe a little bit for the first time in, well, ever, it seems."

"Why don't you just rest for a while? I'll be right here the whole time."

"OK, that sounds good." Eliane let out the first sigh of true relief I'd heard in a long time, and she was out within minutes.

Her mother stood there rubbing her hair, tears welling in her eyes, gazing down at her daughter.

When she was good and asleep the cop sat down his coffee and asked her mother, "Why didn't you tell her the truth?"

"What do you mean?" She asked, standing up a little straighter and looking him in the eye.

"Larry Matthew Demyun *is* her father. We did a rush order DNA request testing his against hers the day of the explosion to help positively identify him. That came back this morning. I know it's not my place, but I'm curious. Why didn't you tell her that?"

She shrugged just like Eliane, then said, "Because the truth doesn't always set you free."

"In my line of work, we tend to believe the opposite, Ma'am," he replied. "She could find out, then she'll know you lied to her."

"Well, this ain't your line of work. And I'll make sure she doesn't find out. She's gonna go to Paris, far away from all this." She paused, gazing at her daughter. "This is a girl who's been through a lot. This is someone who will never stop lookin' for pieces of him in everything she does if she knows the truth. She will find what she's lookin' for, and that needs to be good things, not traces of a man who killed her friend and stalked her since she was in diapers. I was able to take that away from her, and I did. Now she doesn't have to be a serial killer's daughter."

"She's still a serial killer's daughter, whether she knows it or not."

"You're only what you believe you are, sir. I'm finally goin' to give her somethin' worth believin' in."

CHAPTER 43

AFTER

Paris, France

Her apartment sat on top of a small hill on the farthest outskirt of Paris proper and was in the attic of a rock building four stories up that didn't have an elevator. The stairs were too narrow for a couch, so she had decorated the place with a collection of eclectic chairs found mostly at flea markets outside the city. She'd gone to Paris alone (well, almost alone; I'm still here), after working as a waitress at two different restaurants for nearly two years back in North Carolina with her mother. She earned the money herself even though a check from Domino Records eventually came at the request of Jett Jorgenson. She was happy that the tin man finally grew a heart, but she never cashed that check. That, she did decide to burn.

When it was time to go, she found a place that had come furnished with a bed and old wooden kitchen table. But the windows were the kind you could throw open, like the ones everyone poked their heads out of when shouting their most excited "bonjour" in *Beauty and the Beast*. That was enough to sell Eliane on it, that and the fact that she could be in the thick of things with just one quick train ride. Besides that, she could bike anywhere she needed to go. On her side of the street there was a winery, a market, a tiny book shop and the boulangerie Paris, Texas had failed to provide. On the other side, was a small park and pond, which is where she finished the third novel she'd tried to write, the one that was *the* one.

Nearly another pair of years had passed since she finished it, and life was far from perfect. She hadn't had any relationship to speak of, besides the ones with her new literary agent and publicity team. Her nails were almost always chewed to the nub, and her skin had faded more pale than ever from the lack of sunlight. But she was happy. She hadn't had a panic attack since Texas, and she had just the right amount of ease to feel good about it. Anymore would have been too perfect and scared the hell out of her. She was living in her Paris, and it was all real, a perfectly imperfect, only slightly dramatic life.

She was sitting in a Tiffany-blue antique chair by her favorite of the windows, eating a chocolate chip crepe and gazing at the barely visible top of the actual Eiffel Tower in the far distance, checking her email before getting ready for the biggest day of her life.

> *Hey El,*
>
> *I thought I'd shoot you an email since it costs me a million dollars to send off a text. Forget trying to call. I wish I could though, because I miss you, you quirky little thing. I might have to get over my fear of flying and get across the big pond to see you one of these days. It's killing me to miss your book launch today. I've never been so proud of anybody in my life. It's good that you never listened to me. I just wish I was there to see where it got you. I wish I was there just so you could rub it all in my face. You think Vitale could help me get on a plane one of these days?*
>
> *Please have the very best day of your whole life today. Enjoy being in the spotlight, then tell me what that feels like. Be confident when you sign*

the books, too. Know that you earned it. I wasn't perfect but seeing you like this today makes me regret nothing I ever did. You're exactly what you should be. You're finally happy.

Love,

Mama

P.S. It's the best book I ever read. And I also thought about it, and who you are right now is "my Paris." You were always my Paris.

El shut the laptop and took another bite of her crepe. She let one tear fall down her face after about five minutes of stillness. I wish I could have done the same, because I'm pretty sure we felt exactly the same way. And I began to wonder what I'd been waiting on. Why was I still here?

When she finally wiped the tear away, she stood up, sighed once, and then made her way to the shower. The tub sat back almost tunnel-like, in the dark, blocking out all light and sound. The showerhead came out of the ceiling so that it would pour down on her like rain. She turned the water on, then stepped in to let it fall over her bare body. At first, she cried with it, the tears she'd held in before all streaming out of her now, a lot like Jett had cried alone in his hotel room that night, a decade's worth running down the drain with her shedding skin and falling hair. Then she stopped. She let the warm water and soundproof walls embrace her. She let them soothe her and cleanse her. Then she put thirteen tiny squirts of body wash on her loofa, because, well, some of the habits are much harder to break than others, and she washed it all away. With each scrub she pictured on more tear, one more memory, one more hardship going down that drain at her feet. She ran her hands down her arms, her skin feeling soft and renewed. Then she reached for her towel, dried off, and looked at herself in the mirror. She wasn't perfectly tanned and adorned in jewels like she had been back in Texas on the morning of her auditions. It hadn't been adding all that garb that fixed her. It was, instead, stripping it all away. She continued to stare at herself, naked, no make-up, nothing to tame her hair, and she only saw herself. Nothing more.

"You've got a big day ahead, El," she said to herself. "You have it *all* ahead."

CHAPTER 44

She wore an airy floral dress and large stud earrings, brown daisies, just like the dead ones in the box she'd now carted with her across continents, to the event. She stopped outside 5 Rue Daunou in the heart of Paris, France and gazed up at the iconic sign that said Harry's Bar. The American Bar founded in the middle of the city of love on Thanksgiving Day in 1911 was the perfect prohibition era escape for Americans. The Fitzgeralds, and so many others, found it quickly when it moved from its home in Manhattan to the artistic hub of the world, and they enjoyed it together—that lost little sweet spot—in between the world wars. There was nowhere else Eliane was willing to host the launch of her debut novel, *Flowers Never Die*. I'd heard her on the phone with her agent discussing the whole thing about a year before.

"I really think we should hold the launch back in the states since that's our initial market." The agent with the thick New York accent persuaded.

"OK, first of all, there still might be a warrant out for me in Texas. It could be for stalking or obstructing justice. I'm not sure which. Second of all, I just can't. This is where I'm home. I have to do it here. This is like the source of everything that inspired it. It would be like having a Yankees exhibition at Wrigley field to do it anywhere else." El protested.

"You do realize that you'll have to do a U.S. tour at some point to promote this thing, regardless. You need to at least tour the Southeast. We're going to have to fix this outlaw-in-Texas thing. I hope you're exaggerating."

"I was joking. I don't think the warrant was ever actually taken out. I mean, I'm not positive." Eliane paused and thought about it seriously. "Of course, I'll come back to do my tour. The American South is part of it; it's most of it. I just feel strongly that the launch should happen here. I am an American in Paris. Harry's Bar is an iconic haunt for the greatest figures in American literature. It's not just poetic, it feels like my destiny. It was going to end here, well maybe begin here, the whole time."

"Fine," the New Yorker sighed. "We just have to be very strategic with the marketing for this. It needs to be very clear why we're doing it. It should be an ode to the past with a nod to the future. It has to be emotional and nostalgic. We should invite some descendants of The Fitzgeralds and Hemmingways."

"Yes." Chills ran down Eliane's spine. "The refreshments should be taken from their favorite meals, but with some random southernisms thrown in, like deviled eggs and mini jello molds in cupcake papers with sprigs of mint thrown on top. It'll be perfect. The book is really just a love letter to both places, both eras."

"That's one twisted love letter, then," her agent laughed.

"Yes. Yes, it is."

And now, almost a year after that conversation, Eliane stood ready to make her grand entrance to the exact party she'd described. It wasn't just an entrance into a famous bar, or an entrance into a book signing. It was the entrance into her life, the one she'd chosen at long last.

She had her hand on the door, ready to pull it open and see the stacks of books waiting for her to sign, the cover depicting a young girl sitting by a painting of Zelda's flowers that would never be lost again. She was ready to smell the gin in the famous cocktail called the White Lady that she planned to sip as she signed. She was ready for the hum of jazz playing quietly in the background, and she was ready to share all of her secrets—and some of Zelda's too—in a parallel story about them the world was about to read.

"Excuse me, Miss?" A small voice, purely American, but nowhere near full-grown stopped her as her hand reached for the door.

"Oh, hi? Are you speaking to me?" She turned and looked at the girl who couldn't have been more than 10 or 11 standing behind her. Her skin was fair, and her dress was neatly pressed. Her hair, however, was unruly. She'd done her best with it, but it was falling out of the ponytail and onto her small and curious face.

"My name is Denver, and I'm a huge fan of yours. I'm too young to get into the bar for the signing. So, I begged my dad to bring me early in hopes that I would catch you. I have a copy of your book here, if you'll sign it for me. I got it on pre-order."

Eliane paused for a second, eyeing the child, her hands on her hips. "Did you read it already?"

"I did. It's the best thing I've ever read, but I hope that when I grow up that I write one even better. It's my dream."

"It's a very adult book. Were your parents OK with letting you read this?"

Her father chuckled which was when Eliane first noticed him, "Denver has been reading "very adult" books since she was six. We couldn't stop her. Now she's writing them, well trying to, at least. She reads everything that hits the shelves. I couldn't have stopped her if I tried. She went online and pre-ordered it herself. I don't know that I ever had a say in the matter."

"I knew a little girl a lot like that once, myself," Eliane responded, trying to make eye contact with the girl instead of her bookishly handsome but also noticeably fit father with the wavy hair. "We're a rare breed, but it's best to just let us do our thing, isn't it, Miss Denver?"

The younger girl nodded then looked up at her father.

"Denver, that's a really interesting name." Eliane said as she pulled the marker from her pocket to sign the very first book she'd ever signed. She was trying so hard to be cool about it, but her hands trembled a bit.

"It's where we're from. I was named for the city I was born in where my parents first met. My Dad and I moved here about two years ago after my mom passed away. We needed a fresh start, and we looked at the map and picked out Paris together."

"Well, it wasn't exactly together. Denver chose Paris because she said she wanted to be close to the ghosts." He laughed, shaking his head. "But Paris was hard to argue with."

"I wanted to be close to the ghosts, too. Which one is your favorite, Denver?"

"Probably Ernest. He's the most tortured. I tried to get Dad to take me to Key West to see his house and six-toed cats when I was seven, but he said I was too young for Key West. But, I don't think I was too young. I was there for Hemmingway, not all the drunks."

"Hemingway. Interesting. Are you sure you're a little girl?" Eliane cocked her head sideways.

"Not really." She answered in monotone.

"We were never sure," her dad answered. "This is who she's always been. We just always shook our heads, then stood back to admire her. I've gotten good at learning to let go and just watch. That's all there is to do with girls like Denver."

"Smart choice." Eliane agreed. "So, what do you do here, um, I'm sorry, I didn't catch your name."

"Oh, I'm Bodhi. Bodhi Smith. I had such a common last name that my parents said they had to give me a really unique first name. I think it means enlightment or light or something like that. But I have a gallery over by all the old bookshops on the

Seine. I was an art history major. I don't paint myself; I wish. I don't have that creative bug. I just really have a thing for people who do. I'm kind of the yin to their yang I suppose. I'm the guy that looks at the painting, listens to the music, reads the books, you know? It's a passion that no one thought would get me anywhere, but we're here now, so I feel OK about it." He grinned. "Oh, and I'm also apparently the guy that rambles when asked a simple question. I'm sorry. I don't meet that many Americans, let alone famous ones."

Eliane said nothing. She only stared at him for a second. I expected her to blush and tell him how she wasn't *famous*. But she didn't. She owned it because she'd earned it.

"And have you read my book, Bodhi, lover of arts, reader of books?" She finally asked, handing the signed copy back to a beaming Denver.

He sucked some air through his bottom teeth. "I haven't gotten around to it just yet. I read the blurb. I really do want to read it. It's mental illness and murder and messed up love. It sounds incredible, truly. And I love the nods to the Fitzgeralds, now that I'm in Paris and all. I think I might be a little scared to learn about whatever I just let my daughter read. Maybe that's why I was dragging my feet. My apologies." He chuckled awkwardly, but somehow confidently at the same time. Maybe it was the eye contact. Neither of them could tear their eyes away, his deep brown, hers murky blue.

"Well, whenever you get around to reading it, you let me know and we'll discuss it over good gin."

"I—I would love that. How will I get a hold of you?"

"You'll figure it out." She winked at him "Read the book first. If you love it enough, I'll look up from a scone outside a little boulangerie one morning, or I'll glance up from my laptop to look over the river one afternoon and I'll find you standing there. And, I don't know, I'm also known to wander into galleries near my favorite bookstores from time to time."

He laughed and bit the edge of his lip a little bit. "I'll meet you there."

With that, El gave Bodhi a quick nod, then blew Denver a little air kiss. She then turned and entered the door of Harry's Bar, her vintage heels clicking on the slightly sticky floor, ushering her into part two of her life, the next act in her tale. Her beautiful silhouette faded into the dimly lit space that reached its arms out and welcomed her home.

Then I felt the strange pull on my own body again, stronger than ever this time. I saw her moving into the distance at incredible speed, a speed which mortals weren't capable of achieving. But then, I realized it wasn't her moving away from me at all. It was me who was travelling. The place I'd been before disappeared quickly and then I was somewhere new, somewhere free of the earth, of Jett, of Larry Matthew Demyun, of Eliane, and then of even my memories. I watched them all fall off of me one-by-one. Then I stood in a place where light was all that there was, the embodiment of everything that could be seen, touched, tasted, smelled, or heard; and there, I knew a thing I'd never truly known before. There, I was finally free.

"I remember every single spot of light that ever gouged a shadow beside your bones."
–Zelda Fitzgerald

DISCUSSION QUESTIONS

1. Why are names so important in the book? How do the names like Lux, Eliane, and even Bohdi contribute the author's message? How does Eliane's last name, "Pangolin" create a symbol for the type of women the book explores?

2. Everyone is watching someone else in this book. Is that how we all live our lives, vicariously through others?

3. Who is the villain in this novel? Who is the hero?

4. Do you love, love to hate, or hate Jett Jorgenson. Why?

5. Which female in the novel do you most identify with and why?

6. Discuss the lines between uniqueness and unhealthy actions. Where is that line? Is anyone truly "normal?"

7. Think of the people you've admired in your own life. What drew you to them? Was it always good for you?

8. If you could write a letter to anyone in your life, and say anything, who would you write to?

9. What, in your mind, did this book aim to achieve?

10. Does this novel have a happy ending? What does Eliane's future hold?

ACKNOWLEDGEMENTS

I have too many people to thank for this book. First, I'd like to thank God for giving me the desire and know-how to show all the good, bad, ugly, and in-between that floats through my head. I've always been a writer, and though it's been a frustrating thing to be at times, I've never been sorry. And I've never been anything else (except that one year I was mad at my career and decided to try out to be a Carolina Panthers cheerleader).

I'd also like to thank my husband, Kimsey, for always supporting me. If I need time to write, money to travel, a shoulder to cry on, a beta reader, or just someone to believe when I don't, he's there. Every time. I'd like to think my daughter, Allyn, for being so proud of Mommy for writing books. I'd also like to thank every person I grew up with. My early years in Candler, NC always stay with me. I had a whole community believing in a quirky little cheerleader with a dream. They're always so very proud, and I cherish the village that raised me.

I'd like to extend a huge thanks to Reagan Rothe and the entire team at Black Rose Writing. The editing, marketing and PR departments have all believed in this project, and I will be eternally grateful. Also, a big thanks to Patti Callahan Henry for reading and endorsing this novel despite her busy literary life. The same to fellow author Stephanie Alexander, and dear friend and journalist, Sarah Rose. Thanks to my friend and book lover, Stephanie Lee, for being one of the first readers and for giving me so much confidence. Thank you to Charleston Women Magazine for being behind me with all my outside endeavors. I'll never stop being proud of what I do.

Finally, I have to thank all the band members of OneRepublic who unknowingly inspired this novel when they told me over the airwaves to "give all my secrets away" while I was driving down I-26, wondering what the world of literature wanted from me.

The song is over a decade old, but on a random weekday in rush hour traffic, it told me exactly what to write. Most of this book is fiction, but a lot of it is inspired by parts of myself I never had the guts to share before. Finally, like Eliane, I wrote what I knew. And here we are.

And thank you, readers, my heart and soulmates!

ABOUT THE AUTHOR

Courtesy of Mark Staff Photography

South Carolina author, Lorna Hollifield, has penned three novels and serves as the managing editor of *Charleston Women Magazine*. A native of Asheville, NC, where she began her writing career as a tourism blogger, Hollifield now enjoys the Lowcountry life. Combing beaches, sipping good rye whiskeys, volunteering in community events, and creating memories with her husband, daughter, and spunky spaniel (and writing buddy) are her favorite parts of life.

NOTE FROM LORNA HOLLIFIELD

Word-of-mouth is crucial for any author to succeed. If you enjoyed *Bright Little Girls*, please leave a review online—anywhere you are able. Even if it's just a sentence or two. It would make all the difference and would be very much appreciated.

Thanks!
Lorna Hollifield

We hope you enjoyed reading this title from:

www.blackrosewriting.com

Subscribe to our mailing list – *The Rosevine* – and receive **FREE** books, daily
deals, and stay current with news about upcoming
releases and our hottest authors.
Scan the QR code below to sign up.

Already a subscriber? Please accept a sincere thank you for being a fan of
Black Rose Writing authors.

View other Black Rose Writing titles at
www.blackrosewriting.com/books and use promo code
PRINT to receive a **20% discount** when purchasing.